PURRFECT JACUZZI

THE MYSTERIES OF MAX 86

NIC SAINT

PURRFECT JACUZZI

The Mysteries of Max 86

Copyright © 2024 by Nic Saint

All rights reserved. No part of this book may be reproduced in any form by any electronic or mechanical means including photocopying, recording, or information storage and retrieval without permission in writing from the author.

This is a work of fiction. Names, characters, places, brands, media, and incidents are either the product of the author's imagination or are used fictitiously. The author acknowledges the trademarked status and trademark owners of various products referenced in this work of fiction, which have been used without permission. The publication/use of these trademarks is not authorized, associated with, or sponsored by the trademark owners.

Edited by Chereese Graves

www.nicsaint.com

Give feedback on the book at: info@nicsaint.com

facebook.com/nicsaintauthor
@nicsaintauthor

First Edition

Printed in the U.S.A

PURRFECT JACUZZI

The War of the Beaus

When local businessman Nathanial Tindell was found murdered in a run-down apartment in a seedy part of town, it raised a lot of questions. Why was he living under an assumed name, pretending to be poor? And why did he suddenly quit the billion-dollar company he built from scratch, just so he could be closer to his new neighbors Rita MacKereth and her mom Georgia? Suspects galore, not least of which were his business competitors, but also an old man and his dog, Miss MacKereth herself, and three of that young lady's male admirers. Was this a war of the beaus?

While Odelia and Chase conducted their investigation, with the assistance of myself and Dooley, Harriet and Brutus decided to launch a new project: shooting ASMR videos. Before long, they had landed themselves in hot water by filming friends, family members and neighbors in embarrassing situations and posting the videos on YouTube.

CHAPTER 1

Rita MacKereth crouched down next to her car and slid her finger across the scratch that someone had made there. She cursed. A brand-new car, and already it was ruined. She glanced around and wondered who could have done this. Possibly the person who had parked next to her but was gone now. She did notice that whoever this person was had looked at her askance when she had returned from the supermarket pushing a shopping cart. Possibly figuring she had parked too close to her own car. But then she couldn't help it. It wasn't her fault that the powers that be made these parking slots so tiny that people had a hard time slipping in and avoiding bumping into the next car.

She rose again and shook her blond mane. Looked as if she'd have to make a trip to the garage again. Last week it had been someone hitting her rear fender when she was having her nails done at the salon, and now this. The people at the garage would give her a funny look—again!

She got into her car and was about to back out of the parking space when she heard a sort of crunching sound and closed her eyes in dismay. Getting out, she saw she had accidentally backed into another car, this one of the more expensive variety. A BMW. The driver was already getting out of his car and judging from the look on his face and the color of that same face, he wasn't happy with this state of affairs.

She held up her hands in a bid to stave off a possible case of road rage. "I'm so sorry. I didn't see you there."

"No, I got that!" said the guy with some irritation, but then much to her surprise she saw that his face was still as red as it had been before, or possibly even redder, but that the look of rage had morphed into one of astonishment. And as his eyes dipped down her body and clocked her curvy shape with a certain relish, she understood what was going on here.

From an early age, she'd had that effect on men, and even though it had often been annoying to say the least, especially when her classmates had behaved like hormonal teenagers around her—possibly because they had been hormonal teenagers—she had also derived certain benefits from the effect she had on the opposite sex. Like now, for instance, with this hapless BMW driver, victim of a moment's carelessness on her part.

"Let's exchange insurance information, shall we?" she said therefore, and ducked into her glove compartment to collect the leather wallet filled with the necessary paperwork for these contingencies. When she re-emerged from the car, she saw that the man was still glued to the same spot he had been before, and staring at her all googly-eyed. As she walked up to him, she tripped over a piece of detritus and in an effort to regain her balance, accidentally stepped on the man's toe.

"Ow!" he yelled. "Owowow!"

"I'm so sorry!" she cried, horrified.

"It's... all right," he groaned.

"I'm not normally this clumsy."

"Good to know," he said as he ground his teeth in pain.

"So... do you have your papers?" she asked him.

"Yes, yes, yes," he said, and hobbled to his BMW to retrieve the documents. He was a bespectacled man in his early thirties, and quite good-looking, she thought. Not that it mattered, of course. Moments later they were exchanging information and filling out the necessary paperwork, with the man darting the occasional glance in her direction when he thought she wasn't looking—and even when he thought she was. But in spite of the fact that she was relieved he hadn't gone all Incredible Hulk on her, she decided to ignore his glances and get through this awkwardness as fast as possible.

The moment he had moved his car, she was off at a speed that must have surprised him, judging by the strange look on his face as she pulled out past him and was gone.

The last thing she needed was to get involved with random strangers that she met by bumping into them. Her love life was complicated enough as it was, with her recently discovering she was pregnant, and trying to work up the courage to tell her boyfriend about it. She hoped he would welcome the news, though she didn't hold out much hope, as they hadn't been getting along all that well lately, or in fact at all. If he didn't respond well to the news he was going to be a dad, she might be forced to bring this baby into the world as a single mom. Then again, since her own mom had been a single mom, she knew it could be done. Nevertheless, if Harvey wanted give their relationship another chance, that would probably be for the best—both for her and the baby.

She placed her hand on her belly and smiled. Even if Harvey wasn't prepared to give them another chance, she knew things would be fine. Odd how such a tiny little thing, no bigger than a pea according to the gynecologist during her check-up, could make such a big change in every respect.

She indicated left and soon was cruising along the main road into town. Which is when she became aware that a car was right on her tail, and behaving very dangerously and very strangely, honking its horn and flashing its lights as if to tell her something. When she glanced in the rear-view mirror, she saw to her surprise that it was the same BMW she had hit at the supermarket parking lot. And the man behind the wheel was the same man who hadn't been able to keep his eyes off her.

She wondered if she shouldn't simply ignore him. For all she knew, he might have had second thoughts about amicably arranging things between them and without involving the police. But then again, he hadn't come across as a weirdo or a homicidal maniac, and so she parked the car on the shoulder of the road and got out to see what the guy wanted this time.

"Miss MacKereth," he said, kind of breathlessly, and smiling a wide smile. He was holding something in his hand, and she now saw that it was her bag, which contained her wallet and all her personal stuff. "You forgot this," he added as he handed over the bag.

"Oh, god," she said as she took the cherished item from the man's hands. "Thank you so much. I hadn't even noticed."

"It was on the hood of your car, and when you drove off, it fell to the ground," he specified as he rocked back on his heels, looking extremely pleased with himself. He jerked his finger in the direction she had been going. "Driving home, huh?"

She smiled. "How did you guess?" She wondered if he had gone through her stuff, but then realized that he must have gleaned her address from the insurance documents.

"I also live in Hampton Cove," he intimated, suddenly looking extremely shy. "Close to the library, in fact." When she didn't volunteer the information on where she lived, even though he probably knew, he must have realized that small talk wasn't on the cards today. And held up his hand. "Well, I must be off now. Open my store. See you around, Miss MacKereth."

"Yeah, see you around," she said, though she sincerely hoped that wouldn't be the case.

Five minutes later, she was passing the sign that said, "Welcome to Hampton Cove," and once again found her thoughts drifting to the same idle speculation about Harvey's reaction to the news that he was about to become a dad. She bit her lower lip. Even though she sincerely hoped he would be over the moon, like she was, she had to consider the fact that he might not react too favorably. Lately he'd been in such a lousy mood that anything was possible. But however he reacted, he needed to be told. His reaction would tell her whether she would be raising this baby all by herself or with the baby's daddy by her side. She truly hoped for the latter.

CHAPTER 2

For some reason I found hard to grasp, Dooley and Brutus were locked in a staring contest and had been for the past five minutes. The entire concept, as I understood it, revolved around the capacity to look someone in the eye without blinking. The person who blinked first, lost. And since thus far neither Brutus nor Dooley were giving an inch, the outcome was still up in the air.

Surrounding the two competitors, a sort of supporters' club had sprung up, consisting of myself, Harriet, Fifi, and Rufus. In other words: the collected pets of Harrington Street numbers 42 to 44. The place to be was our backyard, and tickets hadn't been sold, nor had the match been announced on social media, or else the entire neighborhood might have come out to see the show.

"I don't think this is healthy, Max," said Harriet as she squeezed my arm a little too tightly, I felt. "I mean, the eyes need lubrication, don't they? What if they suffer permanent damage from this silly nonsense?"

"I'm sure it won't be as bad as that," I assured her. "The

eyes can go without lubrication for quite a while without suffering adverse effects."

"But what if the tissue shrivels up and dies, Max?" she insisted. "It happens, you know. The eyes need that tear fluid or they will DIE!"

"I don't think that's the case," said Rufus as he blinked a few times. "I think the eyes are very strong and don't need any tear fluid at all. In fact, I think that if Brutus and Dooley keep this up, they can go on for days, maybe even weeks."

"They'll need to be fed," said Fifi. "If they want to do this for days, I mean. And someone will need to make sure they get a bathroom break." She sniffed Dooley's butt, and nodded sagely. "I think he's good. Nothing seems to be coming down the pike just yet."

I rolled my eyes, and made sure to lubricate them in the process, as I'm not a big believer in torturing oneself for the pleasure of besting a fellow cat at some silly game. "Look, this will all be over within minutes," I assured my friends. "Nobody can keep their eyes open for days or weeks. It's simply not possible."

"And a good thing, too," said Harriet as she gave Rufus a stern-faced look of reproach. "Putting these silly ideas in pets' heads," she said as she shook her head. "If Brutus ruins his eyes, I'm blaming you, you know," she said in no uncertain terms.

"Eh?" said Rufus.

"Yes, you!" said Harriet fiercely. "This was your idea in the first place."

"It wasn't! All I said was that humans sometimes like to play silly games. Like arm wrestling or trying to see who can pee the farthest. And also a staring contest."

"And now see what happened," said Harriet.

"Good thing they didn't try to see who could pee the

farthest," said Fifi. "Imagine if they did that? Your lawn wouldn't like it, Max."

"It isn't technically my lawn, Fifi," I said. "But I share your sentiment."

"I think the lawn *would* like it," said Rufus. "Peeing on the lawn is good for the grass. It will make it grow at least twice as fast. Or at least that's what Ted always said," he added quickly, before he could be accused of putting ideas in cats' heads again.

"Ted pees on his own lawn?" asked Fifi.

"He does," said Rufus. "Only he does it when Marcie isn't looking, you know. I don't think she would like it."

We all shared a look of surprise. "So Ted pees on his own lawn?" I asked, just to make sure I hadn't misheard.

Rufus nodded. "He does it early in the morning, when Marcie is still asleep. And he makes sure he pees on a different part of the lawn every morning, to make sure that every blade of grass gets equal benefit of this liquid of the gods, as he calls it."

We all smiled at this. Only Ted could call his urine the liquid of the gods. But then the man had always been slightly eccentric.

"I personally blame it on being an accountant," said Rufus. "Sitting there poring over those numbers every day from morning till night, and that for however many years, must have messed with his head. Scrambled his brain, you know."

We all nodded in agreement. I found it hard to imagine that a person would willingly sit in front of a computer entering numbers and crunching data all his life. It sounded like torture.

"I think my snuggle bear is going to win," Harriet said. "Just look at him. Fully focused and not giving an inch. Poor Dooley. He never stood a chance."

"Don't say that," said Fifi. "I see what you're doing, Harriet, and it's not going to work."

"What am I doing?" asked Harriet.

"Psychological warfare!" said Fifi. "You're trying to turn the odds in favor of your boyfriend, and it's not fair."

Harriet's jaw had dropped out of sheer indignation. "I did no such thing!"

"It's practically tantamount to cheating," said Fifi, not pulling her punches. "And I won't stand for it. As the official referee of this battle, I'm telling you to stand down."

Harriet's mouth closed with a soft click and she gave Fifi furious looks, but she did comply and didn't try to sway the competition in Brutus's favor. Instead, she now started staring Dooley in the eyes as well, moving behind Brutus to add more stress to my friend. Fifi wasn't fooled, though, and as she gestured to Harriet to stop doing that, the white Persian finally relented and returned to her position on the sidelines, just like the rest of us.

I couldn't really tell if Dooley was in trouble or not. He didn't seem to be weakening, that was for sure. I could tell that Brutus had a hard time keeping his eyes open though, for his eyelids were trembling, and his eyes were watering. Finally, he uttered a loud cry of anguish and squeezed his peepers tightly shut.

"I'm sorry, but I can't take it anymore!" he cried, much to Harriet's dismay.

"Oh, pookie!" she cried. "Why give up now? You almost had him!"

We all glanced at Dooley, and he certainly didn't look like a cat who was about to flinch. In fact, he was still looking straight ahead of him, and so I got the impression that he hadn't even noticed that he had won.

Who had noticed was Fifi, for she grabbed our friend's

paw and held it up in the air. "Winner of this competition: Dooley!"

Suddenly Dooley seemed to wake up from some kind of slumber, which wasn't possible, since his eyes had been open the entire time. "Hm?" he said, and shook his head. "I think I fell asleep. What did I miss?"

"But Dooley," I said. "You can't have fallen asleep. Your eyes were open!"

He yawned. "Oh, didn't you know? I can sleep with my eyes open. Not sure why, though I remember that my dad could do the same. Mom always said it was a little creepy, for she would wake up in the middle of the night and think my dad was awake and would start talking to him, only to realize ten minutes in that he was still asleep. Made her feel silly."

We all laughed, except for Brutus, who gave our friend a look of dismay. "So... you were asleep this entire time?"

"Not at first, no," said Dooley. "But after a while I got bored, and I must have dozed off."

The big black cat shook his head. "That's so not fair."

"Oh, but you should try it," said Dooley. "It's very easy. You just sleep but keep your eyes open."

And since cats are naturals at trying out new things, we all tried to do what Dooley had just described. Try as I might, though, I simply couldn't do it. The moment I started to doze off, my eyes invariably closed of their own accord. It was the darnedest thing.

"I can't do it," Harriet confessed.

"Me neither," said Brutus as he blinked a few times to prevent his eyes from going all dry and atrophying, just like Harriet had predicted would happen.

"I can do it, you guys!" said Rufus. He had closed his eyes and looked triumphant. "See? My eyes are open, and I'm fast asleep!"

"First of all, you're not asleep since you're talking to us," said Fifi. "And second, your eyes are closed, buddy boy."

"No, but they're... Oh, gee, I guess you're right," said the big sheepdog. "Bummer."

Dooley yawned. "I guess that nap wasn't long enough. I think I'll go and lie down some." And with these words, he trotted off in the direction of the pet flap and moments later was gone.

"You know, we could probably monetize this skill," said Harriet thoughtfully.

"What skill, what are you talking about?" asked Brutus, whose eyes were still watering from the ordeal he had suffered.

"Well, Dooley's capacity to sleep with his eyes open, of course. I'll bet people would pay good money to watch a TikTok video of him demonstrating this unique skill."

I smiled as I imagined people watching a YouTube video of a cat just sitting there with his eyes open. Like watching paint dry. But when I told Harriet, she wasn't impressed.

"It's ASMR and it's a thing, Max," she assured me. "It's very relaxing to watch paint dry. In fact it's all the rage. And since people are all stressed out lately, a video of Dooley sleeping with his eyes open would be a big hit, just you wait and see." With these words, she hurried in after Dooley, possibly hoping to convince him to star in said video.

I turned to Fifi. "What's ASMR?" I asked, feeling silly for having to ask the question.

"Oh, it's videos of the wind rustling in the trees," she said. "Snails creeping through the grass. Water babbling in a brook. Fire crackling in the hearth. Peaceful sounds, you know."

"Okay," I said, even though I still failed to see the big attraction. But then I guess I'm not as *au courant* as I would like to be sometimes. The world does move at a rapid pace, and it's hard to keep up.

Brutus suddenly brought his face up close to mine. "Look at my eyes, Max," he implored. "Are they all right, you think?"

I stared into my friend's eyes. "They look fine," I assured him.

"They sting, Max!" he cried as he squeezed them shut. "They sting something real bad!"

I patted him on the shoulder. "Maybe have a lie-down," I suggested. "You'll feel much better afterwards." I know I always feel refreshed after a lie-down. Which is probably why it might be my favorite thing in the world. And since I felt my advice was pretty solid, I also returned indoors to sample some of my own medicine. All this talk of ASMR had made me very sleepy.

I settled in on the couch and was asleep in seconds.

CHAPTER 3

Tex glanced through his bedroom window and wondered if what he was seeing could possibly be true. Out there, on the lawn, his mother-in-law was performing some kind of dance. She was wielding a soup ladle and was slicing the air with it, all the while hopping up and down like a show pony on steroids and chanting some strange song.

He even rubbed his eyes to make sure he was awake and not still asleep. But when he looked again, the woman was still there, and howling away like a banshee!

He swallowed with some difficulty. He'd always known that this day would come. The day that Vesta finally lost her final marble and went stir-crazy.

"Marge," he said quietly.

"Mh?" said his wife of twenty-five years from the bed, where she was reading *Star Magazine* about the latest juicy gossip from the Hollywood mill.

"Come here a minute, will you?"

"What is it?" she asked as she languidly stretched.

It was Saturday morning, and as was the couple's habit, they liked to linger in bed a little longer than usual.

"Your mother is behaving really strangely," he said. Though 'strange' was probably an understatement for the kind of behavior Vesta was displaying.

Marge finally rose from the bed and tiptoed barefoot to the window. When she saw her mother hacking at the air with her soup ladle, she went perfectly still. "What is she doing?" she asked finally.

"I'm afraid it must have finally happened, sweetness," he said as gently as he could. To break the news to a patient that their mother or dad has gone bananas was hard enough, but having to spring that same news to his wife was even harder. But still, it had to be done. "I think your mother may have developed dementia."

"Nonsense," said Marge, wiping his words off the table in one fell swoop. "I think it's this show she saw last night."

"What show?" he asked.

"There was something on the Discovery Channel about rain dances, so she must have figured she'd try it out for herself."

He took a deep breath. "Ah," he said, and now remembered a conversation he and Vesta had had last night, where she complained that the crops were going to hell in a handbasket because of the lingering drought they had been experiencing in the area. "If this keeps up," she had told Tex, "Farmer Giles won't be Farmer Giles for much longer. I saw him a couple of days ago and he complained that he can't work under these conditions. His crops are going to die if we don't get some rain very soon now."

It was true that they hadn't had a drop of rain for weeks, and that there was even talk about cutting down on watering your lawn, washing your car, or filling up paddling pools if this kept up. Already their gardens were feeling the strain, and even though nobody likes rain, it was true that it had a very important role to fulfill.

Marge had opened the window and shouted, "Ma! What are you doing!"

"Can't you see? I'm doing a rain dance!" Vesta yelled back. "It's supposed to work like a charm." She held her face up to the sky, which was already a clear blue with a sun that was hoisting itself to new heights. "Nothing yet," she said after a moment. "But just you wait and see! Pretty soon now it'll start raining!" And with these words, she continued jumping around and slicing at the air with her makeshift weapon, shouting strange oaths.

Marge smiled as she closed the window. "At least while she's doing this she's not getting into trouble," she said with satisfaction. She gave her husband a kiss on the lips and moved swiftly off. "I'm taking a shower," she announced. Moments later he heard the shower running and wondered if the governor would soon forbid them to do that, too.

He certainly hoped not. He liked his shower in the morning, and the occasional bubble bath. He had even planned to purchase a jacuzzi, along with Chase, and have it installed when both their wives were out, so they could spring it on them as a surprise.

If they couldn't wash their cars or water their lawns, he guessed jacuzzis would be a big no-no, too. But since he didn't have a crystal ball, and a politician's ways are as erratic and unpredictable as the weather itself, he decided not to worry too much about it for now. So he picked up his wife's magazine and was soon up to date on all things Tinseltown. Which is how his son-in-law Chase found him ten minutes later.

* * *

"DAD," said the policeman as he surveyed the scene with his keen cop eye. Man dressed in pajamas reading *Star Magazine* in bed on a Saturday morning while his wife is taking a shower. Cozy scene, he thought. Very family-friendly. And exactly the kind of scene that had played out next door, except it was him that was taking the shower with Odelia reading *People Magazine* in bed to find out all about Oprah's latest weight loss scheme.

Tex looked up and immediately shoved the magazine under the pillow, looking caught. "Oh, hey, Chase," he said as he bounced up from the bed and into a standing position. Immediately he started doing some push-ups. "I was working out a little," he explained as he huffed and puffed his way through the exercise, obviously never having done it in his life. "Important to stay fit, you know," he said, panting heavily.

"Absolutely right," said Chase, who couldn't suppress a smile. "If you want me to give you some pointers…"

"Oh, no, that's fine," said Tex. "I got this."

"I'd only be too glad to."

"I've still got an old Richard Simmons video lying around somewhere," he assured him. "So I'm good."

"Excellent," said Chase as he took a seat on the edge of the bed. "Dad, I figure now might be a good time to talk about that jacuzzi. I mean, if we're going to do this, we probably should do it now. Before the weather turns again."

"The weather isn't going to turn," said the doctor as he sprang up from his awkward position on the floor and did some token stretches. He gestured with his head to the window. "Haven't you seen your grandmother-in-law?"

Chase got up to take a look and nodded. "Oh, yeah. I asked her about it when I passed. She told me it's a rain dance."

"Take it from me, buddy," said his father-in-law. "When

women like Vesta are starting to do rain dances, it's going to be a very long summer."

Chase smiled broadly. "Great," he said. "That means we'll have all summer to enjoy our jacuzzi, Dad."

Tex winced a little, but then seemed to see the wisdom in his son-in-law's words. "Maybe you're right. If we're going to do this, better we do it now. So what did you have in mind?"

"Well, I saw they've got one on sale at Target. And there are several great deals at Walmart, too. Quality-wise, I don't think we can go wrong by installing the exact same one Alec and Charlene got for themselves."

Tex looked up at this. "Alec and Charlene got themselves a jacuzzi?"

"They did," Chase confirmed. "And a great one, too. Though Alec hasn't invited me yet to try it out, I keep seeing great things about it."

Tex's face had taken on a thoughtful look. "He hasn't invited me either," he said, rubbing his chin. "I wonder why that is."

"He probably wants to enjoy it a little longer before he starts inviting others over," Chase suggested. "But I know for a fact that he and Charlene have been soaking in that thing every night for weeks now. It's all over the police station WhatsApp."

"Is that so?" said Tex, and he didn't look happy about it. Which was only to be understood, as the doctor believed in sharing the spoils of his own modest success with the rest of his family, and assumed that they would return the favor. Only Alec and Charlene clearly didn't feel that same way.

"Look, why don't we check it out later today? I'm sure Alec will agree. And then if we like it, we can get us the exact same model," Chase suggested.

Tex nodded. "Great idea, Chase," he said, his voice a little choked up now. "Set it up."

He clapped the man on the shoulder. "Oh, don't be like that, Dad. I'm sure it's just an oversight on Alec's part. Or maybe Charlene doesn't like it when her husband's family is all over their brand-new jacuzzi. You know what Charlene is like sometimes."

Tex nodded, but he still seemed to feel that it wasn't right to purchase an expensive new jacuzzi and not tell your family all about it and invite them over for a great evening of fun.

As he left the doctor to ruminate on this injustice, Chase hoped he hadn't stirred a hornet's nest by mentioning his boss's jacuzzi to his father-in-law. He didn't think he had, but he would still tell Alec that maybe now was a good time to invite the family over. Best not to start a feud over such a silly thing.

CHAPTER 4

Rita arrived home sans car, since she had dropped it off at the same garage where Harvey had got it for her. As expected, the salesman had smirked when he'd seen her arrive on the lot and had barely been able to contain his glee when he had inspected the damage. Clearly, he was of the 'women are lousy drivers' school of thought, though she could have told him that her mom had been driving the family car for forty years with nary a hitch—except for that one time she had accidentally driven it into a lake. A small miracle that it had still functioned after that, and a testament to the fine automobile it was.

The moment she stepped into the apartment, her poodle Shelley jumped up against her, ecstatic to see her. Of her boyfriend Harvey, there was no trace, but then she hadn't expected him to be there, since he hated Rita's mom with a vengeance—and it had to be said the feeling was mutual.

Mom wasn't home either, but then she was probably out with a friend—or maybe visiting their neighbor Morgan.

Rita headed into the kitchen to provide Shelley with some much-desired food and to fix herself a sandwich, since she was starving after the events of that morning. She checked the big clock over the door and saw that she needed to get a move on if she wanted to make it on time for work. Even though today was Saturday, that didn't mean she could laze about as a lot of people did. Saturdays were workdays at the clinic, and she was determined to clock in on time, no matter what.

She had found this job online after a long search, and she was darned if she was going to ruin things by being late. And so after she had fed both herself and Shelly, she grabbed her bag and was off again, this time taking the bus. Her car should be finished on Monday, and she was going to hold them to it since she needed the vehicle to get to and from the clinic.

Arriving right on the dot, she punched in and went in search of her boss, the inimitable Rose Scullion, who had founded the clinic fifteen years ago and still ran it with the same passion she had used to find the necessary donors to start the one and only clinic in Hampton Cove that catered to the owners of pets too sick to remain at home. Some people called it a palliative pet center, but that wasn't all they did. And it wasn't as sad as most people thought it was. A lot of the pets that had been given only days or weeks to live actually beat those expectations and lingered on for months and in a few cases even years. A lot of times the owners were to blame for the bad state their pets found themselves in, whether due to a lack of care or proper nourishment, and the moment the pets were transferred to the Rose Clinic, they suddenly and miraculously went through a complete reversal and in some cases a remission and got their health back.

Rita found Rose tending with loving care to a turtle that had been left in their care by its owner, who claimed the animal was terminal and she didn't have the funds to pay the medical bills. After the turtle, whose name was Barbra, had been examined by their in-house vet Lucy, she had determined that the turtle was far from dying. Barbra was severely undernourished and dehydrated, and clearly hadn't been fed for days, the poor thing.

"How is she doing?" asked Rita as she joined her boss, who was bottle-feeding the turtle, who was also much too tiny for her age.

"I think she's going to pull through," said Rose, who was a real warrior for all the pets in their care. "And if she doesn't, I'm personally going over to that horrible woman and murder her myself."

"Better don't," Rita advised, who wasn't just one of the people taking care of the animals but also their in-house legal aid. "Though if you want to press charges, you could."

Rose's jaw took on that formidable and determined set that she often got, and Rita knew exactly what she was thinking. If people took as much care of their pets as they did of themselves, the world would be a much better place, and places like the Rose Clinic wouldn't see as much heartache and pain as they saw on a daily basis.

"Let's wait and see if Barbra pulls through," Rose said as she squirted another dropper full of vitamin-enlaced water between the turtle's lips. "But if she doesn't..." Her eyes blazed. "All bets are off, and I want you to make sure that woman pays."

"Will do," said Rita, even though litigation wasn't exactly her forte. They could always file a complaint with the police, though, and usually that was enough. They were in luck with the fact that the chief of police's mother had personally given her name to their local shelter. The Vesta Muffin Animal Shelter took in pets that had been found wandering along the street, and in that sense, the Rose Clinic and the shelter were perfectly compatible. It didn't hurt that Vesta Muffin was a self-declared pet nut and never afraid to go to bat for their town's pet population.

Rita left Rose to fight for the life of the tiny turtle, and a moment later was entering her office, where a pile of work awaited her. Not only did they have to draw up a contract with the owners of the pets that were left at the clinic, but they also had sponsors to find and agreements to draw up with those sponsors, of whom fortunately there were many, and a lot of them with deep pockets and big hearts for the pets.

The door opened, and Ken walked in. One of the volunteers who helped out at the clinic, he was a tall and rail-thin teenager who spent his weekends and vacations helping out, which was commendable and something that Rita now wished she had done when she was his age. Instead, she had spent her teenage years dating a series of good-for-nothing boys and hanging out at the mall with her friends. Important, but perhaps not as important as the work that Ken did.

The pimple-faced teenager gawked at her for a moment, as he usually did. According to Rose, he was madly in love with Rita, which gave Rita a frisson of enjoyment mingled with embarrassment since the kid was young enough to be her kid brother. After he had gulped once or twice and pushed his glasses further up his nose, he finally opened his mouth to speak. "There was someone in here to see you earlier," he announced. "A man," he added, and for a moment, he looked angry, as if no man had any right to drop by and introduce himself to the woman he loved. Then he collected himself and continued delivering his message. "He said he'd be back. Something to do with a car you destroyed this morning?"

She rolled her eyes. "For your information, Ken, I didn't destroy any car, and also, I thought everything was arranged." She wondered what the guy wanted from her, and to come to her place of work at that. Too bad she had missed him, or she would have given him a piece of her mind.

"Oh, and this little fella has received a clean bill of health from Lucy," said Ken, and placed a hedgehog on her desk.

They had named him Patrick, and part of his spines were missing, and also part of his foot, courtesy of the man who'd accidentally driven over him as he backed out of his driveway. The vet had nursed him back to health and now he was ready to return home or be adopted by a new pet parent, though the vet had also said he would probably never be the same. And since his previous owner had chosen not to keep him, Rita had volunteered to take the hedgehog home to live with her. It would be quite an adjustment for Shelley, but she'd soon get over having to share her home with this prickly new friend.

"So have you told Harvey yet?" asked Ken, staring at her from behind those bottle-bottom glasses he always wore.

Rita shook her head. "No, I haven't. But like I told Rose yesterday, I'm sure he'll be fine with it."

"And what if he isn't?" asked Ken. He started and brought a hand to his mouth. "He's not going to hurt Patrick, is he? Cause if he is, maybe I should adopt him instead."

"Of course Harvey isn't going to hurt Patrick," she said, putting a touch of dismay in her voice. For some reason, Ken had taken an irrevocable dislike to Rita's boyfriend, possibly because he felt that he didn't deserve to be with a woman as amazing as Rita—Rose's words, not hers, but she had a feeling her boss was probably right. "He's not like that, Ken."

"No, of course not," said Ken, though he didn't look convinced. "Anyway, I guess I'll get back to work," he said after a pause and a minute of awkward silence. Every conversation with Ken was marked by awkward pauses—they were his specialty.

"See you, Ken," she said as the kid let himself out of her

office, but only after another long glance at Rita, as if he wanted to imprint her likeness on his memory, just in case he never saw her again. The kid was nice, but boy oh boy was he weird.

The morning mainly consisted of drawing up a couple of contracts with people whose pets they had taken in, and also a phone call from an irate pet owner who expected them to pay for the pet he had dropped off when by all rights, it should be the other way around, since caring for a sick and dying pet was often expensive. And she had just finished answering an email from a council member about the presence of the clinic at the next county fair when the door swung open again and Harvey walked in.

He didn't look happy, she noticed, and that was quite the understatement.

"Hey, Harvey," she said, bracing herself for a confrontation, of the kind they'd suffered through a lot in the past couple of weeks. "What brings you out here?"

"I just got a call from the garage to tell me that your car will take longer to fix. What did you do this time, Rita?"

"Just a minor fender bender," she said lightly. "It's a funny story, actually—"

"I don't want to hear it," he said, holding up his hand like a traffic cop. He closed his eyes and pinched the bridge of his nose. "You only got that car, what, a month ago? And already you've managed to put it in the shop twice." He spread his eyes open and she watched his nostrils flare. "What is wrong with you!"

"It wasn't my fault!" she cried, also getting worked up, stunned by the injustice of it all. "That guy showed up out of nowhere!"

"They always do, don't they?" said Harvey acerbically. He pointed a finger at her, a habit she truly and thoroughly hated and which put her hackles up something terrific. "I just want you to know I'm not paying a cent this time, you hear!"

"You won't have to pay. The insurance will take care of everything." Hopefully.

"I'll believe that when I see it," he grumbled. He crossed his arms in front of his chest. "So what was it you wanted to see me about?"

She thought for a moment about not telling him, since clearly this wasn't the best time to spring such momentous news on him, but since she was also worked up by his attitude and the whole unfairness of the thing, she decided to just throw it out there.

"I'm pregnant," she said, without further preamble. "And it's yours," she added for good measure, just in case he would ask that ridiculous question, like she knew he would.

He opened and closed his mouth several times, staring at her in horror and shock all the while, and she got the sinking feeling he wasn't entirely happy with the news.

"You're *pregnant*?!" he asked, as if it was the most ridiculous thing he'd ever heard.

"That's right. Six weeks, and according to the gynecologist I saw, everything is fine, both with me and the baby."

Suddenly, he closed his mouth, and she could see his jaw tensing. It was the moment she decided that maybe, just maybe, it was better for her unborn child not to have this man in her life as a dad. And probably a lot better for her as well.

But instead of giving it to her with both barrels, as was his habit, he just shook his head. "We're going to talk about this later." It wasn't a suggestion but a statement. "And then we're going to make a couple of decisions. Is that understood?"

"Perfectly," she said.

She watched him stalk out of her office and slam the

door, and sank back down on her chair. Moments later Ken came in again, looking eager. "So how did it go?" he asked. "Did you tell him about the turtle?"

"Oh, Ken, please leave," she said as she buried her face in her hands.

"Yes, ma'am," said the kid, but when she looked up a minute later, he was still there, and giving her a look of such compassion that she actually got tears in her eyes.

"He didn't pass the pet test," said Ken when she made a 'Well?' gesture.

"The what test?" she asked with a touch of exasperation.

"The pet test. Any man who isn't over the moon when his girlfriend suggests they get a pet isn't a good man." He nodded seriously. "You should break up with him."

In spite of her sense of despair over the impending implosion of her relationship, she smiled. "Thanks, Ken. That may very well be the most sensible thing anyone has said to me in quite a while."

He beamed. "If you want, I could say a lot more things to you, Rita."

"I'll bet you could. Maybe not now, though, okay?"

"Later," he declared solemnly, and left her office again.

Which is when she decided that now was the time for a good cry. And when Rose walked in ten minutes later, that's how she found her: crying her eyes out and surrounded by a large pile of tissues. Her boss didn't even look remotely surprised.

CHAPTER 5

He stared down at the body of the man he had just slain and wondered why he didn't experience more of an emotional response. But then he reflected that maybe he would feel something later. After the shock had worn off and he realized what he had done. He had killed a man, and even though he now regretted his actions, he also knew that it couldn't have happened any other way. In a sense, it had been preordained. Everything leading up to this moment. He glanced down at his hands, still clutching the knife that had ended the man's life. It clattered to the floor as his fingers started trembling violently. He gripped his right hand with his left and squeezed hard to stop the terrifying shakes. Soon they had held his entire body in their grip, and he staggered from the room. His head was pounding and he felt nauseous. He stumbled into the bathroom and stared at himself in the mirror. He wondered what would happen now. There was punishment for murder, a capital crime. Not the death penalty, fortunately, but possibly life imprisonment, not something to sniff at either. And so he methodically started removing every last trace of his presence from the apartment.

The last thing he needed now was to be caught. It was one thing that stood out in his mind. He couldn't be caught.

One hour later, he snuck out the door and down the stairs. The only person he met was an old man and his dog, but since he had his hoodie up, he was pretty sure he wouldn't be recognized. At least there weren't any CCTV cameras covering the old building—an expense the owners didn't want to make. The moment he was out on the street, he hurried away from the scene, just another faceless, hooded figure among many.

Now all he could do was wait, and hope that the police wouldn't solve the case. Knowing how dumb the cops in this town were, the chances of that happening were slim to none.

* * *

Cesar, who spent most of his days roaming the streets of Hampton Cove, looking for something to eat from the many dumpsters and public trash cans that littered the place, and sleeping in the park on one of the benches, almost fell over when a man bumped into him and simply kept on hurrying down the stairs without looking back. Falling on his bum, he cursed wildly. Wasn't it enough that he had to go through the indignity of living an anonymous life that people actually stopped paying attention to him entirely? He shook his fist at the man who had disappeared, and figured it was another one of those young people who didn't seem to mind that their fellow man was suffering.

The man had dropped something, and he picked it up. It was a room key, like the ones they issue at hotels. He put it in his pocket and got back on his feet, then continued to mount those stairs. Rock Tower was where he liked to spend his nights when it was too cold outside. It was also where he often 'found' the odd trifle he could drop off at the pawn shop. The police would have called it stealing, but he simply liked to think of it as recycling stuff people had discarded and didn't need anymore. In other words, doing his bit for the climate.

Most of the hundreds of apartments in the Rock Tower had seen better days, as had the building itself, which had been erected in the sixties and hadn't seen a comprehensive renovation in years. As his dog joined him, he patted the animal fondly and saw that Nicholas, as he had christened the creature, held something clasped between his teeth that looked as if it just might be a nice big sandwich. And so he carefully took it from between the mutt's teeth and fairly divided it in half: half for him and half for Nicholas, who was a real blessing since he had adopted the little mongrel.

Friends of his had told him for years that he should get a dog and double his earnings, but so far he had always held off on the idea since he didn't think it was fair on any dog to have to live the kind of life he lived. But one day he had woken up with Nicholas seated on his chest, and the dog had never left, in spite of the many attempts that Cesar had made to shift him. And ever since then, they had been inseparable.

As he munched on the sandwich, one of the tenants passed him by and threw something in his direction that Nicholas deftly snapped up and deposited in Cesar's eager hand. A buck—not a thing to sniff at. He nodded his thanks to the man, who went on his way. The moment he had passed, he left the landing to go exploring.

Even though he wasn't a thief, he still didn't think it was prudent for a man in his position to ignore the gifts that could be found by being enterprising and paying attention to any opportunities coming his way. Over the years, he had come across so much richness it had made all the difference.

Like that time he hit upon a gold necklace. Since it had an engraving, he decided to find the person it belonged to instead of pawning it. Eventually, he had located the woman, and she had been so grateful that she had given him no less than a hundred bucks as a finder's fee. The bracelet had belonged to her late mother and held a lot of emotional value.

It had warmed his heart, and later that night also his stomach when he had enjoyed a real feast at the local diner.

He carefully mounted the staircase that led all the way to the top of the fifty-floor building and kept his eyes glued to the floor, just in case he found more riches. Nicholas was right by his side, and he would have sworn that the dog knew exactly what he was looking for and did his best to accommodate Cesar by sniffing here and there.

They had arrived on the sixth floor when Nicholas suddenly began barking up a storm, much to Cesar's surprise since the mutt wasn't much for barking. He only ever barked at people he sensed might hurt his human, which was a good thing for a vagrant like Cesar who was mostly in a pretty precarious position and had to be careful at all times.

The dog was scratching at a door and kept up his barking, which wasn't a good idea, for any moment now one of the tenants might appear and kick them both out of there—or worse, call the police and complain about intruders.

"Shush, Nicholas," he told the doggie, and even picked him up to try to take him away from whatever lurked behind that door that had set him off like that.

But the dog simply slipped from his grasp and started pawing at the door again. To the extent that Cesar started to believe that maybe he should take a closer look at what was going on. Nicholas was a smart dog, and if he thought there was something that warranted Cesar's attention, he probably should look into the thing.

And so he practiced the skills of a lifetime by applying one of his nifty little gadgets and gained access to the apartment. The moment the door opened, Nicholas was off like a spear, with Cesar following at a slower pace, inspecting room after room. It was when he arrived in the living room that he got the shock of a lifetime: Nicholas was sitting next to the body of a man who was very obviously dead. And judging from the blood that was coagulating on the floor, until very recently he had still been alive.

CHAPTER 6

Alec Lip was enjoying a nice soak in his new jacuzzi, relaxing alongside his wife Charlene. It was a rare moment of leisure for Hampton Cove's power couple. Both of them had the kind of high-octane jobs that required a lot of energy and time dedicated to them, and so whenever they had the chance to soak in their newest acquisition, they gladly took it. It was also the reason he hadn't yet invited his family to partake in the singular pleasure that a jacuzzi could award. He hadn't even told them yet, and he figured he might keep it that way.

Alec leaned back with a luxurious sigh. "This is the life, isn't it," he said.

"That, it most definitely is," said Charlene, also enjoying their soak with her eyes closed.

"Now all we have to do is install a pool," he said, "and a sauna and we're in business."

She laughed. "Are you serious? You want to install a pool?"

"Why not? We've got the space, we've got the funds… and I know how much you love to swim, baby cakes."

"Well, that's true enough," she admitted. "But where are we going to put it?"

"Right here," he said. Ever since he had moved into the villa that Charlene had purchased many moons ago, back when she was still married to her first husband, he had been thinking how to improve on the place. The pool was only one idea. What they really needed was a spa. But for that he'd need to build an extension, something he was looking forward to. It was a project he was eager to put his back into. Then when it was finished he and Charlene could live through those winter months without suffering that winter blues.

"Or we could put it closer to the fence," he suggested, gesturing to the plot of land that was located right next to the fence that divided their garden from the next.

"I'm not so sure Gregg would agree," said Charlene, referring to their next-door neighbor Gregg Watkiss, a retired decorated colonel with a penchant for keeping his plot of land as squeaky clean and spotless as he could.

"Gregg doesn't feature into this," he said.

"He could always protest," said Charlene. "I remember when the Cormacks wanted to install a pool and Gregg filed a complaint with the planning department. Claimed it would create too much noise and was an infringement on his right to be at peace in his own backyard."

"What noise? It's just the two of us!"

"You know it won't stay that way for long," said Charlene as she studied her big toe, which had bobbed up along with her very shapely leg. "The moment your sister finds out about the pool, she'll be down here every weekend, and so will Odelia and Chase and Grace. And your mother, and your mother's friends. And Gregg will blow his top every time."

"We don't have to tell them," Alec suggested. "Just like with the jacuzzi. If they don't know, they won't come."

"You can't keep a thing like that a secret, Alec," she said.

"Why not? We kept the jacuzzi a secret, didn't we?"

"They'll find out. People talk."

"Gregg won't talk. He's army. They're trained to stay quiet, even under torture."

Charlene laughed. "What are you saying? That your mom would torture pour Gregg to find out about our jacuzzi?"

"I wouldn't put it past her," he grunted.

"Sooner or later, they're bound to find out, honey. And then your whole family will know that we got this wonderful, delicious, amazing contraption all to ourselves, and they'll be chomping at the bit for a chance to join us in here." She let her head fall back into the water and sighed a happy smile. "Maybe we should buy that condo you mentioned. The one in Florida? Now *that* we would be able to keep a secret, for sure."

Charlene was probably right. A jacuzzi and a pool were hard to keep a secret in this town. But a condo in Florida? They could always say they were taking a vacation there. No need to tell anyone they had actually bought a place. That's what you got from getting married to the most wonderful woman on the face of the planet. It had made him feel twenty years younger, and bubbling with ideas and plans for them.

Just then his phone chimed and he lazily grabbed it from the table next to the jacuzzi. When he saw that it was Dolores, the station dispatcher, he sighed. "Yes, Dolores," he said, reluctantly picking up.

"You better get out of that jacuzzi, chief," said the woman, much to his chagrin.

"What jacuzzi?!" he said, scanning his surroundings and expecting to see the dispatcher's face pop out from behind a tree.

"Oh, don't be like that, boss," said the dispatcher. "The whole station knows about that jacuzzi you and the mayor put in her backyard. So when are you going to invite us? The boys at the station have drawn up a list and I'm at the top. So the moment you give us the go-ahead, I'm there with bells on!"

"Who told you?" he snapped.

"Nobody told me," said Dolores. "Randal saw you pick it up from Walmart two weeks ago and took a piccy. He posted it on the station WhatsApp and the rest, as they say, is history. So when are you going to start issuing invites, boss?"

"What WhatsApp!" he cried. "How come I'm not on it!"

"Oops," said Dolores, as if she had let him in on a big secret.

"Is that why you called me on a Saturday morning? To ask about my jacuzzi?" he said. "My *alleged* jacuzzi," he quickly corrected himself.

"Nothing alleged about it, boss," said Dolores. "I saw the picture myself, and it looks pretty great, I gotta say. Can't wait to drop by and have a nice soak in your sweet—"

"Dolores!" he bellowed.

"Okay, fine! There's been a murder. Guy by the name of Nathanial Tindell. Well-known billionaire, apparently. Though he wasn't found in his billionaire mansion but in some crappy apartment in the Rock Tower. Don't ask me why, but then I'm just a dispatcher who can't afford a snazzy jacuzzi and you're the big cheese who can!" And with these words, she hung up.

He stared dumbly at his phone. Had his own dispatcher just told him off? When he looked up, he found himself staring into the sparkling eyes of Charlene, brimming with merriment. "I told you," she said. "Once the secret is out, that's the end of our jacuzzi fun!"

"Darn it," he grumbled, and immediately dialed the

number for Chase. If his Saturday was going to be ruined, at least he could share the fun with his detective.

CHAPTER 7

Rita glanced left and right before crossing the street. Rose had been so kind to drop her off at home since her car was still at the garage and would take a couple of days to get fixed. And since Rita's mom didn't own a car, it was either a lift from her boss or public transport. Considering Patrick, she was glad Rose had found it in her heart to drive her home. Bus drivers might look askance at a passenger transporting a prickly pet, and so might the passengers, even though Patrick was the sweetest and cutest animal she had ever encountered.

"Thanks, honey," she said as Rose waved, pulling into traffic once more. She hurried across the busy street and trotted up to the building where she had lived all her life, as had Mom. It might be odd for outsiders that she would opt to live with her mom, but it was easier this way and definitely a lot more cost-effective. Mom worked as a cashier at their local supermarket, and since Rose had a heart of gold but not exactly a purse made of the precious metal, she couldn't afford to pay Rita a lot of money. She made up for it in the love she poured into her clinic, though, and the kindness she spread to both the pets in her care and the people who chose to work for her. It was, in other words, a labor of love, one that Rita knew she would never get rich from. But she didn't care. She'd rather do something she enjoyed and felt made a difference in the world than make a bundle working for a boss she hated and doing something she utterly disliked.

When she arrived at the front entrance to the building, she was surprised to see all the police cars parked there, their lights still flashing. A police officer was stationed at the entrance, and when she tried to gain access, he stopped her with an imperious gesture.

"But... I live here," she explained.

This seemed to mollify the officer, but he still wanted to see some ID to prove she actually did live there. When she showed him her driver's license and he had checked her name on his list of residents, he waved her through.

"What happened?" she asked.

"Please proceed, ma'am," he said, clearly one of those strong and silent types.

She wondered what could possibly have happened this time. It was a fact that the building her mom had once chosen as their living place was rife with all manner of minor crime and drug offenses, but it was rare that the police would descend on the neighborhood en masse like they had now. Possibly some drug dealer being arrested, she figured, and decided that it was absolutely none of her business.

She rode the elevator up to the sixth floor, and when she got out, she saw that the activity was centered on the apartment where their nice neighbor lived. Morgan Sears had moved in only five months ago but had quickly made himself indispensable in both Rita and her mother's lives by being the best neighbor they'd had in years. He'd put out the trash for them, would invite them over for dinner, and spend evenings playing board games with Rita's mother, something she loved, or watching television with them. In some ways, he had quickly become like a father figure to Rita, and she knew that her mom was very fond of the man. That was quite an achievement for a woman who was a self-professed critic of all men. And who could blame her, after Rita's father had walked out on her when she was pregnant with her daughter?

"What's going on?" she asked, approaching a police officer parked in front of the open door to Morgan's apartment. She tried to peer past the burly cop, but he quickly closed the door so she couldn't look inside.

"Do you know the person who lives here, Miss…" asked the cop.

"MacKereth," she said. "Rita MacKereth. Yes, I do know Morgan. He's my neighbor. Why, what happened?"

"Can you please wait here a moment, Miss MacKereth?" asked the cop, and without awaiting her response, retreated inside the apartment. Moments later, he returned with a fine-boned blond-haired woman in tow. She was a lot nicer than the cop and actually smiled at her. She held out her hand.

"Hi there, Miss MacKereth," she said. "Odelia Kingsley. I'm a civilian consultant associated with the Hampton Cove police department. Could I ask you a couple of questions?"

"What's going on?" she asked, really starting to get worried now. She had read Odelia Kingsley's articles in the paper and knew she mostly worked with her husband Chase, who was a homicide detective. She also knew she was related to Vesta Muffin, of animal shelter fame. "Is Morgan all right?"

"Let's find a place where we can talk," Mrs. Kingsley suggested and led her into the apartment and into the kitchen where Morgan had cooked for them many times. His specialty was creamy baked mac and cheese, but done in such a way that it made her mouth water.

She now noticed that two cats were seated underneath the kitchen table, looking up at her with a lot of interest. One was very large and red, the other small and fluffy, and she now remembered reading somewhere that the reporter never traveled anywhere without her cats.

"Please take a seat," said Mrs. Kingsley. An officer had made some tea and now poured Rita a cup, which she gratefully accepted. "I'm afraid I have some bad news for you, Rita —can I call you Rita?"

She nodded. "What news? It's Morgan, isn't it? Did something happen to him?"

Mrs. Kingsley put a hand on her arm and gave her a look of compassion. "Prepare yourself for a shock, Rita."

She swallowed and nodded. "Is he… dead?"

"I'm afraid so."

A sob escaped her lips. Odd that she had become so attached to a man she hadn't even known five months ago. "What happened? How did he die?"

"He was murdered," said Odelia, giving her arm a squeeze and studying her closely. "His body was discovered this morning by a homeless person wandering in with his dog."

"Oh, God," she said, and pressed her eyes closed.

"There appears to be some confusion, though. You knew him as Morgan Sears?"

She nodded. "That's right. Morgan. Why?"

The woman hesitated. "Let's get to that later. Did you know Morgan well?"

She nodded as tears sprang to her eyes. "He was our neighbor, though in recent months he had become a friend."

"Could you think of anyone who might have wished to do him harm, Rita?"

She shook her head. "I don't think he knew a lot of

people. He was a widower—his wife died a couple of years ago. And he'd hit on rough times. I don't think he had any other family or relatives—at least he never mentioned them to us."

"Us would be you and your mother?" asked Odelia. She had taken out a notepad and was jotting down a few notes.

"That's right. We live right across the hall." She shook her head. "I don't understand. Who would do such a thing? He was just the sweetest man possible."

She suddenly noticed that the two cats were peering intently at her bag, and now saw that Patrick's head was poking out of the bag. Odelia also seemed surprised. "Is that… a hedgehog?"

"Yes, his name is Patrick," she said. "I adopted him from the clinic where I work. He'll live with me and my mom and Shelley—that's my poodle."

"Don't mind the cats," said Odelia. "They're just curious. I don't think they've ever seen a hedgehog up close like this." She bent down to stroke the smallest cat's fur. "This is Patrick, Dooley. Wanna say hi?"

Dooley seemed reluctant to go anywhere near Patrick, which was understandable, as hedgehogs have been known to sting cats with their spines.

"You said he was found by a vagrant?" she asked, as she sniffled a little and wiped her eyes with the tissue that the police officer had kindly offered her, along with the cup of tea. "This wouldn't be Cesar, would it?"

"You know Cesar?" asked Odelia, sounding surprised.

"Yeah, I do. He's been a fixture in this neighborhood for years. Him and his dog Nicholas. In the winter months, the residents of the blocks sometimes put him up in one of the apartments when it gets too cold to be outside. Nicholas is our mascot." She managed a weak smile. "He and Shelley get along great."

"Looks like the killer left the door open," said Odelia, "and Nicholas followed his nose for a bite to eat and they hit upon the body of your neighbor."

"Did you talk to my mom yet?" asked Rita.

Odelia cast a glance at the officer, who shook her head.

"No, we haven't," said the reporter. "Do you think we could have a chat now?"

Rita nodded and got up. "It's going to be quite a shock to her. Morgan was probably the only man she liked. My dad left us before I was even born," she explained as she led Odelia out of Morgan's apartment and across the little hall to the one she shared with her mom. She let herself in with her key. "So she pretty much hates all men. Except Morgan, whom she adored." She raised her voice. "Mom, I'm home!" she yelled.

"In here!" Mom returned.

She led Odelia into the living room where they found Rita's mom on the sofa, channel-surfing with Shelley keeping her company. When Mom saw Odelia, she seemed surprised. "Oh, you're Rose, aren't you?"

"This isn't Rose, Mom," she said. "This is Odelia Kingsley. She's with the police." She took a deep breath. "Mom, something happened to Morgan."

"Morgan? What do you mean? We saw him last night."

"I'm afraid that Morgan has met with an accident, ma'am," said Odelia.

"An accident? You mean…"

Rita nodded. "Morgan is dead."

Just as she had expected, Mom uttered a startled cry and grasped her hands to her chest and violently yelled, "No!"

CHAPTER 8

"Max?"

"Yes, Dooley?"

"What is that… thing?"

"It's a hedgehog," I said.

"Are you sure? It looks like a rat with a pincushion stuck to its back."

"Oh, no, it's definitely a hedgehog," I said.

Odelia had brought us along to visit the crime scene of a man who had recently suffered a fatal accident—if being stabbed with a knife can be considered an accident, of course—and had expressed the fervent hope we would encounter a few pets along the way so we could make ourselves useful. She definitely had her wish, for we now were confronted with no less than two pets on the scene: the poodle that belonged to the victim's neighbor Rita MacKereth, and this hedgehog.

"Hey there," I said, trying to engage the creature in conversation. "Patrick, is it?"

The hedgehog merely stared at me, not exactly eager to be lured out of its bag.

"My name is Max," I said. "And this is my friend Dooley. We belong to that lady over there, whose name is Odelia. So you have been adopted, huh? That must be very exciting."

The hedgehog still kept to its vow of silence.

"I don't think it's a hedgehog," Dooley opined. "Hedgehogs are more talkative than this. Or maybe it is a hedgehog, but it has died. A dead hedgehog."

"I'm not dead," the hedgehog announced, coming out of its stupor.

"Oh, that's so good to know!" I said. Progress!

"It's just that I don't like cats," said the hedgehog, putting something of a damper on our conversation.

"Well, you don't have to like us to talk to us," I suggested.

"I don't like cats and I don't like to talk to cats," the hedgehog specified, making his position perfectly clear.

In despair, I turned to the poodle, who was also staring at the hedgehog, as if it was the weirdest thing it had ever seen, which was quite possibly the case.

"Hey there," I said by way of introduction. "So you're Shelley, are you?

Shelley looked up. "Huh?"

"So what can you tell us about your neighbor, Shelley?"

"Huh?" the poodle repeated.

"Your neighbor Morgan Sears," I repeated, hoping she wasn't going to state that she hated cats and hated to talk to them also.

"Oh, Morgan," said the little doggie. "Well, he's nice enough, I guess. Though I don't trust him."

"You don't trust Morgan?" I asked, much surprised by this. "But why?"

The poodle shrugged. "Call it a hunch? I don't like his smell. I smell him and I get this churning sensation in the pit of my stomach. It only happens when I'm with a person I don't trust, and so I don't trust him."

I shared a look of surprise with Dooley. "Ominous," said Dooley in a low whisper. "Since Morgan Sears did present himself to his neighbors with a fake story, Max."

"He most certainly did," I said.

"What's all that about a fake story?" asked Shelley, perking up considerably like only a poodle can. "What story? What's fake about it?"

"Well, turns out that your neighbor Morgan Sears wasn't Morgan Sears," I explained. "His real name was Nathanial Tindell, and far from being a poor widower, he was a wealthy divorcee."

"I don't get it," said Shelley, blinking a few times. "Can you run that by me again, please?"

"Morgan Sears's real name was Nathanial Tindell, and he was a billionaire many times over. So why he chose to pretend to be a poor widower and come and live here is a mystery."

"We were hoping that you might shed a light on that," Dooley added.

"He probably hated cats," said the hedgehog. "And so he tried to find a place where he could be free of them." He sighed as he settled down in his bag. "Only it turns out there is no such place. Cats are everywhere. No escape possible."

"I'm sure that Morgan Sears, or Nathanial Tindell as his real name turns out to be, didn't hate cats," I said.

"And how would you know that? The man is dead, so he couldn't possibly have told you," said the hedgehog.

"Because he owned several cats himself," I said. "And even though he didn't bring them along to live with him here at Rock Tower, it proves that he's a cat lover, not a cat hater."

Patrick chewed on this for a moment, then shot back, "Or maybe those cats aren't actually cats but dogs. Just like Morgan Sears wasn't Morgan Sears but Nathanial Tindell. Have you thought about that, cat?"

"I'm sure the police can make the distinction between a cat and a dog," I said.

"I wouldn't be too sure about that," said the hedgehog, who wasn't the most friendly creature I had ever met. But then not every pet can be a ray of sunshine. Some of them are downright annoying.

"Okay, so you're saying that Morgan wasn't poor?" asked Shelley, still trying to wrap her mind around these new and startling revelations we had brought to her attention.

"He was extremely rich," said Dooley. "Like, megabucks rich."

"I don't get it," said the poodle. "Why would he lie about that?"

"Like I said, because he hated cats," said the hedgehog, making no sense at all.

In the meantime, Odelia was interviewing Rita and her mother, whose name was Georgia, and both women seemed extremely surprised when she told them about their neighbor's true identity.

"Of course we didn't know that he was rich," said Georgia. She seemed extremely disappointed that their neighbor would have lied to them. "If we knew, do you really think we wouldn't tell you?"

"But why did he give us a false name?" asked Rita.

"Because he's a man, sweetie," said Georgia, "that's why. Men lie, and that's the long and the short of it."

"But he must have had a reason," Rita insisted. "He wouldn't just lie for the heck of it. Or to make fools of us, would he?"

"No, I'm sure he had a good reason," said Odelia. "Only we haven't discovered it yet. But you didn't know?"

"No, we didn't," said Rita as she handed her mother a pill. I wondered what this pill could be, and Rita must have realized for she said, "It's to calm her down. Mom easily gets upset, and it's bad for her heart."

"It's just herbs," her mom pointed out. "It's basically valerian and some other stuff. It's good against anxiety."

"I'm also going to take one," Rita announced. She looked extremely pale, I saw, which was understandable.

"So is that Patrick?" asked Georgia, taking a closer look at her daughter's bag and its prickly contents.

"Yes, this is Patrick," said Rita. She carefully opened the bag and lifted the hedgehog out, then placed him on the coffee table.

"Cute," said her mother in a raspy smoker's voice. I didn't really see the resemblance between mother and daughter. Rita was an attractive young woman with long blond hair and an amazing complexion, whereas her mother had leathery skin and looked about a hundred years old. When I noticed the pack of cigarettes on the coffee table, I wondered if all of that smoking may have hurt her skin as much as it had her voice.

"I work at the Rose Clinic," Rita explained for Odelia's benefit. "We take in animals that are sick and dying and try to ease their suffering in the final weeks and months when their owners aren't able or willing to. And Patrick here was brought in after he had been run over by a car. But fortunately, he recovered amazingly."

"And his owner didn't want him back?" asked Odelia as she ever so carefully caressed the hedgehog, which he seemed to enjoy very much, judging from the way he closed his eyes.

"No, we got the impression it had been an impulse buy for the kids, and after they got bored with him, they no longer wanted him. It happens," she said. She picked up the hedgehog from the table and held him in her lap. "But now he's got a new family and a new home, don't you, little buddy? And he knows he's going to be loved here and can stay forever."

"He's really cute," said Odelia with a smile.

"But he hates cats," Dooley added for good measure.

"Nobody's perfect," I told my friend.

Chase now walked in, to see if his wife needed any support, and when he saw the hedgehog, seemed touched by the display of affection Rita was showing the tiny animal.

"This is my husband Chase," said Odelia, making the introductions. "He's in charge of the investigation."

"Who did this, detective?" Georgia insisted. "Who murdered that poor man?"

"I'm afraid we don't know that yet, ma'am," said the detective. "But we'll do everything to find out."

"He may have lied to us, but he was a good person. And whatever his reasons were for giving us a false name, I still like to think he was a real friend to me and my daughter. I can spot a liar," she added vehemently. "And the friendship Morgan showed us was real. One hundred percent real!"

CHAPTER 9

Dooley hadn't really enjoyed his visit to the tawdry crime scene. The setting wasn't quite right. Billionaires should live in billionaire mansions, not some tatty apartment in the seedy part of town. And then there was that cat-hating hedgehog, who hadn't struck him as particularly helpful. Even the dog hadn't done anything to contribute to their inquiry. And so the sooner they were out of there, the better. All in all, it reminded him of the kind of crime shows on television that were mostly shot at night in dark alleys, with the kind of underworld characters that he didn't like, doing things that didn't bear thinking about. In other words: not a scene conducive to a positive mental attitude such as the one he liked to maintain.

The moment they were on the ground floor again, and roaming around the area to take in the view and possibly to encounter more pets that could be instrumental in helping them solve this murder, he told his friend what he thought of the experience and he didn't mince words when he did.

"I didn't like it up there, Max," he told the large blorange cat. "I didn't like it at all."

"Patrick?" asked Max, showing what a perspicacious cat he really was.

"Not just Patrick," said Dooley. "The whole scene. The people weren't very nice to us, and the atmosphere was stifling. All in all, I don't think I want to go back there, Max. Can we not go back there?" he implored.

"I'm sure that we've got everything we need, Dooley," said Max. "Though it's still possible that there will be a few things that Odelia needs to check."

"So we'll have to go back there?"

"It's possible," said Max. At least he was being honest about it, Dooley thought. Unlike that billionaire pretending to be poor.

"You know, I don't understand why a man who is richer than Jesus pretended to be poor, Max."

"I think the expression is richer than Croesus, Dooley," his friend corrected him. "But you're right. It is a mystery why he would want to willingly swap lives with a man living in such tawdry circumstances."

For that was another thing that Odelia and Chase's investigation had uncovered: there actually was a man named Morgan Sears, and he had rented that apartment, before the people working for Nathanial Tindell had approached him and offered him a nice cash settlement if he would sublet his apartment to the billionaire and sign an NDA in the process, making sure that everything remained a strict secret.

"So did this Morgan Sears move into Nathanial's mansion, Max?"

"I don't think so," said Max. "Looks like this was a one-way direction kind of thing only. With Nathanial moving into Morgan's apartment but not the other way around."

"So it wasn't like one of those reality shows where a rich family swaps lives with a poor family?"

"No, it was not," said Max with a smile.

They had reached a sort of playground that had seen better days, with a couple of kids playing on the swings, their parents looking on. They both glanced up at the building behind them, and Dooley wondered if nobody would have seen the murderer come and go. Then again, with a building that contained hundreds of apartments, one man or woman coming and going wouldn't attract attention. And since there were no cameras anywhere on the premises, it was going to prove hard going to find out who had killed that poor rich man.

"Maybe someone found out that Morgan Sears wasn't Morgan Sears but Nathanial Tindell," he suggested. "And decided to rob him."

"Nothing seemed to have been stolen," Max pointed out. "And also, to make his deception complete, Nathanial hadn't moved any of his valuables into the apartment."

That was true enough. The man's wardrobe had been decidedly sparse, and his cupboard strangely bare. Looking at things from the outside point of view, he certainly hadn't lived like a billionaire, definitely trying to keep up appearances.

"Let's go and talk to Nicholas," Max suggested, gesturing in the direction of a shabbily-dressed man seated on a bench and talking to a police officer. Underneath the bench, a raggedy sort of canine was seated, wagging his tail.

"I hope he doesn't hate cats, too," said Dooley.

But they shouldn't have worried about that. The moment they came within earshot of the doggie, he shouted his greeting. "Hey there, kitties! Over here!"

The moment they had joined him, he introduced himself with a hearty, "The name is Nicholas, and even though I'm not a saint, I still like to dole out surprises. So what can I gift you?"

"Um…"

The two cats shared a look of uncertainty, and Max said, "What do you have on offer, Nicholas?"

The doggie beamed. "I've got good wishes, good feelings, and good intentions. Which will it be?"

"I'll have the good wishes," said Max.

"And I'll have the good intentions," said Dooley, who liked this game.

"Okay, so good wishes for you," said the doggie. "I wish you good health and everything your little heart desires…"

"Max," said Max.

"And I'm Dooley," Dooley added.

"For you, Dooley," said the doggie, "I will express the good intention of giving you a hug." He proceeded to wrap his paws around Dooley and give him a tight squeeze. "How did that feel, buddy?"

"That felt good," Dooley admitted. "And just what I needed right now."

"I knew it! Nicholas always knows!"

"We met a hedgehog who professed to hate cats," Max explained. "And so Dooley isn't feeling very happy right now."

"I feel a lot happier already," said Dooley. "After that hug you gave me, Nicholas."

"There's more where that came from, little bud," said Nicholas, and proceeded to give him another big hug and even a smacking smooch on the ear!

The man seated on the bench reached down and gave his dog a pat on the head, and the dog seemed mighty pleased with this. "It's all about paying it forward, fellas," he explained. "My human shows affection to me, and I show affection to you, and in return I hope that you will show affection to a random stranger you meet on the street later on."

"We will," Dooley promised fervently. Except if that

PURRFECT JACUZZI

random stranger turned out to be a hedgehog. For some reason, he had become quite prejudiced against the species.

"The thing is, Nicholas," said Max, "that we're investigating the murder of that poor man up there."

"Oh, did that give me a fright!" said Nicholas. "The moment I smelled him, I told Cesar we had to call the cops."

"How did you happen to go up there in the first place?" Max wanted to know.

"A coincidence," said the doggie. "Oftentimes these apartments will organize an open house for the likes of me and Cesar, and so we like to take advantage of that fact."

"So you found the apartment door open and snuck in?"

"Well, not exactly," said the doggie. "The door was closed, but I had the impression that something was wrong. I could smell blood, you see. Human blood. So I barked up a storm and pawed that door until Cesar managed to gain access."

"And how did he do that?" I asked.

"Let's just say he has a knack for that sort of thing," Nicholas said, and gave them a big wink.

"What happened after you entered?"

His face morphed into a mournful expression. "Turns out I was right, Max. We found the dead man in the living room, lying in a pool of his own blood. Quite a shock it gave me."

"How did you know he was dead?" Max wanted to know.

"Oh, you know, experience will tell you that," said Nicholas. "You see, my previous owner passed away, and so I know when life is extinct."

"I'm so sorry to hear that, Nicholas," said Max, who always knew the right thing to say to anyone, whether man or pet.

"It's fine. I've got Cesar now, who's ten times the man that Bernard was—Bernard was my previous human, you see."

"Yes, I got that," said Max. "Did you happen to see the

person responsible for the death of Morgan Sears, Nicholas? Maybe he was still in the apartment?"

"Oh, no. The apartment was empty, apart from the dead man. If anyone had been there, I would have smelled them."

"Maybe you met someone on the stairs on your way up?"

The doggie thought for a moment, then shook his head. "I'm sorry. I didn't see anyone." He gave Max a curious look. "Are you sure that it was murder?"

"It was," Max confirmed. "Morgan Sears, or Nathanial Tindell as his real name turns out to be, was stabbed with a knife. And presumably not long before you and Cesar arrived. Which is why I was wondering if you had seen the killer."

The doggie shook his head. "Nope. Didn't see anyone."

Somehow, Dooley thought that Nicholas wasn't being entirely honest with them. But it's hard to make a dog talk when he doesn't want to, so they decided not to pressure Nicholas. Dooley glanced up at Cesar and wondered if he could have been responsible for the death of the billionaire. But he was sure that if he was, Max would figure it out. He always did.

Odelia's interview seemed to be going about as well as theirs with Nicholas, which was to say: not very well at all. And as Dooley glanced around, he happened to spot a kid sitting in an old car and directing a pair of binoculars at the apartment block. He nudged Max. "Look at that kid over there. What do you think he's doing?"

Max seemed appropriately concerned to alert Odelia, and moments later she was in communication with her husband, talking to him in low, urgent tones. It wasn't long before Dooley became aware of a small army of police officers approaching the vehicle with the kid, arms at the ready.

Oh, boy! Looks like Dooley had found the killer!

CHAPTER 10

Ken had been keeping tabs on Rita since he felt that somebody had to do it, so why not he? He had cared for the woman ever since she had joined the clinic, and had made working there an even better experience than it already was. And since he had gotten to know her better, it wasn't too much to say that he had fallen deeply, irrevocably in love with her and would pretty much give his eye teeth for her. Which is why he was so concerned when that man had dropped by that morning, wanting to see her.

He immediately saw the man for what he was: a serious threat to the love of his life, and possibly to the clinic as well. For hadn't he been wearing a leather jacket? And leather shoes? Clearly an animal hater, and men like that should be punished, not encouraged. And so he had decided to keep a close eye on Rita—even closer than he usually did—by following her around and pretty much acting as her personal bodyguard from that point. Too bad he couldn't look inside her apartment and be there for her when she needed him. But unfortunately their relationship hadn't yet extended beyond the professional level and veered into the deeply personal.

One day she would be his, he knew that. But as long as that day hadn't arrived yet, at least he could keep her safe from harm as much as he could. Even if it took all of his free time, of which luckily he had a lot, since he didn't really have any friends and his family didn't much care what he was up to when he wasn't home. His mom certainly was happy that he didn't get in her way, and his dad had never failed to make it perfectly clear how much of a disappointment this youngest son was to him, with his animal-loving nonsense that he got up to instead of learning an actual profession and getting an actual job that he could make some serious money with.

He aimed his binoculars at the sixth floor, where he knew that Rita and her mom lived, and was in luck: the woman he loved was just passing in front of the window, and was soon joined by her mom, the two women talking animatedly, no doubt discussing what they would have for dinner that night or something of equal importance to them. As he lowered his binoculars for a moment, he saw two cats fixedly staring at him. He had noticed them before: two cats, accompanying a beggar on a bench and a pretty young woman talking to the beggar. He wondered what they were up to, but since he didn't think they posed a threat to Rita, he didn't really care. And neither did he care that the place was buzzing with the boys and girls in blue, no doubt on some kind of drug bust.

Once he was older and Rita saw him for the man that he was, or would be by then, and they were going steady, he would get her and her mother away from here. He and Rita would buy a house, and he would adopt that rug rat of hers and add a couple of their own. And Rita's mom could live with them if she liked—or they could set her up in her own little apartment, conveniently located right around the corner. He didn't know how he was going to accomplish that, since he was still in school, but he was determined to get there. And since his dad was a bank manager, he could give them a loan at favorable conditions once he saw that his son had brought home an amazing girlfriend like Rita. It would definitely make the old man look at him in a different light, he knew.

And he was just about to put those binoculars to his eyes again when all of a sudden a large, solid object blocked out the sun. When he looked closer, he saw that it was a big, burly police officer. He was armed to the teeth and was screaming something at him. The moment he had rolled down the window, he understood that it was a statement along the lines of, 'Get out of the car with your hands up!'

And since he didn't feel like getting shot, he did exactly that.

* * *

Dooley and I watched on from behind the one-way mirror as Chase and Odelia interviewed their first suspect in the Nathanial Tindell murder. The young man they had in the hot seat was sweating bullets, and looking extremely miserable.

"Do you think he's the one, Max?" asked Dooley.

"I don't know, buddy," I said. "But if he is, he's certainly not going to hold out long before he confesses. Just look at his leg."

Dooley studied the legs of the young man under the table, and we could both see they were shaking violently, so much so that the entire table was rattling and moving about. Finally, Chase had to put his hands on the table to keep it stable.

"So tell us, Ken," said the detective. "What were you doing staking out Rita MacKereth's apartment?"

"I wasn't—"

Chase lifted one eyebrow, and the kid broke.

"Okay, so I was totally staking out Rita's apartment, you are absolutely right!" he wailed as he buried his face in his hands. "I know I shouldn't have done it. Oh, am I going to jail now for stalking? Did she file a complaint against me?"

"No one has filed any complaint against you, Ken," Odelia was quick to reassure him. "But we are wondering what you were doing there."

The kid looked up with a tear-streaked face. "I love her, Sergeant," he said.

"Detective," Chase corrected him.

"I love that girl so much! And I want to keep her safe—especially after that weirdo came looking for her this morning, and that creepy boyfriend of hers has been threatening her. Now that Rita is pregnant, she needs all the support and protection she can get. And did you see the apartment she lives in—drug dealers all over the place! You must know, since you were there for a drug bust this morning."

"You thought we were there for a drug bust?" asked Odelia.

"Well, weren't you?" he asked, wiping his tears. She handed him a tissue from the dispenser, which is a fixture in the police interview rooms, and he loudly blew his nose.

"Just tell us in your own words why you were stalking Rita," said Chase.

He wiped at his eyes with his sleeve. "Like I said, I want to make sure those men don't hurt her. I love Rita, Lieutenant."

"Detective," said Chase through gritted teeth. Like any cop, he likes to be addressed with the correct rank.

"I love her so much. She's the most wonderful, sensitive,

beautiful woman in the whole world, and I want to marry her."

"Is Rita aware of your... affection?" asked Odelia, who couldn't suppress a smile, I now saw.

"I'm not sure," said the kid, shaking his head violently. "But if she is, she hides it really well. I wrote her a letter once, but I didn't send it. And I also wrote her an email once, but I deleted it before I could send it. So I don't think she knows."

"What was that you said about a weirdo coming in to see her this morning?" asked Chase.

"It was a man dressed in a leather jacket and wearing leather shoes," said the kid, nodding to himself. "*And* he brought flowers. So you can clearly see he was bad news."

"Name?" asked the detective as he held his pen poised over his notebook.

"Um... Samuel... Dickenson? I think? He said something about Rita bumping into him that morning and how he wanted to arrange everything without involving the insurance. Something about a premium. Though anyone could see that was just a feeble excuse to get close to her."

"And what did Rita say?"

"Oh, she wasn't there."

"When was this?" asked Chase.

"Um... eleven-thirty? Something like that?"

"And what's all this about Rita's boyfriend threatening her, and her being pregnant?"

"Rita wanted to marry that man, can you believe it, and all he can do is storm into the office and shout at her. She doesn't think me and Rose know, but of course we do, and we're both rooting for her that she finally dumps that loser and moves on. But Rose says it's complicated, since he's her baby daddy, and you don't just dump your baby daddy. Though if it was up to me I would do more than dump him.

I'd make sure he never comes near her again. A restraining order maybe."

"Name?" asked Chase curtly.

"Um… Harvey something. Furniss, I think."

"And he was also in the office this morning?"

"Yeah, he came storming in and screaming something about her being involved in an accident." He straightened. "If my girlfriend was pregnant and got involved in an accident I'd be worried sick about her, but this guy started hurling all kinds of accusations at her." He shook his head. "A sick man."

"Where were you at eleven this morning, Ken?" asked Odelia. She had folded her hands on the table in front of her and spoke in gentle tones.

"Well, at the clinic, of course," said Ken, as if it was the most natural thing in the world. "I was feeding the animals, like I always do around that time."

"And Rita was in her office?"

"She was. Only she left around eleven-twenty, to run an errand. I think she said something about picking up some food for dinner tonight. She was back twenty minutes later, which is when that madman of a boyfriend of hers came storming in and making such a big fuss. Even Rose said it was too much, and if he did that again she was going to make sure he never set foot inside the clinic ever again. Which is totally what she should do." He was tapping the table with a nervous finger. "That man is dangerous, Inspector!"

"Detective," Chase said intently. "So is this the reason you decided you needed to become Rita's personal bodyguard?"

"Absolutely!" said the kid. "Someone has to do it, and since nobody else is going to volunteer for the job, it might as well be me." But then he directed a pleading look at the cop. "Please don't tell her? She might take it the wrong way."

"And what way would that be?" asked Odelia.

"She might think I'm a weirdo?"
This time even Chase had to smile.

CHAPTER 11

A meeting had been arranged and was taking place in Uncle Alec's office. In spite of the fact that it was a Saturday and Uncle Alec hadn't wanted to come in at first, the death of one of Hampton Cove's most prominent—and rich—citizens had prompted him to drop whatever he was doing and join us for this urgent meeting.

I saw that his hair—whatever there was left of it—was wet and wondered if he had been taking a bath when he decided to come in for this meeting. He certainly looked as if he had been enjoying a leisurely time, not dressed in his uniform as usual but in a flowery Hawaiian-motif shirt. If I didn't know any better, I would have thought he had flown in straight from Hawaii.

"So what do we have?" he asked.

"Well, the victim is one Nathanial Tindell, sir," said Chase as he placed a picture of the dead man on the chief's desk.

"Hampton Cove's richest man," said the chief unhappily. "You can count on it that there's going to be a lot of attention on this investigation. A lot of scrutiny."

"Apparently, Mr. Tindell made his fortune creating and

selling drones," said Chase. "He runs a company called Iron Eagle and supplies drones to the Department of Defense."

"So can anyone tell me what the richest man in Hampton Cove was doing living under an assumed name in one of the crappiest apartments in town?"

"I talked to Iron Eagle's spokesperson," said Chase. "And she claims that about six months ago Nathanial called a board meeting and announced that he was stepping down as CEO and president, much to everyone's astonishment, as he had been known in the business as the hardest working company executive. He was also the company founder. But all of a sudden he didn't seem as interested in the success of Iron Eagle as he had been. He'd just signed the biggest deal of his career with the Department of Defense, and so the board was quite put out that he wouldn't personally want to see the execution of the deal through, as he had always done."

"We're going over there later today to talk to the CEO," Odelia clarified.

"And what about this kid Ken Torres?" asked the chief.

"He's professed to have an abiding affection for Nathanial's neighbor Rita MacKereth," said Chase. "And has appointed himself her personal bodyguard. He seems totally obsessed with the woman, boss, and so it's not inconceivable that he would see Nathanial as a threat and decided to launch a preemptive strike to take him out of the running."

"You think Nathanial Tindell had a crush on this girl?"

"It's certainly possible," said the detective. "He wouldn't be the first man who falls head over heels in love with a girl and decides to throw everything he's achieved in the toilet for a chance to be close to her."

"So that's the assumption you're working from, is it? That the richest man in town had fallen in love with this girl who works at a pet clinic and decided to rent an apartment next to her so he could be closer to her?"

"It's one theory, sir," said the detective. "Honestly, I don't see why else he would do such a thing."

"She's attractive, is she, this Rita MacKereth?"

"Um..." Chase glanced at his wife, and the latter smiled.

"I think there's no doubt that Rita is a stunningly attractive young lady, uncle," she said, sparing her husband the embarrassment of having to spell it out. "And if she managed to inspire Ken to go all out and turn personal vigilante for her, I can imagine she would have had a similar effect on Nathanial Tindell."

"But why move in next door? Why change his name and pretend to be poor? I don't get it."

"Maybe he wanted to see if she would like him for who he was?" Odelia ventured. "Not for the fact that he was rich?"

"There's also the fact that Rita's mother hates all men."

"She hates all men?"

"That's correct, boss. She was dumped by Rita's dad when she was pregnant with the girl and became a self-professed man-hater ever since. The only man she liked was Nathanial, so maybe the guy had done his research and knew that Rita's mom wouldn't accept him if he approached the girl as himself, but stood more of a chance if he gradually worked his way into their graces."

"He cooked for them, ran errands for them, and generally acted like the perfect neighbor," said Odelia.

"Okay, but that still doesn't explain how they met."

"We think that he must have paid a visit to the clinic and saw Rita there," said Chase.

"And fell head over heels in love," said Odelia.

"So what about this bum?" said Uncle Alec, consulting the preliminary report Chase had delivered to him. "Um... Cesar Tinker, is it?"

"That's right," said Chase. "He's the one who found the body, along with his dog, um..."

"Nicholas," Odelia said. "The odd thing is that Nicholas lied to Max."

"The dog lied to Max?" said Uncle Alec, giving me a scrutinizing look that I didn't like one bit, as if I was personally to blame for being lied to!

"Max thinks the dog was hiding something," said Chase.

"He does, does he?" said the chief, his stare intensifying and making me feel entirely ill at ease.

"He thinks that there's more to this story of Cesar being in that apartment than he says there is. He claims he was looking for stuff people had dropped so he could return it for a small reward, and that when his dog started barking up a storm, he decided to check the apartment since the door was open. And that's when he came upon the body of the victim."

"But why would this Cesar kill Tindell?"

"Possibly the door wasn't open, and Cesar is simply a common thief who saw an opportunity?" Chase suggested.

"We think that Nicholas is Cesar's monkey," said Odelia.

"His monkey?"

"It's a common theme with certain burglars that they employ an animal, typically a monkey, who does the scouting for them. Then when the coast is clear, the thief himself follows and robs the place. Nicholas must have thought the place was empty, only for Cesar to discover that it wasn't. There was a confrontation and Cesar stabbed Tindell."

Uncle Alec rolled his eyes. "If you can't even trust the statement of a dog…"

I got the impression he was being ironic, though I could be wrong. It's hard to know sometimes with Uncle Alec. And definitely now when he wasn't in the best mood, courtesy of Odelia and Chase dragging him into the office on a Saturday.

"You think the dog lied to us, Max?" asked Dooley.

"Yes, I do," I confirmed.

"So he could be an accessory to murder?"

"He could very well be."

It wouldn't be the first time that a dog covered his human's tracks by lying.

"Okay, so as I see it we've got two solid suspects," said the chief. "This Ken Torres kid, because he was in love with Rita and saw Tindell as a love rival. And Cesar Tinker, a burglar caught by the man he was trying to steal from."

"Also Harvey Furniss," Chase added. "Rita's boyfriend. He sounds like the explosive type, according to Ken. So if he figured that Tindell was putting the moves on his girlfriend, he might have decided to do something about it."

"And there's also this mystery man who brought flowers for Rita," Odelia reminded her husband. "Samuel Dickinson."

Uncle Alec slapped the table lightly. "Excellent work, team. Talk to these people, find me the evidence that will seal this case right up, and let's close the investigation quick as we can, before it's all over the papers and this place turns into a circus."

Odelia and Chase shared a look.

"There is something else, boss," said Chase when the chief got up and made to leave and enjoy the rest of what was left of his Saturday.

"What is it?"

"Well, there seems to be some confusion over your jacuzzi," said Chase. "And some talk amongst the men."

The chief froze in situ. "My jacuzzi? What jacuzzi would that be?"

"Oh, come on, boss," said Chase. "We all know that you bought yourself and Charlene a brand-new jacuzzi."

"No, I didn't."

"The pictures of you hauling that contraption out of Walmart and putting it in your truck are all over the WhatsApp group."

"Photoshop," said the chief staunchly. "I do not now and have never owned a jacuzzi. Is that clear?" And he gave his underlings a look of such vehemence that they flinched.

"Yes, boss," Chase murmured.

"Yes, uncle," Odelia muttered.

"Good," said the chief. "And you would do well to remember that, and to spread the news in your WhatsApp group. Of which, through some mysterious oversight, I am not a member." And after raking them some more with fiery eyes, he left the office, slamming the door as he did.

"He didn't look happy, did he, Max?" said Dooley.

"No, he certainly did not, Dooley."

"Is it the jacuzzi, Max?"

"Yeah, looks like he doesn't want to share, buddy."

"I don't mind," said Dooley as we followed our humans out of the office. "I don't like to get wet."

"Neither do I. But that can't be said about them," I said, referring to Chase and Odelia, who were discussing Uncle Alec's vehement denial in what they called 'jacuzzigate.'

CHAPTER 12

Uncle Alec stalked through the office like a bull in a china shop. It wasn't too much to say he was seething. What business was it of his officers whether he had purchased a jacuzzi or not? And who in his right mind would think it was permitted to spy on his superior officer and post pictures of him in his private time shopping and lugging a jacuzzi into his car? He had a good mind to find the culprit and drag him before a court martial. But since this wasn't the military and he wasn't a general, he figured he probably wouldn't be allowed to do that. What he could do was haul that man or woman into his office and read them the riot act.

And so he stomped up to Dolores's desk and stood before the woman, wide-legged, his face spelling storm, and his fists thrust into his sides.

"Well," he said.

"Well what?" riposted the dispatcher.

"Who is the person who took a picture of me shopping?"

"How should I know?" said Dolores, giving him a curious look. Almost mocking, he thought, the way she was smiling.

"I want you to give me the name of that officer!" he

PURRFECT JACUZZI

bellowed, making it perfectly clear that a line had been crossed that shouldn't have been crossed in the first place.

"And I'm telling you I don't know!" she said, rising from behind her desk and taking a stance.

He should have known that he was about to face some stiff resistance. And so he decided to try a different tack.

"How can I get into this group?" he asked, holding up his phone.

"So you can hunt down the person and fire them?" she challenged.

"Of course not! I just don't think it's right for the chief of police to be excluded from the official Hampton Cove PD WhatsApp group."

"Oh, so it's the *official* Hampton Cove PD WhatsApp group you want? I can make you a member right now, boss."

And it was with a lifting of the spirits that he saw how she grabbed her own phone and started messing around with it, tapping here and there and everywhere.

"There," she said finally. "That should do it."

He studied his phone and saw that he had indeed received an invitation to join the group. Well pleased, he accepted the invitation and started walking away when he saw that there were only three members of this particular group.

"Dolores?" he said, frowning. "How come I'm the only member of this group, along with two former police chiefs?"

"Because this is the official Hampton Cove PD WhatsApp group, boss," she said sweetly. "It's the one you wanted."

He had to suppress a sudden urge to drag her from behind that desk, grab her by the neck and squeeze—hard. "I want to be in the *real* HCPD group! The one with all the others!"

"Oh, but why didn't you say so?" she said, and did some more tapping on her screen. Moments later he received another invitation. He clicked and saw that it was indeed a bigger group, but when he looked closer, he also saw that all of the officers were retired.

"This isn't the right group!" he railed. "Again!"

"This is the HCPD group," she assured him.

"But… these people are all retired! Or dead!"

She shrugged. "These are the only two groups I know, boss. Was there anything else? 'Cause some of us have to work on a Saturday, you know."

He balled his fist and waved it in the air for a moment, but since he knew there wasn't anything he could do, apart from grabbing Dolores's phone and finding that group himself, he decided to walk away before he committed grievous bodily harm on the woman.

"Have fun!" she yelled after him. "In your jacuzzi," she added quietly.

He turned back, but when he saw she was innocently talking on the phone, he slammed through the door. He was being trolled by his own people and there was nothing he could do about it!

When he got to his truck, he saw that a poster had been attached to the rear window. As he stared at it, he saw that it was a picture of himself hoisting the jacuzzi into his truck with the assistance of several members of the Walmart staff. He glanced back at the station house and saw that a sizable contingent of his officers were standing at the windows looking at him. So he pulled the picture from the car, balled it up, and threw it on the ground. Then, thinking better of it, and figuring they might be filming him and would be posting a video of the chief of police littering, he picked it up again, held it up in plain view, and got into his truck and drove off.

And all over a silly jacuzzi, he thought. And wondered how he was going to explain to Charlene that their secret was out and would soon be all over town.

PURRFECT JACUZZI

A call came in, and when he saw that it was his brother-in-law, he quickly tapped the button to answer the call.

"Tex!" he said. "What can I do for you, buddy?"

"Rumor has it that you have bought yourself a jacuzzi, Alec," said the doctor, not wasting time getting down to business. He sounded aggrieved, Alec thought. "And rumor also has it that it's supposed to be this big secret."

"I do not and have never owned a jacuzzi," he said, deciding he should be staunch and consistent in his denial.

"So why is there a video of you hoisting a jacuzzi into your car all over the internet?" Tex wanted to know.

He started. "What do you mean?"

"It's all over Facebook. A video of you putting a jacuzzi into your truck and driving off. Looks like a giant one, too."

"Photoshop," he said, though he realized that he was starting to sound pretty ridiculous by now.

"It's a video, Alec!"

"Well, you know they can do anything with the software they've got these days," he tried.

There was silence on the other end of the call, and for a moment he thought Marge's husband had hung up on him.

"Tex, are you still there?" he asked for good measure.

"I'm still here," said Tex finally. "And I want you to know I'm disappointed in you, Alec. I'm not angry, but I'm very, very disappointed. And so is your sister, by the way."

"You shouldn't be disappointed, since I don't have a jacuzzi! This is all some stupid rumor that someone created."

"The video looks pretty real to me."

"It's a fake, all right! Just a stupid fake!"

"All right, if you say so," said Tex, but he could tell that his words hadn't convinced the doctor. "Oh, Marge wants me to tell you that she's coming over later tonight. She's arranged to drop off some books that Charlene asked her to get."

And with these words, he finally hung up.

Alec pounded his steering wheel. "No!" he cried.

CHAPTER 13

"We need sounds, snow pea," said Harriet as she pricked up her ears and raked the backyard with eyes that missed nothing. "Lots and lots of sounds."

"So what sounds would those be, smoochie poo?" asked Brutus. He felt they probably should have heeded Odelia's call when she announced that there had been a murder, but then Harriet had claimed that they had more important things to do, so they had elected to stay put and address these more important things—whatever they could be.

"Sounds that will make you feel relaxed," she clarified. "Like people snoring. Those kind of sounds."

Brutus couldn't imagine what was so appealing about humans snoring, but then he often had to admit that ever since he had moved from the big city of New York to Hampton Cove, he had felt out of his depth. They did things differently here in the Hamptons, that much was true. "So we need people snoring?" he asked as he tried to keep up with his girlfriend as she traipsed from one backyard to the next.

"Not snoring, necessarily," she said. "We need a whole

range of sounds. Like…" Suddenly she halted and stood stiff as a board. And it wasn't hard to understand why: in front of them, a man was peeing on a rose bush. And if he wasn't mistaken, and he didn't think he was, that man was none other than their neighbor Ted Trapper.

"What is he doing?" he asked quietly.

"He's peeing," said Harriet.

"Yes, I can see that. But why?"

"Looks like he's moved on from peeing on his lawn to peeing on his rose bushes," said Harriet. "Humans are weird."

It was certainly a truth firmly established by now that the human race was one of those species that did things a certain way—and their motivations were often hard to fathom.

Ted had a sort of blissful look on his face, and seemed to be enjoying himself tremendously. From time to time he would glance in the direction of the house, then back at the work in progress, which seemed to be progressing to his satisfaction.

Rufus had told them Ted thought peeing on the lawn made the grass grow faster, but Brutus had his doubts. A lot of them.

"I've heard of people peeing on a wound when they've been stung by a jellyfish," said Harriet. "Dooley told me all about that. He'd seen it on the Discovery Channel."

"But he's not peeing on his foot, is he?" said Brutus. "And as far as I know there are no jellyfish here."

"No, I guess not," said Harriet. Then her face brightened. "Snuggle bunny, this is exactly what we need!"

"Ted peeing?"

"Exactly! The sound of a person peeing is very relaxing. Like water babbling in a brook. We need to record this ASAP!" And so she took the contraption she had been lugging around with her from her back and placed it against a nearby tree. It was Gran's smartphone and Harriet had managed to sneak it from the kitchen counter when the old lady wasn't looking, figuring they needed it more than her.

"Okay, hit record," she murmured, and pressed the appropriate button. Moments later, the device was recording their neighbor relieving himself all over his rose bushes. But if the sight and sound were supposed to have a relaxation effect, Brutus wasn't feeling it. Then again, he wasn't human, so maybe it took a human to enjoy another human peeing? Just like Harriet seemed to enjoy the sound of Dooley snoring?

These were very deep waters to plumb, the black cat felt, and so he settled down behind that tree and thought hard.

* * *

Vesta wondered where she could have possibly left her phone. Maybe she should finally get around to installing one of those whatchamacallits. Those apps that tracked your phone. Though Odelia had shown her several times already how to install it on her phone, she still hadn't gotten around to activating it. And now that she needed it, she regretted not having heeded her granddaughter's advice.

She had already searched her room, behind the cushions on the living room couch, underneath the kitchen counter, and even inside the microwave. She was, after all, a certain age, as her son-in-law never failed to point out, and her memory was sometimes not as sharp and reliable as it used to be. But try as she might, the last time she remembered having her phone was when she had looked up where to buy a jacuzzi.

Ever since she had overheard Tex and Chase discussing the topic and announcing they planned to buy one, she had been fascinated with the subject. She could just imagine herself soaking in that hot tub—she and her friend Scarlett.

"Where did I leave that darn thing!" she grumbled as she checked the fridge for good measure.

"What are you doing?" asked Marge.

"Trying to find my phone," she said.

"Have you looked outside? You were on the terrace just now, weren't you?"

"I was measuring," she said.

"Measuring? Measuring what?"

"Well, where we can put that jacuzzi that Tex and Chase are thinking about buying."

Marge stared at her. "Chase and Tex are buying a jacuzzi?"

"Sure. Didn't they tell you?" Technically they hadn't told her either, but then she never bothered with such minor details. "I was thinking we could put it right next to the garden house. That way Ted and Marcie won't be able to look in on us when we're having our soak, Scarlett and me."

"Oh, so Scarlett also knows about this, does she?"

"Or we could put it in the middle," said Vesta as she tried to picture the thing in her mind. "Surrounded by a fence. Though that would probably end up being an eyesore."

"They could have told me," said Marge, as usual only interested in her own line of thought. "Does Odelia know?"

"Hm? No, I think she went out on a case with Chase. Something about a murder. Well, you know the drill. These murderers never do have any respect for a person's weekend."

"I can't believe they wouldn't have told me," said Marge, getting worked up. "It's the same thing as Alec's jacuzzi all over again. Did you know that he bought himself and Charlene a jacuzzi and then didn't tell anyone about it? Worse, he's staunchly refusing to admit that he bought it, even though there's photo *and* video evidence."

"Yeah, I saw it," said Vesta. "Which is why it's such a great idea to get one of our own. I mean, who wants to schlep across town to go and have a soak in Alec's jacuzzi? We are still a democracy, last time I checked."

"What's that got to do with anything?"

"Everyone gets their own jacuzzi, Marge! I get one, you get one, everybody gets one—not just madam mayor."

Just then Harriet and Brutus walked in, and much to her surprise, she saw that Harriet was clasping her phone between her teeth!

"So *you* took my phone!" she cried.

"You have to check this, Gran," said Brutus.

Harriet dropped her phone on the floor in front of Vesta. "We shot some footage of Ted Trapper peeing on his bush."

Vesta shared a look of consternation with her daughter. "Ted Trapper is peeing on his bush?" asked Vesta.

"Now why would he go and do a thing like that?" asked Marge, still quietly fuming about the whole jacuzzi business.

Vesta picked up her phone from the floor and checked the video that Harriet and Brutus had shot. It was as they had said: Ted Trapper, peeing on a rose bush.

"At least he's not peeing on his own bush," she said, trying to make light of the situation.

But Marge didn't think this was funny. "The man has gone completely off his rocker," she said sternly. "Doesn't he realize there could be children watching?"

"What children? He's in his own backyard, minding his own business," said Vesta, who thought that her daughter had a prudish streak from time to time that she didn't like to see.

"Grace could be watching!" Marge cried, and flapped her arms up and down for good measure.

"Grace has the good sense to stay far away from Ted Trapper and his strange habits," she said with a frown as she studied the ecstatic look on their neighbor's face. "And besides, maybe he has his reasons."

And so she vowed to ask him all about it. Her rain dance hadn't worked, so maybe this was another way to deal with this terrible drought they were going through.

Inquiring minds wanted to know.

CHAPTER 14

I probably should have been surprised that we even had the possibility to interview the CEO of Nathanial Tindell's drone company, but then I guess CEOs of big companies work seven days a week, and possibly even spend their nights negotiating deals and making sure their investors and shareholders are satisfied with their profit numbers.

Jason Bourne, the man who had been appointed CEO of Iron Eagle, was a slender man and something of a fitness fanatic if his first words to Chase were any indication.

"Kingsley!" he cried as he slapped the detective on the back. "My gym buddy!"

Chase grinned widely. "When you told me you ran a small business, I didn't realize it was the largest drone business in the state, buddy."

"Oh, we're just one of many," said the man modestly. "So I'm guessing you're not here to discuss next week's gym schedule, huh?"

"No, I'm afraid I have to be the bearer of bad news, Jason.

Your boss—Nathanial Tindell—was found dead this morning."

The news hit the man hard, for he stumbled back and collapsed in his chair, rolling a few feet until he hit the wall behind his desk. He looked stunned. "No way."

"I'm afraid so."

"How…" He swallowed as he looked at Chase with wide-eyed astonishment. "How did he die?"

"Foul play, looks like," said Chase carefully.

"Foul play! You mean… murder?"

Chase nodded. "Stabbed with a knife in the apartment that he was renting in the Rock Tower."

"Were you aware that your former boss had moved into that apartment, Jason?" asked Odelia.

Jason shook his head. "The Rock Tower, you say?"

"That's right."

"No, he never mentioned anything about it."

"The story we heard was that he gave up his job here at the company to go and live under an assumed name," said Chase.

"That's news to me, detective. Though I have to say when he announced he was stepping down as CEO and president, we all figured there had to be a reason. Speculation was rife that it was health-related."

"When did he step down?"

"About six months ago? Something like that? Nate used to live for this company, and then all of a sudden he seemed to have lost interest. As if he didn't care what happened to Iron Eagle anymore, and that as far as he was concerned, we could take it in any direction we liked. Got us all worried, I don't mind telling you. Which is why we all figured maybe he had contracted a disease and wanted to take it easy for a while."

"What did you do before you were appointed CEO?" asked Odelia.

PURRFECT JACUZZI

"I was vice president in charge of the research and development department," said Jason as he got up from his chair. His tanned face displayed the shock he had just endured, and it was obvious that he harbored a lot of respect for his predecessor, who had also been founder and president.

"So Nathanial never told you the exact reason he quit?" asked Chase.

Jason shook his head. "We didn't have that kind of relationship. And since he was the founder, CEO *and* president, he didn't owe us any explanation."

"But surely the board must have asked him what he was up to. Iron Eagle is listed on the stock exchange, isn't it?"

"It is," Jason confirmed as he raked his hand through his prickly mane. "But that doesn't mean that the shareholders have a right to know what goes on in the CEO's personal life. If Nate wanted to take a leave of absence for personal reasons, he didn't have to disclose what those reasons were. All he had to do was make sure that he left the company in good hands, and credit to him, that's exactly what he did. And also, he's still the president—or was," he amended.

"Can you think of anyone who might have wished him harm?" asked Chase, slipping into his role of detective with practiced ease. "A business rival maybe?"

Jason thought for a moment. "We have our competitors, of course, but no one in their right mind would go around murdering the president of a competing company. The business world is a cutthroat world, as everyone knows, but nobody has ever taken that literally. We compete in the marketplace by trying to get the best deals and put out the best products, but stabbings and killings? Nah. That's taking things to the extreme, and I don't see any of our competitors capable of such a thing. Besides, like I said, Nate left the company in good hands, so even with him gone, it's not going to make any difference to Iron Eagle's day-to-day operation."

Chase nodded. "Outside of the business world, did Nathanial have any enemies that you know of?"

He smiled a tight smile. "Like I said, we didn't have that kind of a relationship. We were colleagues, but we didn't socialize. Nate was a very private person, and I didn't even know what kind of hobbies he had."

"What's going to happen to his shares now?" asked Odelia. "They must be worth a lot of money, right?"

"Oh, absolutely," said Jason, happy that the conversation had landed on a topic he was familiar with. "Nate still owned a majority stake in the company, and at the current market price, those shares are worth about ten billion."

Both Chase and Odelia goggled at the man. "Ten billion!"

Jason grinned. "We might be small, but we are successful."

"I'll say," said Chase as he gave the other man a look of admiration.

"Ten billion is a lot of money," said Odelia, and that was quite the understatement. "Any idea who'll inherit?"

Jason shook his head. "No idea, I'm sorry. But I'm sure Nate will have made a will. That man left nothing to chance."

"Who would be familiar with the particulars of that will?" asked Chase.

"Talk to Nathanial's personal assistant. Bella Fuller. She's about the only person in this entire company that Nate trusted with his personal affairs. She pretty much ran his life, personal and business both."

Chase gratefully jotted down Miss Fuller's particulars and thanked his gym buddy profusely. As we rode the elevator down, Dooley asked, "Is ten billion a lot of money, Max?"

"It's a pretty outrageous sum, Dooley," I said.

"So why did a man who was as rich as that live in a shabby apartment and pretend to be poor?"

"Now that," I said, "is the million-dollar question, buddy."
"Or the ten-billion-dollar question," he said.

CHAPTER 15

Rita was worried about her mother. She had made the woman a pot of jasmine tea, which usually helped calm her nerves, but she had a feeling that mere tea or the valerian pills she had given her wouldn't be enough this time. The news that Morgan had lied to them and wasn't the person he claimed to be had hit both women hard. Frankly, Rita couldn't understand what the man had wished to accomplish with his elaborate ruse. She returned to the living room with the pot of tea on a tray and poured her mother a cup. She could see that the woman was still stunned by the stunning revelations. First the murder and then the truth about who the man was.

Rita had quickly googled the name Nathanial Tindell and had been surprised to find he was indeed their neighbor Morgan, only in the pictures she had found, accompanying an article in *Forbes Magazine*, he had looked every inch the successful and flashy businessman, whereas they had known him as a more humble and down-to-earth person. She wondered who of these two the real Nathanial Tindell was. She had a feeling it might be the flashy businessman, with the Porsches and the fancy mansion and the superyacht that he used every summer to travel to the South of France to party with the rich and famous in Saint-Tropez.

She placed a hand on her mother's arm. "How are you feeling?"

"Rotten," her mother confessed. "I just wish that man had never entered our lives. What was he thinking?"

"What did he want?" she said, asking the question that the police hadn't been able to answer, much to her astonishment.

"He can't have been interested in us for our money," said her mom. "That's for sure."

"But then what?" asked Rita.

Her mother gave her a sad look. "The only thing I can think is that he wanted you, sweetie."

"Me! But the man was old enough to be my dad!"

"That has never stopped a man before," she said. "And you know it."

"I very much doubt it, Mom," she said. She had never once sensed that kind of vibe from Morgan. Never once had he looked at her the way men often did. The way Harvey had when they first met, for instance, or even Ken, in all his youthful innocence when she caught him gawking.

"It's the only explanation," said her mom. She shrugged. "Maybe he'll have left you something in his will, if life is fair."

She laughed. "And I very much doubt that!" she said, and took a sip of that same tea herself. It wasn't just her mother who had sustained a nasty blow from the news that their neighbor had been murdered but she as well.

"I think we'd better add a few bolts to that old door of ours," said her mom, proving that she was thinking along the same lines as her daughter. "Make sure that freak doesn't murder us in our beds tonight."

"Now why would anyone want to murder us?"

"Why did they murder Morgan—unless they knew he wasn't Morgan, of course, but that billionaire fellow."

"The police will figure it out," she said, professing a faith in the police that her mother didn't share.

"Maybe we should move," Mom suggested. "Far away from here." She gestured around to their cozy little apartment, a safe haven in a pretty dilapidated apartment block nevertheless filled with a lot of similar cozy apartments. Even though from the outside it didn't look like much, a lot of people had done their utmost to turn their own apartments into pleasant nooks filled with love and warmth, as had they.

"We can't afford to move, Mom," she reminded her mother gently. "And besides, I like it here. It's home to me."

"I know it is, sweetie," said her mother, placing a hand on her cheek. "And I'm very sorry about that. I just wish I had been able to give you more, you know."

She saw that her mother had tears in her eyes now, and it broke her heart.

"You gave me everything I needed, Mom," she assured her mother. "And more. Much more."

"If you say so," said her mother, not convinced.

She gave the older woman a hug. Her mother would never understand that material possessions were no supplement to the love she had given her. The care she had showed all her life was more important than anything money could buy. Maybe that's what Morgan had been looking for: something he hadn't found in his own world, which consisted of the trappings of material wealth. Mansions and yachts and parties with the rich and famous. And still he had moved into the Rock Tower looking for something. Looking for love?

But then she discarded the notion. Of course he hadn't been looking for love. But maybe he had been looking for something to fill a void in his life. Something to give it meaning. Then again, maybe they would never know what had driven the man to adopt a false name and become their neighbor. Maybe Morgan had taken his secret to the grave.

"I'll miss him, you know," she told her mom. "I liked Morgan."

"Me too," said Mom. "He was a good man. Even though maybe it was all a lie, deep down I think his intentions were good. You can't fake a thing like that."

Shelley barked once and settled next to them on the couch. On the floor, Patrick had been moving around, inspecting his new home. She picked the hedgehog up and placed him on her lap.

"So what do you think about our new pet?"

Mom gave him a curious look. "He seems nice. Are you sure they'll let us keep him?"

"Oh, absolutely. I squared it with Rose. Nobody else wants him, and he seems to want us, so…"

It was Patrick who had picked them and not the other way around. The moment the little guy had been placed on her desk, he hadn't wanted to leave, and had made quite a nuisance of himself when she had placed him in his cage. And since she had never owned a hedgehog before, she figured that she might as well take a chance on the little guy. She just hoped that he and Shelley would play nice.

She placed the hedgehog next to her poodle and the two sniffed at each other for a moment, then settled in, amiably sharing the space on the couch.

She smiled. "Looks like they're friends already."

"I hope so. I don't want to have to run to the vet with Shelley after she gets her nose stung."

"That won't happen," she assured her mom. And if it did, she could always take Shelley to the clinic vet. Rose had arranged special rates for staff and friends of the clinic. Which was the only reason she had been able to afford to have Shelley. Otherwise keeping a pet was expensive. Another benefit of working at the pet clinic.

Her phone chimed and she saw that the same person she had bumped into that morning had sent her a message.

'I missed you at the clinic.'

She frowned.

"Who's that?" asked her mom.

"The guy whose car I hit this morning. He came to see me at the clinic but I was out."

"What does he want?"

"Beats me. Rose said he showed up with a bouquet of roses, so your guess is as good as mine."

"Maybe he wants to apologize for bumping into you?"

"I bumped into him, and he wasn't happy about it."

Her mom smiled and tickled her cheek. "Looks like you've got yourself another admirer, honey."

"I just hope he won't make a nuisance of himself," she said. That was the last thing she needed: another man in her life making things hard for her.

"How are things with Harvey?" asked her mom, deciding to broach their favorite topic.

Her lips tightened. "I thought we discussed this."

"I know, I know," said her mom. "The H-word should never be spoken again under this roof. So the wedding is off?"

She nodded. "He dropped by the clinic this morning, ranting and raving because of that fender bender."

"Better cut your losses," her mother advised. "That man has a few screws loose if he thinks he can treat you like that."

She felt her chest constrict all over again when she thought back to the terrible moment in her office. "He practically told me that he doesn't want the baby," she confessed.

"He did what?!" her mom cried, turning to face her. "But honey, that man is a demon!"

"Yeah, he's not on my list of favorite people right now," she admitted.

"Drop him," her mom advised. "Drop that man like a stone! And if you don't have the guts to tell him it's over, I will!"

She smiled. "You never did like him, did you?"

"I had a hunch that he was bad news," her mom confirmed. "And I was right, wasn't I?"

She put her head on her mom's shoulder and sighed. "Why are you so smart, Mom?"

"Because life gave me so many kicks I learned to kick back."

"Maybe I should start kicking back some."

Shelley crawled onto her lap, and so did Patrick. She might not have a lot of luck with men, but at least she had plenty of good fortune when it came to pets.

CHAPTER 16

We met up with Harvey Furniss, Rita's boyfriend, at the garden center where he worked. To say that he wasn't pleased to see us would be an understatement. Dressed in coveralls and rubber boots, he was transferring about a ton of manure from a pickup truck to a bay on the lot, where customers could pick it up and take it home, to fertilize their gardens.

"It stinks, Max," said Dooley, wrinkling up his nose.

And that, it most certainly did, especially for a pair of cats like us, whose noses are more sensitive than our human counterparts' appendages.

Odelia and Chase didn't seem to mind, and Odelia even remarked to Chase, as we walked up to the man, how she loved the smell of fresh manure in the morning. "It has something… comforting and cozy, don't you think?"

Dooley and I shared a look of consternation. "Comforting and cozy!" my friend mouthed, and I shook my head in dismay. But then what can you expect from a species that urinates on its own lawn to make it grow faster?

"Mr. Furniss?" asked Chase, holding up his badge. "Detective Chase Kingsley, Hampton Cove PD. May we have a moment of your time, sir?"

The man gave us a dirty look. "Does it have to be now?" he grumbled, standing there with a pitchfork in his hands. I took a few steps back, just to make sure he wouldn't run us through with that thing. Unhappy garden center workers and pitchforks are never a good combination.

"Yes, it has to be now," said Chase, who can be firm and implacable when he needs to be.

"It's just that this is my busiest time," he said, and gestured to a small group of customers waiting to fill up their carts with manure.

"They can wait," said Chase, and held up a picture of the dead man. "Do you recognize this person, Mr. Furniss?"

Furniss, leaning on his pitchfork, which was something I liked to see, since he couldn't use it if he was leaning on it, studied the picture for a moment, then shook his head. "Can't say that I do. Who is he?"

"His name is Nathanial Tindell," said Chase. "But you probably know him as Rita MacKereth's neighbor Morgan Sears."

A look of recognition spread across the man's face. He pointed at the picture. "That's right. Now I recognize him. Morgan Sears. Moved in a couple of months ago?" Then his face clouded. "Tried to hit on my girl, if memory serves."

"Did he now?"

Furniss nodded. "I once told him in no uncertain terms that I was keeping an eye on him. But he assured me that he had absolutely no intention of going after Rita."

"So you had an altercation with Mr. Tindell?" asked Chase.

"I wouldn't call it an altercation. Simply a straightforward no-nonsense conversation. From man to man, you know. Making sure there were no misunderstandings."

"So you told him to back off, and he said he would? Is that how you would describe this conversation?"

"That's exactly how I would describe it," he said, jutting out his chin like a battering ram. "But what's it to you?"

"Unfortunately, Mr. Tindell was found murdered this morning. Stabbed to death."

"Can you tell us where you were this morning around eleven, Mr. Furniss?" asked Odelia, not missing a beat.

The man seemed taken aback by this sudden shift in the conversation. "Why? What does this have to do with me?"

"As you just indicated, you and Mr. Tindell had an altercation," said Chase.

"So that makes me a suspect, does it?"

"Just answer the question, Mr. Tindell. Where were you this morning?"

"I was right here!"

"According to Miss MacKereth, you paid her a visit at the pet clinic where she works," Odelia pointed out. "So at least during that time, you weren't here."

"Okay, so maybe I passed by the clinic on my way over here. But that was way before eleven, I can assure you. By the time that guy was killed, I was hard at work—and if you don't believe me, you can ask my manager. He'll tell you."

"Don't worry, we will," said Chase dryly. "Why did you pay a visit to Miss MacKereth, may I ask?"

"None of your business," said the man gruffly.

I saw he was fiddling with that pitchfork again, and I didn't like to see it. So Dooley and I took another couple of steps back, making sure that when he started stabbing at us, we would be out of range of that dangerous instrument.

"This is a murder investigation, Mr. Furniss," said Chase. "So everything is my business. Let's try this again. Why did you pay a visit to Rita MacKereth this morning?"

The man shot a dirty look at the cop but finally relented.

"My insurance broker called me. Said she had been involved in an accident, so I wanted to make sure she was okay."

"That's not the story that we heard," said Chase. "According to our information, you stormed into Miss MacKereth's office and started screaming at her about the accident and generally behaving like a bully." His expression darkened. "I don't like bullies, Mr. Furniss. Never have—never will."

"I don't like bullies either," Odelia indicated.

"Okay, fine. So maybe I flew off the handle a little. But wouldn't you do the same when you have just arranged a brand-new car for your girlfriend and a couple of weeks in she's already totaling it? I'm not made of money, you know."

"We also have it on good authority that you don't approve of the fact that she is pregnant?" asked Odelia, not hiding her lack of sympathy for a man who would behave like that.

He shrugged. "What's it to you?"

"Like I said, this is a murder investi—"

"This got nothing to do with the dead guy!" the man screamed. "Nothing at all, is that clear!"

"It paints a picture," Chase clarified.

"What picture? What are you talking about?"

"The picture of a man who can't control his temper, who is extremely jealous, who gets into fights with complete strangers because he suspects them of hitting on his girlfriend. A man, in other words," Chase explained, "who would stab that man if he suspected him of having an affair with her."

The man offered the detective a vicious grin. "Prove it!" he spat, and with these words, picked up the pitchfork and stuck it into the pile of manure with such vehemence both Dooley and I reeled a little.

I could see that Chase's hands were itching to wrap a nice pair of shiny handcuffs on this suspect, but Odelia held him back. Even though Mr. Furniss was the perfect suspect for the murder of Nathanial Tindell, he also had an alibi. And unless his manager couldn't confirm that he had been present at the garden center at the time of the murder, he was innocent.

And so the couple went in search of Harvey Furniss's manager while Dooley and I decided to return to the car. A garden center teeming with people on a Saturday afternoon is the perfect place to get trampled underfoot, and the last thing we needed was for some amateur gardeners to stomp all over us with their soil-enriched boots!

As we took up position near the car, Dooley gave me a nudge. "Look there, Max," he said.

I looked there and saw that Uncle Alec had shown up, accompanied by Charlene Butterwick. The couple both entered the garden center, and I wondered what they had come there to buy. But then I saw that the garden center had an entire range of jacuzzis on display in the outdoor section of the store, and wondered if they were going to buy themselves another secret jacuzzi. Though what anyone would do with two jacuzzis is beyond me. But when I offered this question to Dooley, he had a simple answer.

"They're two people, Max, so obviously they need two jacuzzis. Just like they need two toothbrushes and two bottles of shampoo."

"There's a big difference between a toothbrush and a jacuzzi, Dooley," I said. "For one thing, the price. Jacuzzis are expensive."

"Oh, but I'm sure that the mayor and the chief of police can afford two jacuzzis," he assured me. "They're probably paid very well. Especially since Charlene is technically Alec's boss, so she decides how much he gets paid."

It was a matter I hadn't yet looked into, but he was right. Technically, the mayor appoints the chief of police, or at least in Hampton Cove she did. And so she possibly had a say in his salary as well. "But… isn't that a conflict of interest?"

"I don't think so, Max," he said. "They're married, you see. So there can't be a conflict of interest. Married couples aren't allowed to have a conflict of interest. They're always united."

I smiled. "I hadn't looked at it like that, but you're probably right."

"Of course I'm right! When Father Reilly asked Uncle Alec if he was interested in taking Charlene as his lawfully wedded wife, and he said why not, that was the end of any conflicts of interest. Their interests are always aligned now."

It certainly was a novel way of looking at things, I had to say. Also, there are probably laws in place that decide how much a chief of police is paid, whether Charlene likes it or not.

The couple now exited the garden house with a salesman in tow, and just as I had suspected they started looking at one of the jacuzzis on display. It was a very large model, and they seemed extremely interested.

"Maybe they're simply trading up," I said, and decided that the matter didn't warrant any interest. After all, Uncle Alec and Charlene are grownups, and what they wanted to do with their money was their own business. So if they wanted to start collecting jacuzzis, that was entirely up to them.

Chase and Odelia came walking out of the store, and the oddest thing happened: the moment Uncle Alec and Charlene spotted them, they quickly hid behind the jacuzzi, making sure they kept well out of sight.

"They're behaving very strangely," I said.

"Maybe they don't want anyone to know they're buying another jacuzzi?" said Dooley.

"It certainly looks that way," I said.

But then Uncle Alec suddenly spotted us, and as our eyes

met, I could tell that he wasn't happy about us being there. I could even see him utter a few choice curse words to Charlene. The mayor also looked over, and when she saw that Dooley and I were intently looking at them, her face turned grim. I'm not a lip reader, per se, but even to an amateur like me, it was clear what she said to Uncle Alec: "We're busted!"

CHAPTER 17

We met up with Samuel Dickenson, the man who had dropped by Rita's office carrying a bouquet of roses, in his shop on Main Street. The shop was called The Honey Comb, and Samuel turned out to be one of Wilbur Vickery's colleagues and fellow Main Street shopkeepers. In particular, the man sold honey and honey-related products. As Dooley and I stepped into the store, in our humans' wake, I marveled at the number of products one could use honey for. There were cookies, candy, beer, yoghurt, crackers, cereal, but also candles, teas, and even wax figurines you could use for decoration purposes. All in all, it turned out that those busy bees were at the heart of a very diversified product portfolio.

"I didn't even know there were so many different kinds of honey, Max," said Dooley as we found ourselves in front of a rack filled with dozens of different types of honey.

"It all seems to depend on the types of flowers the bees frequent," I explained.

"Oh, but I know all about that!" Dooley assured me, and I shouldn't have been surprised, since he's been a loyal viewer of the Discovery Channel for years. "Though I don't see what's all that special about honey, Max."

"No, me neither," I said. "It has this weird texture."

"Our humans seem to like it," he said.

We both looked at Chase and Odelia, who were being given a tour of the store by Samuel himself, who seemed extremely excited about this visit from the constabulary, contrary to our previous visit where we had faced death by pitchfork. Also, honey smells a lot nicer than manure.

"And here we have our honey pralines," he said, holding up a box of the stuff and offering Odelia one.

"Mm, they're delicious," she said.

The man beamed. "I know, right? They're probably our most popular product, though the candles are also big sellers."

"So what can you tell us about this man, Mr. Dickenson?" asked Chase, and held up his phone. He may have enjoyed touring the store, but now it was back to business.

Mr. Dickenson studied the picture on Chase's phone for a moment, then shook his head. "I don't think I've had the pleasure. Is he a customer?"

"No, he's Rita MacKereth's neighbor," Chase clarified, and when the name didn't immediately ring a bell, he added, "The woman who bumped into your car at the supermarket this morning?"

The man's face broke into a big smile. "Oh, Miss MacKereth, of course! Such a lovely young lady. I went to her apartment earlier, but unfortunately, I didn't find her on the premises."

"You also paid a visit to the Rose Clinic, didn't you?" asked Odelia.

"I did. I wanted to suggest we don't involve the insurance, as it would only lead to them upping her premium. I checked the damage to my car again, and it's not a big deal.

So I figured we could come to some kind of an arrangement."

"That's very considerate of you. Is that why you added the twelve long-stemmed red roses?"

The man blushed. "I hear news travels fast." Then he seemed to realize something. "Is that what you wanted to talk to me about? The accident from this morning? Because I can assure you that Miss MacKereth and myself have agreed to arrange everything between ourselves."

"This is not about the accident," Chase said tersely. "This is about the death of this man." He held up his phone again.

"Oh, Miss MacKereth's neighbor died? That's such a shame."

"What time did you drop by the apartment this morning?" asked Odelia.

"Um… I guess around eleven? Something like that?"

"Did you enter the apartment?" asked Chase, towering over the man and giving him the benefit of one of his glowering looks.

The bee salesman shrunk a little and stammered, "A-a-as a matter of fact, I didn't. I rang the bell and when no one answered I put a message in the mailbox and left."

"Are you sure you didn't enter the building? According to our information, the door doesn't function as it should. One good push and it's open."

"I didn't try," he said. "I mean, I didn't push."

"The thing I don't understand," said Chase thoughtfully, "is why a man whose car was damaged by someone would suddenly decide to buy her a bunch of roses and show up at her doorstep and at her office."

"Well…"

"You have to admit that's not typical behavior, Mr. Dickenson."

"No, I guess it isn't. It's just that… I wasn't very nice to

Miss MacKereth this morning, after she hit my car. In fact, I was downright unfriendly to her. And so I wanted to apologize for my behavior by offering her flowers."

Chase fixed the man with a look. "Are you in love with Rita MacKereth, Mr. Dickenson?"

"I-I-I'm not sure what you mean," said the man. But when Chase's look didn't waver, he relented. "The thought may have crossed my mind that she's a very nice-looking young lady, yes. Though I wouldn't say that I'm in love with her, necessarily. Though I had thought that maybe I could ask her out. Get to know her a little better, you know. And apologize in person for my appalling behavior this morning."

"Mm," said Chase, not convinced.

"Had you met Miss MacKereth before?" asked Odelia.

The man switched his attention from Chase to Odelia. "Um… No. No, I hadn't." He didn't sound very convincing, I thought, and I got the impression that Chase felt he was lying.

"So you hadn't met her at the clinic at some point and decided to pursue her?" he asked.

"No!" said the man. "God, no, of course not. I met her for the first time this morning, when she hit my car in the supermarket parking lot, I swear."

"Do you always buy flowers for the people who hit your car?"

He seemed already to regret having offered Odelia those pralines, for he now took the box away from her and tucked it back into its proper place on the shelf. "Look, I don't know what's going on here. Did Miss MacKereth file a complaint against me with the police? Because I can assure you that she hit me, and not the other way around. And we both filled out those insurance papers and she signed them."

"This isn't about that," said Chase.

"Then what is it about?" he asked, and pushed his glasses further up his nose as he gave the cop a nervous look.

"This is about the murder of Rita MacKereth's neighbor," Odelia explained. "He was murdered around eleven o'clock this morning, and as we have established, you were there at that time, eager to renew Miss MacKereth's acquaintance."

"You *are* in love with her, aren't you?" asked Chase, stabbing the man's chest with an implacable index finger. "And you *had* met her before at the clinic. So when you discovered that you weren't the only one vying for her affections, you decided to get rid of the competition!"

"No!" cried the man. "Absolutely not! Whoever killed that man, it wasn't me! You have to believe me! I didn't do it!"

"If I had a nickel for every person who has ever said that," Dooley murmured, "I would be as rich as Nathanial Tindell."

CHAPTER 18

In the end, Chase decided not to place Samuel Dickenson under arrest. I guess he felt that the evidence they had against the man was too thin. Though before we left The Honey Comb, he pointed to the man and uttered the fateful words, "I'll be back."

The man nodded, but the moment we had left the store, he locked the door and turned over the Closed sign. I guess he wasn't in the mood to sell any more honey products that day.

"Maybe you shouldn't have been so hard on the guy," said Odelia as we walked back to the car.

"I think he did it," said Chase. "I don't know why, but I can smell it."

"I think it's the honey that you smelled." She popped another one of the pralines that Samuel had offered her before their good cop/bad cop routine had commenced into her mouth. "He may be a killer, but he definitely sells some pretty tasty stuff. I'll have to tell Mom. She loves honey."

"Better tell her to hurry up. The moment he's under arrest and goes down for murder, that shop will be closed."

"Too bad," Odelia said, earning herself a critical look from her husband.

The moment we were back in the car, Dooley and I felt it was time to fill them in on the sighting we'd had of Uncle Alec and Charlene at the garden center. Odelia didn't seem surprised.

"Sometimes it's like that," she explained. "You buy one jacuzzi, and the habit forms, and the next thing you know, you can't stop buying more and more until you realize you're addicted."

I smiled. "Very funny, Odelia."

"No, but I'm not even kidding. I mean, why else would they buy a second jacuzzi?"

"Your uncle is buying a second jacuzzi?" asked Chase.

"The cats saw him and Charlene at the garden center. They were checking out the jacuzzis. And when they realized they'd been seen, Charlene said, 'We're busted.'"

Chase grinned. "Looks like your uncle is into jacuzzis big time these days."

"Yeah, and the worst thing is that he's lying about it, and I cannot understand why. What's so shameful about owning up to the fact that you like jacuzzis?"

"I guess they don't want us to join them in their jacuzzi? That's the only thing I can think of."

"But why? We've been inviting Uncle Alec over for dinner for years now. So the least he can do is to return the favor and invite us over so we can check out his jacuzzi."

"He doesn't want us to check out his jacuzzi, babe."

Odelia settled down in her seat while her husband drove us out of town. "It's not fair," she lamented. "Especially to Mom."

"Life isn't fair." He checked his GPS and soon was en route to the house where Nathanial Tindell used to live before he decided that a life of abject poverty in a rundown apartment at the Rock Tower was better suited to a billionaire like him.

A call came in, and Odelia picked up. Moments later, she was chewing the fat with her mother, the way she often did.

"Yeah, they saw him. At the garden center. Checking out the jacuzzis. And when they saw the cats, Charlene said, 'We're busted.' Can you believe it?"

Chase glanced and shared a glance with us in the rearview mirror, and I rolled my eyes. I guess one gets used to these long conversations, and so did Chase. But I had a feeling he would much rather have discussed the case instead of his boss's jacuzzi addiction.

It wasn't long before we arrived at our destination, and I have to say that if I had been in Nathanial's shoes, I wouldn't have moved out of my old house. The mansion we saw before us was pretty spectacular. Even Odelia paused chatting with her mother for a moment to check it out. "Jeez," she said.

"You can say that again," Chase agreed. And then he was driving up the long drive that led to the house. Nathanial may have moved out, but apparently his personal assistant had decided not to share her boss's new lodgings. And I couldn't blame her.

Chase parked in front of the house, which looked more like a small castle, minus the turrets and battlements, and we walked up to the front door. Our arrival had been announced, for even before we got there, the door swung open and a middle-aged lady appeared, clasping her hands together, then ushering us in, but not before darting a curious look down at Dooley and me.

"I didn't know you were going to bring your cats," she announced. "We also have cats, you know."

"Yes, Nathanial's neighbor told us about that."

I had wondered if that would have been another one of

Nathanial's lies, but apparently that part of his story was true.

And since we didn't want to miss making these cats' acquaintance, we eagerly followed Nathanial's PA into the drawing room, where she bade us to take a seat—or at least Odelia and Chase. The two of us could remain seated on the carpet, which was of the high-pile and comfortable variety. I had to resist the urge to dig my claws in and really go to town on that thing. But since I'm a well-bred cat, I have a firm policy never to destroy other people's carpets and so has Dooley.

"So what can I help you with, detectives?" asked the woman. She sat primly on one couch while our humans sat on the other. Then she seemed to realize something, and brought a distraught hand to her face. "Oh, my God. Where are my manners? Can I offer you anything? Tea, coffee, refreshments?"

"Coffee is fine," said Chase, who's a real coffee nut.

"Same for me, thanks," said Odelia, who shares this affliction with her husband.

"And a donut, right?" said the PA as she gave Chase a smile. "I know what you cops are like. Or is that just in the movies?"

"No, I like donuts," said Chase.

"I won't be a minute," said the woman, and briskly walked off. We hadn't been alone for ten seconds before the first cat stalked in, tail up and looking down her nose at the two of us.

"Will you look at that?" she said. "Two intruders."

"I see them," said a second cat as she followed in after the first one, "and I don't like them."

I could tell that both of them were purebred Siamese cats, and they looked absolutely gorgeous, albeit a little scary—or a lot!

"Dooley, get behind me," I said quietly.

I had noticed the look of menace in both cats' eyes.

"But why, Max?" said my friend. "They look nice."

"Just do as I tell you," I urged.

And so, despite his misgivings, he got behind me. If these cats attacked, the least I could do was to shield my friend and bear the brunt of the attack. At least until this lady returned and made sure her boss's cats didn't rip us all to shreds.

"I don't like tabbies," said the first one as she directed a scathing look at me. "Especially fat tabbies."

"Fat *red* tabbies," the second cat specified.

"They are the absolute worst," said her friend.

Dooley stuck his head from behind my broad back. "Excuse me," he said. "Max isn't red. He's blorange."

This made the two cats burst into a bout of sniggers. "Blorange!" said the first one. "I've never heard of anything so ridiculous!"

"Well, it's true," said Dooley. "Max's color is blorange. A mix of blond and orange. And he's not fat—he's big-boned!"

More hilarity ensued, and for a moment both cats rolled on the floor laughing. Then they straightened and approached us in a menacing fashion. "As I said, we don't like intruders here," said the first one as she held up a paw and unsheathed a set of very sharp-looking claws. "So if I were you, I'd get out of here while you still can."

"Run, kitties," urged the second one. "Run for your lives!"

"Look, we're here to investigate the murder of your human," I explained. "So I'm afraid we're not going anywhere."

They needed a moment to digest this, but finally one of the twosome said, in a vicious sort of undertone, "You're lying, tabby. Our human wasn't murdered, surely!"

"Of course not," said her friend. "Our human is the richest

man on the planet. You can't *murder* a person like that. He's got security."

"Plenty of security."

"Bodyguards up the wazoo."

"More bodyguards than the president of the United States."

"He wasn't living with his bodyguards," I said.

"He had decided to renounce his wealth and live a life of poverty," Dooley explained. "Under a different name in a different part of town."

The two cats shared a look, then laughed, once again rolling on the floor as they did, a habit that I found extremely disconcerting. Especially since they stopped as quickly as they had begun and approached us in a menacing fashion.

"I believe Red Fatty likes to tell jokes," said the first one.

"But they're not very funny, his jokes," said her friend.

"Not funny at all. Now why would our human suddenly decide to desert his beloved home—his beloved cats—his beloved life—to move across town and live in poverty?"

"It makes no sense."

"No sense at all."

"He was in here all the time."

"But he wasn't sleeping here every night, was he?" I said.

The Siamese gave me a dirty look. "That doesn't prove a thing and you know it!"

"Nathanial has many houses—many properties."

"And he's a busy man—juggling many balls."

"That may very well be, but the fact of the matter is that he was murdered, and that he had been living under an assumed name."

"Nonsense!"

"Poppycock!"

"You're a filthy liar, Red Fatty!"

Just then, the PA returned, carrying a tray with cups and

saucers and a pot of steaming hot coffee. There was also a selection of cookies, I saw, and… kibble. Cat kibble!

When she saw that Dooley and I were hiding under the sofa at this point, with the two Siamese dangerously close to attacking us, she barked, "Mia! Tia! Get away from there at once!"

And much to our surprise, both cats immediately came to heel! It was the strangest thing. One moment they had looked as if they were about to rip us to shreds, and the next they were sitting next to Bella on the couch, sweet as can be. At least we could re-emerge from our hiding place and not be afraid for our lives.

"That was close, Max," said Dooley, who understood that Mia and Tia weren't the sweet kitties he had taken them for.

"You can say that again," I said, as we both directed a look of admiration and extreme gratitude at Bella Fuller.

"I think I've just fallen in love," Dooley confessed.

"Me too!" I exclaimed.

And so we decided to stay very close to this woman!

CHAPTER 19

"Of course I knew why Nate wanted to move into that apartment," said Bella in answer to Chase's question. "He felt that he had achieved all he had set out to achieve and that he had reached a sort of ceiling in his professional life that he couldn't possibly top, and he wanted to make some changes."

"But why renounce all of this?" asked Odelia, gesturing to the surrounding visitor's room, which was as opulent as I imagined the rest of the house to be. "And that," she added in reference to Mia and Tia.

Bella smiled. "Look, the thing you have to understand about Nate is that he had started in business at a very young age. At fourteen, he was already building his inventions in the backyard of his parental home. He launched his first company at sixteen, and by the time he was nineteen, he was a multi-millionaire several times over. I guess you could say that he had done it all, seen it all, and felt bored by the whole thing. In other words, in spite of all of his achievements, the one thing that eluded him was to feel truly happy."

"So he decided that moving into a rundown apartment

would help him find that?" asked Chase, not hiding his incredulity.

"It may seem strange to you, but it was his way of trying to find meaning in life, beyond the material. And since he figured he could never do it while staying tethered to his old life, his old identity, he wanted to go all the way and adopt an entirely new persona. Though I have to say he still dropped by the mansion from time to time to touch base. Iron Eagle was his baby and he couldn't let go completely. But yes, he spent most of his time at the Rock Tower as Morgan Sears."

"And you helped him with that?"

"I did, yes. I rented the apartment for him, helped him change his appearance to some extent, and also made sure that none of his old circle of friends and associates knew."

"What about family?" asked Odelia.

"They were in the dark as well."

"So you were the only person Nathanial told about this?"

"That's right. He felt it was the only way to make sure that this experiment of his stood a chance of success."

"Who selected the Rock Tower?" asked Chase.

"Well, he did, actually."

"Why this particular apartment in this particular building?"

"No reason," said Bella with a slight shrug. "He wanted to live the kind of life most people live. And so he felt the Rock Tower gave him the best chance at accomplishing that."

"So he didn't pick the apartment so he could be closer to Rita MacKereth and her mom—his next-door neighbors?"

"Absolutely not," said the woman with a smile.

"Is it possible that he paid a visit to the clinic where Rita MacKereth worked?" asked Odelia. "And that he fell in love with the girl then, which is why he decided that moving next door to her was an opportunity to get to know her better without having to reveal to her who he really was?"

"Without all of that money and wealth coming between them," Chase added. "To make sure that Rita fell in love with him because of who he was, not because of his money."

Bella displayed a wry smile. "This is all mere conjecture on your part, I hope? I mean, you can't really believe this nonsense? As far as I can tell, Nate never paid a visit to the clinic where Miss MacKereth works. And I should know, since our security team did a full background check on the MacKereths before Nate moved in next door to them. As I said, the decision to rent this particular apartment was made because he wanted to experience what it felt like to live a regular life. The rest is speculation."

"Mh," said Chase, though I could tell he wasn't buying it.

"Look," said the personal assistant. "I've known Nate Tindell for thirty years, and in all that time, he's never had any secrets from me. So if he moved to that apartment because he fell in love with Rita MacKereth, he would have told me."

"Okay, fine," said Chase, reluctantly dropping his promising theory. "Can you think of anyone who would have known about Nathanial moving out there, apart from you?"

"No one," said the woman with absolute conviction. "He made sure that everything remained a secret. He felt it was vital to the success of his experiment, as he called it."

"So you were the only one who knew that Nathanial Tindell, one of the richest men in the country, was living under an assumed name?"

"That's correct, detective."

"And nobody could have found out?"

"Well... there is always a small chance that someone found out, of course. Best-laid plans and all that. But they sure didn't find out from me or Nate. He was determined to succeed."

"There must have been some kind of paper trail," said Chase musingly.

"I tried to be as discreet as I could," said the woman with a touch of defensiveness. Obviously, she was a person who took great pride in her work. "So I don't see how anyone could have known."

"What about the background checks on the MacKereths? The security people you mentioned?"

"They were told that the MacKereths had posted certain derogatory things about Iron Eagle on social media."

"A cover story."

"That's right. Nate wanted to leave nothing to chance."

"Okay, so let's assume for a moment someone did find out somehow," said Chase. "Is there anyone you can think of who would have wished to do harm to your boss, Miss Fuller?"

She thought for a moment as she casually caressed the Siamese cats' necks, to which they responded by closing their eyes and purring contentedly. "Well, there is the competition, of course," she said reluctantly.

"The competition?" asked Odelia.

"These government contracts are worth billions," she explained. "With several companies vying to land them. Nate's main competitor is a company called D-ROHN Technologies, and they were extremely set on getting this particular contract. In the end, Iron Eagle won out, and the people behind D-ROHN weren't happy about that."

"D-ROHN," murmured Chase as he wrote this down.

"But I really can't imagine anyone being stupid enough to go and murder the head of a competing company just because they felt they were being robbed of a business opportunity."

"The new CEO said the same thing," said Odelia. "The

business world may be a cutthroat one, but they don't actually cut each other's throats."

"If they did, they wouldn't be in business very long."

"Anyone else you can think of who would wish to harm Nathanial?"

"Or who would benefit from his inheritance," Chase added.

The woman hesitated, and Odelia urged, "Yes?"

"Well, there is Nate's ex-wife and son."

"Nathanial had an ex-wife?" asked Odelia.

"And a son?" Chase added.

"They got divorced over fifteen years ago," said Bella. "And even though Nate's relationship with his son was solid, he and Hope didn't get along very well. In fact, I don't think they've spoken more than a few words in all that time."

"The wife got custody of the boy?" asked Chase.

"She did, yeah. Not because Nate was a bad dad, but because the boy decided that he wanted to go and live with his mom. She wanted to become an actress and moved to LA."

"And did she become an actress?"

Bella smiled. "She landed a few jobs shooting commercials, and also a role on a reality show about real estate."

"The Real Housewives of LA?" Odelia suggested.

"Not exactly. She works as a realtor, and was featured on a show that only lasted one season. But all in all, she has done well for herself. Even though mostly with Nate's money."

"Is the ex-wife mentioned in Nathanial's will?" asked Odelia.

Bella shook her head. "I'm not sure."

"I thought you said Nathanial didn't have secrets from you?"

She studied her perfectly manicured fingernails. "I guess this is the one area where he did," she said primly. "He made a will, but its contents were between him and his attorney. I guess he felt it was too personal to share with anyone." She seemed unhappy with this, which was understandable.

"He never gave you a hint of what was in his will?"

She heaved a deep sigh. "No, he did not. It was the only time in our professional collaboration that Nate felt he couldn't include me in his decision process. I know about the will because I put him in touch with the attorney. But as to the contents of the will—I'm afraid he kept me out of the loop."

"Could you tell us where you were this morning around eleven, Bella?"

She seemed surprised by this sudden shift in the conversation. "Well, I was here, as usual."

"You live here?"

"Yes, I do. Someone had to look after the house while Nate was away for his life experiment."

"Can anyone vouch for you?" asked Chase.

She pointed to the two cats. "Only Mia and Tia, I'm afraid."

At this moment, Odelia cut a glance at me, and I knew exactly what this glance meant: talk to these cats! Now!

In other words, the exact last thing I wanted to do!

CHAPTER 20

Mia and Tia didn't look all that eager to answer any questions, and definitely not from two 'intruders.' But since Odelia needed us to get this information from the two Siamese cats, I decided we'd better get on with it. And so I cleared my throat and approached the cats a little trepidatiously, followed by Dooley, this time hiding behind my back of his own volition.

"So that's a pretty neat set-up you've got yourself going here," I said by way of breaking the ice, even though the ice was probably already broken—shattered, even. "Nice house, great humans, probably good quality nosh?"

"We can't complain," said Tia haughtily, though it could have been Mia, of course. Hard to keep these two apart.

"Though now that Nathanial is gone, there's no telling what might happen," I continued.

They stared at me. "Again with the lies!" Mia growled.

"Is Nathanial gone, Mia?" asked Tia.

"That's what this young upstart is trying to have us believe," said Mia. She narrowed her eyes into slits and regarded me balefully. "Are you joshing us, Max?"

"Is that what's going on here?" asked Tia. "Is this fat cat joshing us?"

"'Cause if you are, I will cut you like a pig."

"And I will gut you like a pig," Tia added.

The claws had come out again, and I got the impression this conversation had gone off the rails really fast.

"Nathanial died this morning," said Dooley timidly as he peeked from behind my back. "He was murdered, and we're trying to find out who did it. So if you want to help us catch his killer, we would be very appreciative, you guys."

For a moment, they didn't speak, then Tia said, "Bella seems to believe it, Mia. I just heard her mention the M-word in connection to Nate. So maybe these two aren't lying?"

"I'll believe it when I see his dead body!" said Mia.

"I don't *want* to see his dead body," said Tia.

"No, I don't want to see it either," said Mia.

Another pause, with both cats staring us down. I was starting to feel that Odelia had given us an impossible mission here, and one fraught with a certain modicum of danger. Suddenly Tia burst out, "Who did it?! Who killed our human! I'll cut them open! I'll slice and dice them from stem to stern!"

"We don't know who did it," I said. "That's the whole point of our investigation. To find out who the murderer is."

"I don't like this, Tia," said Mia.

"I don't like it either, Mia," said Tia.

"Life without Nate won't be the same."

"It most definitely won't."

"But you have Bella to look after you," I reminded them.

They looked up at the personal assistant, and a hint of a smile seemed to lift the corners of their mouths. "Yeah, I guess that's true," said Mia. "We will always have Bella."

"Good old Bella," said Tia.

"Fat, ugly Bella," said Mia viciously.

"Stupid fat cow Bella!" said Tia.

"They don't seem to think very highly of Bella, Max," said Dooley.

"No, I get that impression," I replied. I raised my voice. "So was she here this morning? Bella, I mean?"

Tia looked without much enthusiasm. "Mh?"

"Bella? Was she here this morning, would you say?"

"Around eleven?" Dooley added.

Mia shrugged. "Who cares?"

"Why do you want to know?" asked Tia suspiciously.

"Oh, it's just one of those routine questions that crop up in every investigation," I explained.

"We have to delude her from our inquiries," Dooley added.

"Exclude," I quietly corrected him.

"So... let me get this straight," said Tia. "You guys think that Bella may have murdered Nate? Our Bella?"

A cruel smile spread across Mia's face. "Bella wouldn't murder anyone. She's too chicken."

"Afraid of blood," Tia specified.

"Afraid of everything. Not the right spirit."

"Too timid to lift a finger against anyone."

"Is that what Nate said about her?" I asked. "That Bella doesn't have the right spirit? And that she's too chicken?"

"And what if he did?" asked Mia.

"He was right, wasn't he? Bella isn't the kind of person anyone would choose as his second-in-command. But Nate did, and he regretted it all the time. Complained endlessly about Bella on the phone. Said she didn't have what it took to make it in business. Didn't have that killer instinct."

"That she was only good for one thing, and that was to handle his personal agenda."

"Pick up this laundry."

"Organize his shopping."

"Make sure the house was clean."

"Small chores. Limited responsibility."

They both laughed. "Poor Bella," said Tia.

"Poor, poor Bella."

"What a sap."

"What a chump!"

They both flashed their eyelashes at us. "Anything else you wanted to know, Maxie?" asked Tia. "Or you, Doo-ooley? Such a funny name, isn't it? Doo-lee? Reminds me of a dog I once knew. Dumbest dog I ever met. When you asked him to do something, he did it. Even when I told him to take a running leap off the roof."

"Off he went," said Mia, giggling at the recollection.

"Off the roof he flew—like a little birdie!"

"Splat! On the lawn. Never was the same again."

"What happened to the doggie?" asked Dooley, who had followed the tale with rising indignation, as had I.

"Oh, they brought him to the vet," said Tia.

"To put down. Only the vet couldn't bring himself to do it."

"A sap, just like Bella," Tia said with a shrug.

"So where did the dog end up?" I asked.

"How should I know? And besides, what do you care? He was just a stupid dog."

"All dogs are stupid, Tia," said Mia.

"I know that, Mia. But this one was stupider than most."

Odelia and Chase had gotten up from their position on the couch, and I had the impression that the interview was over. And we still didn't have the answer to our question! So I decided to give it one last shot.

"So where was Bella this morning?" I asked.

"Around eleven?" Dooley added.

Tia smirked. "You think that she did it, don't you?" she

rolled her eyes. "If I didn't know any better, I'd think you guys were dogs."

"So stupid," Mia sighed.

"But was she here?" I insisted. "Here at the house?"

Tia smiled victoriously. "That's for us to know and for you to find out, isn't it, Maxie?"

"Well put, Mia," said her housemate, and the two cats slapped paws on it.

And so it was that I had to admit to Odelia, when we were driving back to town, that for possibly the first time in my life as an assistant detective, I hadn't been able to get a witness to give me an honest testimony.

After Odelia had told Chase the bad news, he gave her a grim-faced look. "You know what that means, don't you, babe?"

"That Bella Fuller is on our list of suspects?"

"It wouldn't surprise me if the things Tia and Mia said about Bella are all statements they heard Nathanial say about his personal assistant. And if Bella knew what her boss really thought about her, she had every reason to get rid of him."

And so in a sense, our recent conversation with Tia and Mia hadn't been a total disaster after all. We had added one more suspect to the list, and a strong motive to murder Nathanial.

CHAPTER 21

We arrived home just in time to see a minor procession in progress: Tex, Marge, and Gran had just gotten into the car, along with Brutus and Harriet, and were about to take off. Also present was Grace, who looked excited about this field trip, as she called it.

"We're going to shoot videos," she announced happily. "ASMR videos, no less!"

"What is an ASMR video again?" I asked.

She rolled her eyes. "Oh, Max. You really should make an effort to stay up to date. An ASMR video is a video that makes the viewer relax. It can be water running or a person brushing their hair or whispering something. It's all the rage."

"So you're all going out to shoot these... AMR videos?"

"ASMR," she said emphatically. "Try to keep up, Max."

Odelia's mom and dad had stepped out of the car the moment they saw Odelia and her husband pull up, and Marge explained they were going over to Uncle Alec's place since she had promised Charlene to drop by a book from the library.

"We're also going to take a look at their new jacuzzi," Tex announced.

"We saw them just before," said Odelia. "At the garden center. Checking out a second jacuzzi."

Gran rolled her eyes. "How many jacuzzis does a person need! They must be rolling in money!"

Harriet raised her head sniffily. "I was just telling Brutus all about it. Since Charlene is Uncle Alec's boss, she probably gave him a big pay raise since they got married. A groom bonus."

Dooley's eyes widened considerably. "I was telling Max the exact same thing! But he said that technically that's a conflict of interest, but I said that since they're married, they can't have a conflict of interest, unless they get divorced, of course."

"So are we going or what?" asked Gran, slapping the side of the car.

"I'm going to shoot a video," Harriet announced. "I'm going to shoot lots and lots of videos and post them online."

"Harriet shot a video of Ted Trapper peeing," Brutus said proudly. "It came out very nicely, didn't it, sugar lips?"

"It did! Even Gran said it was amazing how well I had captured Ted on video."

"Are you sure it's all right to post that video?" I asked with a touch of concern. "Ted may not like it."

"Oh, that's fine," said Harriet with a throwaway gesture of her paw. "Ted won't mind. In fact, he'll probably thank us for making him famous. Once that video goes viral, he'll be happy."

I had my doubts about that, but since Gran didn't want to waste any more time listening to us flapping our gums, as she called it, they all filed back into the car, and we got back into Chase's squad car, and soon the circus was on the road.

"So nice of Uncle Alec to finally invite us to go and see his jacuzzi," said Odelia as she buckled up. "When we talked to him earlier, he seemed adamant that he didn't have a jacuzzi."

"He must have finally realized that he couldn't keep a thing like that a secret anymore," said Chase. "And since we are his family, after all, he figured we might as well get first dibs on that famous jacuzzi of his."

"Oh, shoot," said Odelia as she thunked her forehead.

"What is it?"

"I forgot to grab my bathing suit."

"Maybe you can borrow one from Charlene," the cop suggested.

"She's not my size, I don't think, but I guess it will have to do." She smiled happily. "If the jacuzzi is as big as I think it is, Grace will be happy playing in that thing. Though she will have to wear swimming bands. It's too deep for her otherwise."

"We'll get her some," Chase assured her. "Though we'll have to ask Alec to turn off the jets. I don't like the idea of Grace being in that thing with the jets going full blast."

"Oh, no, absolutely," said Odelia.

"I don't really understand all the fuss," Dooley intimated. "It's just a big box filled with water, Max. Why do they all like it so much?"

"I'm not sure," I confessed. "But humans do seem to like bodies of water a lot. Whether they be big, like a sea or an ocean, or small, like a pool or a jacuzzi. I guess they've got a kind of affinity with water."

"They do say that the human body consists mainly of water," he said.

"Is that a fact?"

"Oh, it's true," he assured me. "It was all over the Discovery Channel last week. Though I don't really see where they put all of that water. When I look at Odelia, for instance, she doesn't look wet at all. She looks mostly dry, at least on the surface. Maybe inside she's all water?"

"Humans are very wet inside," I said. "Just look at what happens when they get cut, like that poor billionaire. A lot of water leaks out in the form of blood."

He shivered. "It doesn't bear thinking about, does it? That the moment you stick a knife in a human they simply empty out like a water balloon? Must be terrible to have to live like that, always in fear of getting cut and deflating like a balloon."

"I don't think it works like that, Dooley," I said. "I'm sure that if you stick a knife in a human they don't fully deflate."

"And I think they do. That's why they try their best to patch up these holes the moment they get them. Like last week, for instance, when Marge cut herself chopping those onions. And immediately she put a band-aid on it, to make sure she wouldn't keep leaking. Tex was worried."

"Tex wasn't worried about his wife losing all of her water," I told him. "But about her getting an infection."

"Be that as it may," he professed, like the professional Discovery Channel watcher or viewer that he is, "I still think it must put an awfully big strain on our poor humans."

We had arrived at the house where Uncle Alec and Charlene Butterwick live. Ever since they got married, Alec had decided to move in with his wife and not the other way around, possibly because she always did have the nicer house. Uncle Alec told us he sold his own house, and that's probably why he can afford to buy as many jacuzzis as he wants.

"Maybe we should have stayed home," I said as we hopped out of the car. "I'm not all that interested in these jacuzzis."

"Me neither," said Dooley. "But then I guess we need to show our solidarity. Our humans are so happy with these bubble-producing machines that we should probably pretend to like it also. That's what a good pet does, Max."

"Yeah, you're probably right," I said. As long as they didn't try to drag us into these jacuzzis with them, it was fine with me.

The entire family gathered on the front lawn, and it was Marge who put her finger on the buzzer and rang the bell. It didn't take long for Charlene to appear. She seemed surprised to see us, but when Marge offered her the book, she was glad.

"Ooh, that's so sweet!" she cooed as she took receipt of the reading material. "I've been wanting to read the new Jackie Cooper for the longest time. Come on in." She frowned at the long procession that filed into her home—all to drop off this one book. And she was even more surprised when the entire family made a beeline for the sliding glass doors, passed through them and into the backyard, where they stood looking around, in search of that fabled jacuzzi.

"Where is it?" asked Gran, never one to beat about the bush.

"Where is what?" asked Charlene innocently.

"Well, the jacuzzi, of course," said Gran.

Charlene seemed embarrassed by the directness of the question. "What jacuzzi would this be?" she asked, but I could tell that even though she was a politician, lying wasn't her forte.

Just then, a familiar face popped up from behind a nearby bush. It was Uncle Alec, and he was dressed in nothing more than a Speedo, wet from top to bottom, and looking perfectly happy and relaxed. "Aren't you coming, baby?" he asked. "The water is great."

The moment he saw his collected family standing on the deck, his smile vanished.

"Oh," he said.

"So that's where you've been hiding!" Gran cried, and immediately tiptoed off in the direction of those bushes. The rest of the family followed suit, but not before both Marge and Tex had shot their relative a look of disappointment.

Odelia patted her uncle on the chest. "I'm so glad you invited us, Uncle Alec."

"Took you long enough, chief," said Chase as he gave his superior officer a light slap on the back. "Got enough towels? We didn't bring our own."

"Oh, and can I borrow one of your bathing suits, Charlene?" asked Odelia.

"And armbands for me, Uncle Alec!" said Grace. "Nice pink ones with dolphins, please!"

Uncle Alec closed his eyes in dismay, and I got the impression he wasn't as happy with us as he could have been.

CHAPTER 22

With their humans all splashing in the new jacuzzi that Uncle Alec and Charlene had bought, there wasn't a lot of ASMR to shoot. Too noisy. Not relaxing enough in her professional opinion as one of YouTube's up and coming influencers. And so Harriet decided to go in search of something more suitable for her channel. She had asked Gran if she could borrow her phone again, and Gran had reluctantly agreed and had strapped her phone to Harriet with the aid of a rubber band. It wasn't ideal, but then a videographer and rising star has to make sacrifices to get what she wants.

And since neither Max nor Dooley had any interest in paddling in that pool—or jacuzzi as the technical term seemed to be—the four cats now roamed the gardens and backyards of Charlene Butterwick's neighborhood in search of some great stuff they could use for ASMR purposes. It wasn't long before they had arrived in a familiar-looking backyard, and Harriet realized they had been there before.

"You guys!" she cried excitedly. "This is Uncle Alec's old house!"

And so it was. And even though the police chief had told everyone that he had sold the house, as far as she could tell it still looked exactly the same as it had before, with no new tenants having moved in. She could see the same big surfboard stuck on its hook to the side of the house, dating back to a time when Uncle Alec liked to go surfing from time to time. And also the plastic plants he loved so much, since they didn't take any work at all to maintain. She could even see the big-screen television in the living room, where he and Chase had enjoyed watching football games when they used to live together. Maybe they still did, she thought, as Chase did have a habit of sneaking out of the house of an evening, supposedly to work late at the office or go to the gym.

"Looks like Uncle Alec hasn't moved out yet," said Max as they looked around.

"I didn't know Charlene and Uncle Alec lived on the same street," said Dooley. "They could have gotten married a lot sooner."

"He's definitely made the right choice to move in with Charlene," said Brutus. "This place looks like a dump in comparison."

It was true that Charlene's house was the nicer of the two. It was also a lot bigger and featured more modern architecture. It also featured a very large backyard, perfect for such pastimes as frolicking in the jacuzzi.

Speaking of jacuzzis, Harriet suddenly thought she spotted one. Which wasn't possible, since Uncle Alec had never owned one as far as she knew. But as she looked a little closer, she definitely detected a similar structure to the jacuzzi installed a couple of houses down the road.

"You guys," she said as she pointed to the contraption. "Isn't that..."

"That's a jacuzzi," said Max knowingly. "And if I'm not

mistaken, it's exactly the same model Uncle Alec and Charlene were checking out at that garden center earlier."

"Oh," said Dooley. "Do you think Uncle Alec bought one for the new people that are about to move in?"

"It's done all the time," Brutus knew. "They want to make sure that the house looks its absolute best before putting it on the market, and adding a few extras like a jacuzzi or a new kitchen or bathroom will up the value considerably."

And since they were by nature curious animals, the four decided to take a closer look at this strange contraption that by rights had no business being there. It was as they approached that Harriet thought she heard someone softly singing. And when they mounted those few steps up to the jacuzzi and she carefully stuck her head above the parapet, great was her surprise when she saw that none other than Uncle Alec was lounging in the jacuzzi, his eyes closed and humming a pleasant song.

Immediately she ducked her head back down, and she realized what this was: the perfect setting for another one of her ASMR videos! And so she motioned the others to keep their tongues and remain out of sight, and with the assistance of her Assistant Director Brutus, managed to stick the phone over the edge of the jacuzzi and hit Record.

She let the recording go on as long as possible, since that was exactly the point of these ASMR videos: people needed to get in the mood and be able to relax, so the longer these videos were, the better and the more views and likes she would get.

But then Uncle Alec stirred, and she got the impression he felt he had soaked in there long enough. And so she immediately stopped the recording and lowered the phone. Ten seconds later they were already hiding underneath some nearby bushes, and watching the police chief descend from the jacuzzi, towel himself off, stick his feet into his plastic toe slippers and amble off towards the house.

After he had let himself in, she shook her head. "I don't know, you guys, but something tells me he hasn't sold the house. Otherwise why would he act as if he still lives here?"

"I think you're right," said Max. "He hasn't sold the house at all. He still lives here."

"But why?" asked Dooley. "A man can't live in two places at the same time, can he?" But then his eyes widened. "Oh no! You guys!"

"What?" asked Harriet.

"They're getting a divorce! Or maybe they already got one, and they haven't told anyone the bad news yet."

"It's possible," Brutus allowed. "Charlene is the mayor, after all. She could easily arrange their divorce to become official and make sure no one finds out."

"Oh, no!" said Dooley. "And I really liked them as a couple. And now they've already broken up again!"

"Good thing that he hadn't sold the house yet," said Brutus. "Or else he wouldn't have a place to stay."

"But then why were they looking at jacuzzis together?" asked Max.

"I'll bet they're still great friends," said Dooley. "It happens all the time. It's called an amicable divorce. They separate but they remain friends. Mostly for the kids. Though in this case that doesn't apply, since they don't have any kids, do they?"

"No, I don't think they have," Harriet agreed.

It was sad, she thought. "Just look at that poor man," she said as they all watched Uncle Alec grab a brewski from the fridge and settle down on the couch. Moments later he was watching a football game on the big television while he sipped from his beer. "All alone and nowhere to go."

"We have to tell Marge," said Dooley. "She can start

inviting him to have dinner at the house again. Make sure that he doesn't feel lonely."

"And maybe Chase can drop by from time to time to keep him company," Max suggested. "He won't mind, will he, Brutus?"

"Chase will love it," said Brutus. "He really loves his godfather, so he'll want to see him through these tough times he's experiencing right now." He shook his head. "And to think that we were all giving him such a hard time about that jacuzzi of his. And all the while he was suffering in silence."

"It takes a great man to suffer and not tell a soul," said Dooley.

"You know what?" said Harriet. "I'm going to post that video right now. And I'm going to add a few notes about Uncle Alec needing a friend. And I'm going to post his address so the people who want to can drop by and keep him company. He needs friends now more than ever, doesn't he?"

"Great idea, Harriet," said Brutus. "I like it."

"I had my doubts about this new channel of yours, Harriet," said Max. "But this is the best idea you've had in a long time. Uncle Alec will be so happy with you."

"And while we wait for Uncle Alec's friends to arrive, maybe *we* can keep him company," Dooley suggested.

They all agreed this was an excellent idea, and so she quickly posted the video they had just shot, along with the video of Ted Trapper peeing—also a great ASMR video—and she added a few notes about Uncle Alec having recently gone through a terrible divorce from the woman he loved, and if anyone was in the area to drop by and give the man a hug.

By the time she was done, she actually had goosebumps.

Now she understood why people said that giving is much more satisfying than receiving. And since she was in a giving mood, she hurried after her friends, and as they stepped into the house and hopped up onto the couch next to Uncle Alec, they decided to give the word 'love bomb' new meaning by showering that poor lonely man with as many cuddles as they could give.

The look on his face was priceless.

Pure and unadulterated gratitude.

CHAPTER 23

Marge was surprised to find that the new jacuzzi her brother had bought was so nice and big. She still didn't understand why he had insisted on keeping it a secret but thought that maybe he was keeping it as a surprise and would spring it on them unexpectedly. Just like Tex had when she had told him that she didn't think it was funny that he had decided to buy himself a jacuzzi and hadn't told her about it.

"But that's just the point, honey," he said on the drive over. "It was supposed to be a surprise. Me and Chase were going to buy it for you and Odelia as a surprise for your birthdays."

Thoroughly mollified, she had given him a big kiss, and he had momentarily swerved across the road and almost hit Ida Baumgartner before he had righted the vehicle and had continued the journey with a big smile on his face. The sweet man did love to make his wife happy, didn't he? And he knew exactly what he had to do to accomplish it.

And so she had been in quite the mellow mood by the time they arrived to check out her Alec's new jacuzzi. And it had to be said that if Tex and Chase got her one of these things, it would be the best birthday present ever. Though judging from the look on her husband's face, it wasn't going to be as nice as the one Alec and Charlene had gotten for themselves.

"This is really big, isn't it, bud?" said Tex.

"It sure is, Dad," said the cop as he studied the gargantuan contraption. "Alec splurged."

"He did," Tex confirmed. He darted a surreptitious look at his wife. "Maybe we should upgrade?"

"Maybe," Chase agreed. "By a lot!"

Charlene had also walked up and seemed relieved somehow that their secret was finally out. "I wanted to tell you about it, but Alec felt that we should wait until we'd had a chance to test it out properly."

"You were absolutely right," said Marge immediately. She believed in live and let live, and not making unnecessary trouble, especially with members of her own family. "And I think you got yourself a gorgeous jacuzzi, honey. It must be nice to soak in it, mustn't it?"

"Oh, absolutely," said Charlene as she handed a bathing suit to Odelia and told her where she could go and change. "It's so nice to be able to soak in the tub of an evening. Glass of wine, turn on the jacuzzi and in we go. Alec even told me he believes it's the best investment we've made."

"So it's an investment, is it?" asked Tex as he sidled up to them.

"How much, would you say?" asked Chase.

"Oh, I wouldn't know," said the mayor. "Alec arranged everything. He researched different systems and different stores, then he bought it and moved it over here. He even installed it himself, if you can believe it. Figured it was worth the time spent on it. And he was absolutely right."

Grace couldn't wait to get in the jacuzzi, but Marge held

her back. As long as she wasn't properly outfitted, she didn't want the little girl to go in the thing. After all, she couldn't swim yet. "So where is Alec?" she asked, glancing around.

"Oh, he went into town to run a quick errand," said Charlene.

"Pity," said Tex as he rubbed his chin and studied the hot tub from every angle. "I have about a thousand questions I would like to ask him."

Just then, Chase's phone chimed a funny tinkling bell sound that reminded Marge of the kind of sound an elf makes. He casually took his phone from his pocket and cast a quick glance at the screen. But when his jaw dropped and he quickly opened the message, she had a feeling that something important must have happened—probably connected to one of the cases he was working on.

"Um… I'm afraid I have to go," he said, and before supplying them with any more details, hurried off.

"A cop's life," she said.

"Yeah, work never stops," said Charlene. "It's the same with Alec. Just when you're settled in for the night, the phone will ring and he's off again. But then I knew that when I married the man."

Charlene's phone chimed, and she gave Marge an apologetic look. "It's my mom."

"Oh, please," she said. "Go ahead," and watched as the mayor picked up the phone and walked away a few paces to talk to her mother. She watched as the woman's face suddenly clouded and she started conducting an urgent conversation, gesticulating wildly and clearly in a state of distress.

"Tough call?" asked Odelia, who had joined them again. She was dressed in one of her aunt's bathing suits and looked gorgeous, Marge thought.

"Her mother," she explained. "Looks like bad news."

"Aren't you going to try out the hot tub?"

Marge smiled. "Are you kidding? Of course I'm going to try out the hot tub!" And since she didn't think anybody would be watching, she ducked behind the jacuzzi and quickly changed. And she was just pulling on her bathing suit when she saw that a man was watching her intently from behind the fence. He was an elderly man and she recognized him as Gregg Watkiss, Charlene and Alec's neighbor. Oops!

So she gave him a friendly wave, and then hurried after her daughter and into the hot tub. And she had to admit that Charlene was right. This was simply heavenly!

The third person to join them was her mother, and the three ladies settled back and agreed that life just wasn't the same without a hot tub in it.

"God bless Alec!" said Ma, and Marge couldn't have agreed more with the sentiment.

"And here we all thought he was holding out on us," said Odelia. "When all the time he couldn't wait to spring this surprise! What a blessing to have Alec as an uncle!"

"He's the best son a woman could hope to have," Ma said. "I just knew he wouldn't want to deprive his sick old mother of this little pleasure. God bless a son like my dear Alec."

"God bless a brother like Alec!" Marge added.

The Alec love fest lasted about five minutes. Then Tex's head popped up over the edge of the hot tub. He was holding up his phone. "Um… there's something I think you need to see, honey," he said. He pressed Play on a YouTube video, and that's when all three women realized that Alec wasn't the best uncle/son/brother in the world. Quite the contrary, in fact!

CHAPTER 24

There are certain misconceptions that people have about cats that are very hard to fight. One of those is that we enjoy being cuddled and stroked and patted. Another is that we enjoy the company of humans even more than that of our brethren. Neither of these notions is even remotely true. And so when the home of Uncle Alec suddenly became a sort of beehive or zoo filled with people from all walks of life, we decided it was time for us to say goodbye and hit the road.

We had done our bit for the good of this beloved police chief and felt that we could safely leave him in the capable and loving hands of his neighbors, friends, and family. To support him in his time of need and heartache. Even though he and Charlene were still on speaking terms, and possibly even still friendly to one another, it was clear that the chief once again had been unlucky in love.

"It's just like that time with Tracy Sting, Max," said Dooley. "Remember her?"

"I do, yeah," I said.

Uncle Alec had enjoyed a brief fling with Tracy Sting, that

hadn't led to anything serious, since Miss Sting was one of those cosmopolitan and peripatetic people who live in their suitcases and are always on the move. Tough to have a relationship with a person when you can't even pin them down for five seconds to have a conversation or enjoy dinner together. And now this second heartache with Charlene, though judging from the way he had been singing a song in his jacuzzi, I got the impression that the break-up had happened weeks ago and he was already getting over it.

The house was filled with voices and people, all of them highly complimentary to Uncle Alec, and even though the man didn't look happy now—I even thought I could detect a tear glistening in his eye—at least he would not be alone, which is important under these tragic circumstances.

"We did a good thing," said Harriet. "And I'm glad for it." She sighed happily. "I wonder if there are other people we can do something for. It just makes you feel so warm and happy inside, you know."

I smiled. "It's always nice to be there for a person," I agreed.

"So how are you getting along with this murder case of yours?" asked Brutus.

The four of us had legged it from Uncle Alec's old house and were en route to the old homestead since we didn't want to trouble our humans, who were all frolicking in the jacuzzi.

"Oh, you know," I said. "It's still early days. So far, we've established that the dead man wasn't who he said he was."

"He was a billionaire!" said Dooley. "A real billionaire!"

"We've identified a few suspects, but so far we haven't been able to determine which one of them was responsible."

"There's a homeless man with a lying dog," said Dooley. "They're the ones who found the body, and we think they may be involved. And then there's the billionaire's personal assistant, who was treated very badly by him, so maybe she was out for revenge. Also, a jealous boyfriend, a jealous admirer, and a jealous fan—all three in love with Rita, the billionaire's neighbor. She works at a pet clinic."

"What is a pet clinic?" asked Brutus curiously.

"It's a clinic for pets," said Dooley.

"I know that, doofus," said our friend. "But what do they do, exactly? I mean, is it like a hospital or something?"

"Not... exactly," I said. "More like a hospice for pets."

"Pets that are dying," Dooley clarified. "Though not all of them actually do die. One of them didn't die, a hedgehog that was adopted by Rita. He hates cats," he added sadly.

"A cat-hating hedgehog, huh? I'll bet he's the killer," Brutus quipped.

Our conversation seemed to have sparked Harriet's interest. So far she had been wrapped up in her own thoughts, but now she came out of her meditations on all things ASMR to regale us with her latest idea. "A hedgehog! That's perfect! We have to go and pay a visit to this hedgehog, you guys!"

"He hates cats," I reiterated. "So he won't like it when we pay him a visit. At least not if our last conversation is any indication."

She gave me a smile. "He hasn't met Harriet, has he?"

"So who else have you got for this murder?" asked Brutus.

"Well, there's also the billionaire's ex-wife and son, but they live in LA," Dooley explained. "So they couldn't have done it. But just to make sure, Chase and Odelia will talk to them soon. They're flying in for the funeral and will be here tomorrow."

"Tomorrow is Sunday," Brutus reminded him. "They won't like it when two cops bust in on them on a Sunday."

"Didn't you know, Brutus? The police never rest!"

And neither did Harriet, for she was already making plans to capture this hedgehog for one of her ASMR videos. I could have told her this was a bad idea, but since I knew she wouldn't believe me, I decided that if she was going to go through with it, best she did it with the support of her three friends. If the hedgehog attacked, at least we could protect her.

And since with Harriet there's no time like the present, she decided that we needed to find this hedgehog immediately and capture his ASMR-inducing qualities for posterity.

Which is how we ended up back at the Rock Tower. Gazing up at the imposing structure, Harriet sighed happily. "This is so ASMR, you guys! The sound of the wind whipping around a high structure like this is exactly what we need!"

I didn't fully agree, but then I'm no ASMR expert. And so moments later we were climbing the fire escape to the sixth floor, hoping to catch Patrick in a good mood.

CHAPTER 25

Patrick was dozing on top of the couch when he became aware of a strange sight. Four cats were waving at him from the fire escape, and seemed to have some urgent desire to speak with him. He shook his head and was determined to simply ignore them until they went away—like a bad dream—but that wasn't what his new human had in mind.

Georgia felt that she couldn't just let those kitties sit there all by themselves, and so she just had to go and open the window so they could enter the apartment. Big mistake!

"Go away," he said as they all trooped around him.

"There's something I would like to ask you, Mr. Hedgehog," said a white Persian. She seemed to be the one in charge, even though formerly he had assumed that the large orange one was the boss. Clearly, that wasn't the case.

"I said, go away," he repeated.

"Oh, aren't you the cats belonging to Odelia Kingsley?" asked Georgia as she placed a saucer of milk on the floor.

"Thanks, but we don't drink milk," said the red one.

This was too much for Patrick. He directed a scathing

look at the big cat. "That's extremely rude of you!" he said. "When a person offers you a saucer of milk, you accept that saucer of milk and you say thank you!"

"But I don't drink milk," said the big cat, whose name, if he remembered correctly, was Max. "It gives me diarrhea."

"Even so. You should never refuse a gift. It's not done."

"I like milk," said the Persian. "But Odelia has told me never to drink milk offered by a stranger, or food for that matter. It could be poisoned."

The hedgehog raised himself up to his full height, which wasn't very high, and said, "Where are your manners! How dare you think my human would offer you poisoned milk?"

"No, but I'm not saying *this* milk is poisoned," the Persian clarified. "Just that it *could* be poisoned, you see."

"And I'm telling you that my human would never do such a thing. So either you will drink this milk right now, or you will leave the same way you just came."

The cats all stared at the milk, and gulped. "I'll drink it," said the smallest of the foursome. "I'll sacrifice myself for the team."

"No, I'll drink it," said the big black one. "I've had milk before and it hasn't killed me yet." He approached the milk with visible reluctance. "It doesn't smell bad," he said after taking a sniff. He took a lick. "It doesn't taste bad."

"Brutus, don't do it!" the Persian cried passionately, and actually swiped the saucer of milk away from the black cat, causing all of the milk to spill on the floor.

Georgia, who had witnessed this, seemed surprised. "Has the milk gone off? Oh, that's too bad. I only bought it a couple of days ago. I'm sorry, kitties. I'll give you some of Shelley's kibble."

The poodle came tripping into the room from the bedroom, where she liked to sleep on the bed. When she saw the cats, she seemed surprised, but then her tail started wagging, a sure sign of how she really felt about these cats—the traitor.

"Ooh, it's you again!" she cried. "I was just wondering when you would pop in for another visit. So have you found out who killed poor Morgan? I mean, like I told you last time you were here, I didn't like him, but that doesn't mean he deserved to die."

"We haven't discovered who killed him yet," Max said. "But we have identified several suspects."

"Three of them are in love with your human," said the small fluffy one proudly.

"In love with my human?" asked Shelley as she darted a hesitant look at Georgia.

"Not that human," said the cat. "The other one."

"Oh, Rita!" said Shelley. "Yes, I can believe that people would fall in love with her. She's lovely. In fact, I think I'm also in love with her, and so is Patrick. Aren't you, Patrick?"

"I'm too old and set in my ways to fall in love with anyone," Patrick grumbled. Though it was true that Rita was very nice. So nice, in fact, that he felt immediately protective of her. "Who are these bozos who are in love with Rita?" he demanded.

"Well, there's Harvey," said the small fluffy cat. "Who likes to shovel manure at the garden center and isn't very nice. And also Samuel Dickenson, who sells honey and liked it very much that Rita bumped into his car this morning. So much so that he bought her a bouquet of long-stemmed red roses. And finally, there's Ken, who's probably a little young for Rita, but who's been keeping tabs on her and looking at her through his binoculars and thinks of himself as her personal bodyguard."

"In other words, three weirdoes," said Patrick. "But what else did I expect? Men are weird—all of them."

"That's definitely true," said Shelley.

They both looked up at their human, who had written the book on men and never failed to point out to them that the first man who could be trusted had yet to be born. She had trusted Morgan, and he had turned out to be a liar. The fact that Patrick was a man didn't seem to bother Georgia, though. But then Patrick wasn't a *human* man but a *hedgehog* man, and to Georgia that made all the difference in the world.

"Look, all we want is to shoot a video," said the Persian. "And then we'll be out of your hair—or out of your spines."

"You want to shoot a video of me?" asked Patrick.

"Absolutely. I run a YouTube channel, you see, posting ASMR videos. And I'm sure that my viewers will just love to watch a video starring a hedgehog. You guys are *so* ASMR!"

He had no idea what the cat was talking about, but since Georgia seemed determined not to shoo this annoying foursome away, he felt that the sooner he gave them what they wanted, the sooner they'd leave. And so he sighed and said, "Do your worst, cat."

"Harriet," she said. "And these are my friends Brutus, Max, and Dooley."

"Yeah, we met," he said, giving the big red one an unhappy look. And as he watched on, the black cat removed a phone from behind a rubber band tied around the Persian, and they worked together to set the phone up so that he was perfectly framed. Moments later she pressed Record, and gave him two paws up. So he closed his eyes and went to sleep, hoping sincerely that by the time he woke up, they'd be gone.

CHAPTER 26

I didn't know what the big deal was about watching a hedgehog sleep, but Harriet seemed to love it, for she kept that recording going for as long as she could. In the meantime, she instructed us not to make a sound or even move a muscle. Which was a little hard, since I like to stretch my legs from time to time, and also, our hostess kept walking up and down to the kitchen to supply us with different types of kibble that she thought we might like. She really was a superb hostess.

"We're not going to eat all of your kibble, Shelley," I assured the poodle, when she looked sad at the prospect of us eating all of her precious food.

"No, it's fine," she said. "Eat as much as you like. I've got plenty more. Plenty… more…" she said, but didn't look convinced. I had the impression that the MacKereth women, mother and daughter, weren't the richest people in town, and that kibble wasn't the kind of food they got on a daily basis, since it's not all that cheap. And the stuff they gave Shelley was definitely not the finest kibble on sale. Quite possibly the worst I had ever tasted, and my friends all felt the same way.

"Shhhh!" Harriet exhorted us not for the first time. "I'm trying to shoot a video here!"

Brutus grinned. "Steven Spielberg at work," he whispered.

"I heard that," said Harriet icily.

Twenty minutes into the recording, Rita arrived home, carrying an envelope and looking excited. "Mom, look what arrived!"

Her mother checked the letter and seemed surprised. "I don't understand," she said. "What is this?"

"An invitation to attend the reading of the last will and testament of Nathanial Tindell. Monday morning at ten o'clock at his lawyer's office in town."

"But... I don't understand. Why us?"

"Morgan—or rather Nathanial—must have left us a little something," said Rita. "Maybe some souvenir to remember him by."

"I guess," said Georgia as she reread the letter. "Says here that our presence is required. Without us, they won't proceed."

"Legalese," said her daughter as she disappeared into the kitchen. "Lawyers always write these funny phrases into their official letters, just to make sure you can't sue them. Or something." When she returned, she was carrying a glass of orange juice. Only now did she notice that four cats were seated around her hedgehog, with one of those cats giving her angry looks.

"And that's my video ruined!" Harriet cried as she stopped the recording.

"Good," said Patrick without opening his eyes. "Who has ever heard of a hedgehog featuring in a YouTube video? Not me, that's for sure."

"Well, whether you like it or not, you will be in this

video," said Harriet stubbornly. The hedgehog opened one eye and it happened to meet mine. A silent communication passed between us, and I was pretty sure that he understood that Harriet isn't the kind of cat you can deny anything.

"Max, is it?" he asked.

"That's right," I said. "At your service."

He gave me a crooked smile. "You know? You may just be the first cat I've ever met who isn't half bad."

Strangely though it was formulated, I decided to take this as a compliment. "Thanks, Patrick," I said therefore.

"I don't have anything to wear to this lawyer's meeting," said Georgia. "What do you even wear to these occasions? Does it have to be black? I don't have anything black. Will there be many people? Probably there will be. He was a billionaire, for crying out loud. Probably all of his billionaire friends will be there! And I can't afford to buy a decent dress!"

"Just wear whatever you like to wear, Mom," said her daughter. "I don't think there will be many people there. Only the ones who have been left something in his will."

"Like who?"

"I don't know. His ex-wife and son, probably his personal assistant. Maybe his business partner?"

"I didn't even know that Morgan had a wife and son," her mother grumbled. "He could have told us."

"There are a lot of things we didn't know about Morgan. But what we do know is that he was a good and decent man."

"Was he? Was he really? Then why did he lie to us, huh? Can you explain that?"

Her daughter shrugged. Clearly she couldn't. We could have told her, but then nobody ever listens to a cat. I was sure that once the investigation was concluded, Odelia and Chase would sit down with Rita and her mother and tell them all about what was going on with Mr. Tindell. How he felt he had missed out on what real life was like and wanted to experience it firsthand. And that presumably he had fallen in love with Rita at some point and wanted to get to know her before he revealed to her he was a billionaire several times over—something he feared would cloud her judgment of him.

Harriet had been waiting for the perfect opportunity to shoot some more footage of Patrick, but with Rita and her mother settling down on the couch to talk more about this Morgan Sears business, it soon became clear that wasn't happening. And so we decided to take our leave.

"See you around," said Patrick, giving me a salute.

"Yeah, see you, Patrick," I said.

"I hope you'll drop by again," said Shelley fervently.

"We will," I promised.

As we passed onto the fire escape, I had a feeling we were being watched. And as I searched the horizon, it wasn't long before I located Ken, seated in his car and studying the apartment with his binoculars. Rita's self-appointed bodyguard and admirer was at it again. And as I scanned the parking lot, I saw another man seated in his car. It was Samuel Dickenson, and he was also staring fervently up at Rita's apartment, clutching a bouquet of flowers in his hand.

As we watched, he got out of his car and set foot for the entrance to the apartment block. And he probably would have made it, if Ken hadn't stepped out of his car and taken a running leap at the man, tackling him to the ground!

Rita and her mother came hurrying out of their apartment at the altercation that was taking place, and Rita even clutched at her head as she cried, "What is going on!"

The two men grappled with one another, with Ken hitting Samuel with the flowers, giving him a good thrashing. After the roses had lost their edge—and their thorns—he tried using his binoculars as a weapon. Only he wasn't exactly a skilled fighter, for as he swung them at the other man, he missed, and they ended up hitting him in the face. He went down hard.

"We better call an ambulance," Rita's mother said, and hurried in to grab her phone.

Ten minutes later the ambulance arrived, and Ken was carted off to a nearby hospital while the paramedics dressed the wounds Samuel Dickenson had sustained. By the time we had descended the fire escape and watched the scene from the vantage point of the hood of a nearby car, Rita had also come down to see what was going on, and when she saw the scratches and blood on Samuel's face, she seemed horrified.

"Did Ken do this?"

"Is that his name?" asked Samuel as the paramedic put some antiseptic on the cuts.

"This is going to sting," he announced, and judging from the expression of pain on the honey salesman's face, he hadn't exaggerated.

"He works with me at the clinic," said Rita. "Oh, I'm so sorry, Mr. Dickenson."

"Samuel, please," he said as he checked another wound on his arm, as well as his ruined shirt. He glanced unhappily at the bouquet of flowers, now lying discarded on the ground. "I wanted to give you these," he said.

"I know. You were at the clinic, weren't you?"

"I was," he confirmed. "And also here, but you weren't there."

"I'm so sorry about the car," she said.

"And I'm sorry for being so rude this morning," he said. "I should never have said the things I did. I was mad, and I lashed out."

"I hit your car and destroyed your door."

"A minor scratch."

"You will need a new door."

"I never liked the old one," he assured her.

"And I stepped on your foot."

"It doesn't hurt. Well, it hurts a little, but only when I smile." He smiled and winced. "See? It's the strangest thing."

She laughed. "So why did you want to give me these flowers?"

"Like I said, I wanted to apologize for my rude and frankly inexcusable behavior this morning."

"I'm the one who should apologize."

"Have you eaten yet, Miss MacKereth?"

"Um... no, not yet. We were about to start preparing dinner, but then this letter came and..." She waved her hand. "But that's neither here nor there. Why do you ask?"

"Could I... could I invite you out to dinner? With me? To apologize for my behavior, I mean? Could be just pizza, if you like," he hastened to add when she gave him a curious look. "Or a burger at your favorite burger place. Or I could ask you both out—you and your mother. I'm sure she's nice."

"She *is* nice," Rita confirmed. She thought for a moment as she studied him. Then finally seemed to feel that he wasn't dangerous in any way. "Okay, I'll go out to dinner with you. But maybe not my mother. She thinks all men are evil, and I'm not sure she's willing to make an exception for you."

The smile of relief that lit up the honey salesman's face was something to behold. "Oh, that's great! And please tell your mom that not all men are evil—I'm not evil—or at least I don't think I'm evil. Well, not very evil, at least. Maybe just a smidgen. But not dangerously so." He was babbling a little, and it seemed to amuse Rita to no end.

"Pick me up at eight?" she suggested.

And he nodded about ten times in quick succession. As we watched her return to her apartment, I don't think I've ever seen a man with scratches all over his face look as happy as this honey man did at that moment.

"Love," said Harriet. "It's very ASMR, isn't it?"

Only now did I notice she had filmed the entire scene.

"You're not seriously thinking about putting that online, are you?" I asked.

"And why not? People will love it."

"It was a private moment between two people, Harriet!"

"Not very private," she argued. "Seeing as we're in a public place."

"Tootsie roll, for once I agree with Max. Better don't put that online unless you want to get into a heap of trouble. People don't like it when you throw their private conversations onto the internet."

She rolled her eyes. "Oh, all right. Have it your way. But I still think it's a fine piece of footage and will make a lot of people happy."

"Except Rita and Samuel," I pointed out.

"Spoilsports," she said and started to walk away.

"Do you think Rita and Samuel will become a couple, Max?" asked Dooley as we walked after her.

"I'm sure I don't know, buddy," I said.

"I hope they will. I like Rita, and this man seems all right. In spite of the fact that he's something of a doofus."

"Maybe Rita likes a doofus," said Brutus. "Maybe a doofus is exactly what she needs right now."

Truer words had never been spoken, and as we trailed after our indignant and incandescent Persian friend, we freely speculated about the budding love affair between this honey man and the hedgehog-loving girl.

CHAPTER 27

Alec realized he should have known that his day was about to turn bad when he saw Chase and his niece at the garden center. But he hadn't known just how bad it would get. The first inkling was when he suddenly found that the four cats belonging to his sister had entered the house and jumped him on the couch, for some reason finding it important that they show their love and affection to him in a way that he didn't think was entirely appropriate. Harriet even gave him a sort of lick across the nose, for crying out loud!

The moment he had managed to shake them off, the first person showed up. It was his neighbor Gregg Watkiss, carrying a bottle of wine and actually giving him a hug!

"I like you, Alec," said the guy. "I like you a lot!"

The second person was one of his oldest neighbors, Yvonne Boyle, who said she had baked him a cake and wanted him to know that he had her full support and that of her husband Hubert, who had also joined her and stood stiff as a board for a moment, before actually slapping his arms around him and giving him a bear hug!

Plenty of people did the same thing after that, and it became something of a ritual. Dozens and dozens of neighbors showed up, and also members of his police force, all of them giving him their best wishes and patting him on the back and offering him food and drink in abundant quantities. So much so that before long his dinner table was groaning under the weight of pot roast and cake and pie and all manner of hearty foodstuffs.

But it was only when his sister Marge showed up, accompanied by their mother, and also Tex, Chase and Odelia, that he finally got an idea of what was going on, exactly.

"You should have told us, Alec," said Marge, and he saw she actually had tears in her eyes. She gave him a heartfelt hug and said, "You can always eat at ours again, just like you used to do after Ginny died."

"Our door is always open, buddy," said Tex.

"I'm going to make it a habit of visiting you every night," said Chase. "We're going to watch the game together, and I'm going to be there for you every step of the way, boss."

"But... I don't understand," he said. "What is going on?"

"The divorce," said Tex. "I understand now why you didn't say anything. And why you bought that jacuzzi. To drown your sorrows, right? It's just that..." He took him by the arm and led him aside. "Please tell me you weren't thinking of actually drowning yourself in that thing?"

"What... what divorce?!" he cried. Just then, he saw that Charlene herself had entered the house, which was filled with people, all talking and drinking and exchanging whispered conversation, just like at a funeral.

"What's the meaning of this?" she asked.

"I don't know!" he cried. "First the cats attacked me, and then suddenly all of this bunch showed up!"

She held out her phone and showed him a video. Much to

his surprise, he saw that it was him in that video, taking a nice soak in his new jacuzzi and having a ball—alone and in peace, just like God intended.

"Look at the message, Alec," she insisted.

He read the message, and saw that someone had written that he needed a lot of support right now because he was getting a divorce!

"But... who wrote this?" he asked. "Who shot this video? I don't understand!"

"The cats," said Tex. "They shot the video and posted the message."

"It's Harriet's new YouTube channel," his mother explained. "She's into ASMR at the moment and likes to post stuff that she thinks people will find relaxing."

"What's so relaxing about me sitting in my tub?!"

She shrugged and held up her hands. "To each their own, son. I don't find it remotely relaxing to see a naked middle-aged man in a hot tub. But then who am I?"

"You have to ask them to take this offline," said Charlene.

"I can ask," said Ma. "But why should I? If it's the truth, and you guys are getting a divorce."

"But we're not getting a divorce!" said Alec.

"Then why did you make up that story about selling the house when it's obvious that you haven't sold the house and you're still living here?" asked Ma sternly.

"Because from time to time I like to be alone!" he cried. "Is that so hard to understand?"

"Alec wanted a man cave," Charlene explained. "But I don't have the space at my house, and so we figured he might as well keep his own house for now, so he can come here and have some time to himself."

"And a second jacuzzi?" asked Tex. "Why, Alec?"

"Because I knew that you were going to find out about

my first jacuzzi, all right?" he said. "And that you were all going to spend all summer in my hot tub, and sometimes a man just likes to be alone and soak in his hot tub all by himself!"

It was certainly a sentiment that he knew wasn't going to win him any points in popularity, but it was the truth. He saw that Marge and his mother didn't like the notion that he didn't feel like sharing his hot tub with them, but he could also see that both Chase and Tex understood all too well the need for any man—especially a married man—to have his own space.

"You're such a child, Alec," said Ma. "A real baby."

"Yes, this is very selfish of you, Alec," said Marge.

"Two hot tubs and still you don't want to share?" asked Ma. She patted his chest. "I raised you better than that."

"Okay, fine. You can have the first hot tub, but please let me keep the second one? Pretty please?"

"It's not just *your* hot tub, Alec," Charlene reminded him. "It's *our* hot tub—the both of them." She turned to the others. "We arranged that we would keep this second hot tub just for us—so we would have it all to ourselves. But the cats must have found out, and drew the wrong conclusions."

"And now the whole town thinks we're getting a divorce!" Alec cried as he pulled at the last remaining strands of hair on his scalp. "This is a nightmare!"

"It's not that bad," said Marge. "As soon as Harriet removes that video, and you put out a statement that everything is fine between the two of you, I'm sure this whole hubbub will die down quickly."

"And if you feel so terrible about your family using your hot tub, all you had to do was say the word," said Ma. "And we wouldn't have darkened your doorstep. In fact," she said, as she drew herself up. "We should probably leave, since our presence clearly isn't wanted. Come on, Marge—let's go."

"Oh, don't be like that!" said Alec.

"I'm sure that Alec didn't mean it like that," said Marge.

"No, I'm sure that Uncle Alec loves our company," said Odelia, possibly the only sensible person in this town of theirs, "but just like all of us, he needs his personal space from time to time. And so we should give it to him." She darted an anxious eye at her husband. "Maybe we should all give some space to the people we love."

"I know what you're thinking, and I'm good, babe," said Chase as he put an arm around her shoulder. "I don't need my own personal hot tub, if that's what you're worried about."

"You can soak in *our* very own hot tub soon," said Tex. And when Odelia looked up in surprise, her dad added, "As a surprise for your birthday and Marge's, Chase and I have arranged to buy a hot tub for you—for us—for the family."

"See?" said Ma, raising her chin. "We don't need your stinking hot tub, mister. Cause soon we'll have our own!"

And with these words, she took off, like a galleon under steam. Or rather a rickety old schooner, he thought.

"Don't mind her," said Tex, clapping a hand on his shoulder. "You know Vesta. She'll come round soon enough."

"I hope so," he said. The last thing he needed was to get into some kind of imbroglio with his family. "Look, if I insulted anyone, I'm sorry," he said. "It wasn't my intention."

Just then, Dolores came walking up to him. "So where is this famous hot tub, chief?" she asked. She held up her bathing suit. "I've been wanting to take a soak in that thing for ages."

He sighed deeply and pointed to his hot tub, out in his backyard. "Please, be my guest," he said.

"Thanks, chief!" she said, and bellowed, "Follow me, you guys! It's hot tub time!"

And before his astonished eyes, about half of the men and

women on the force hurried after the dispatcher, eager to take a dip in his now-famous hot tub.

So much for some time alone for Hampton Cove's embattled chief!

CHAPTER 28

It had been a while since Rita had gone out on a date with a man who wasn't Harvey. But then she and Harvey had spent more time fighting than enjoying each other's company lately, so that wasn't saying much. And since she had selected their local diner to enjoy this bite to eat, she didn't even see it as a date at all. More like an opportunity to allow Samuel to apologize for his behavior, and for her to apologize once again for causing him so much inconvenience.

Her mother had warned her that she was dancing with the devil, and she had assured her that she would be safe at all times, since the diner was a busy place, and they would be surrounded by other people, just in case Samuel turned out to be a psychopath, which she didn't think he was.

"So you sell honey?" she asked after he had told her a little bit about himself and she had told him about her work at the clinic.

"Honey products of every kind," he confirmed. "Up to and including wax candles. In fact, I took the liberty of bringing this." He placed a small gift-wrapped package on the table, and she picked it up with a smile. She loved receiving gifts.

"Let me guess," she said. "A little pot of honey?"

"Open it," he said as he seemed to have relaxed considerably from the moment he had asked her out. Even his stutter had remarkably improved, and he didn't seem as nervous as he was. But then he had enjoyed an aperitif, so that might have been instrumental in settling his first-date jitters.

She wasn't feeling nervous at all since she had absolutely no intention of actually dating this man—or any man, for that matter. She was still dealing with the aftermath of the whole Harvey disaster, and on top of that, she had her pregnancy to deal with and the future of her unborn child to think about. She wasn't ready to get involved with anyone—and might not be for a long time to come.

She had opened the package and saw that it was a little bee blowing kisses to the recipient. "Cute," she said, well pleased as she placed the bee next to her glass. "Very cute."

"I've got a second one just like it for your mother," he said, and handed her a second package. "I hope she likes it."

"Oh, she will," said Rita.

"Even though it comes from a man?" he teased.

"Mom is pragmatic like that. She doesn't mind men if they're serving her at the restaurant or delivering her groceries. What she doesn't want is for any man to enter her personal sphere, or at least not in a romantic setting."

"Is your dad still in the picture?" he asked as he unfolded his napkin and placed it on his knees. The gesture brought back memories of her dates with Harvey, who hadn't been a very clean eater and had never failed to litter the floor with the remnants of his meal—a habit she had never enjoyed, since she was usually the one who had to clean up after him.

"He died," she said. "Before I was even born. And from the stories Mom tells me, it wasn't a great loss to the world."

Oddly enough, she didn't even know what the man had looked like, since Mom had destroyed all his pictures when he left her, pregnant and alone. All she knew was that he had been a shoe salesman, and she had met him when she bought a pair of shoes in his store. In later years, Rita had gone looking for the shoe store, located at the mall, but it hadn't been there anymore, which stood to reason if the owner died.

The only keepsake her mom had kept was a small silver necklace depicting an angel. Rita had found it once when going through her mother's stuff, as kids do, but when she had asked her mom where it came from, her mom had snatched it from her hands and insisted she should probably have thrown it out years ago. Later, she had told her that it was a gift from her dad, and had even gifted it to her daughter at some point. Rita had always kept it as one of her most prized possessions. The engraving on the necklace read 'to G from R,' which was also how she had found out that her dad's name began with an R. No last name, and her mother had never divulged it to her, and since the topic was so sensitive, Rita had learned not to touch it. And so she hadn't.

"I wanted to apologize once again," Samuel began.

"I wanted to apologize for this morning," Rita said simultaneously. They both laughed. "Okay, so maybe we've done all the apologizing we need for now," she said.

"Why don't we order dinner?" he suggested. He seemed apologetic again when they checked the specials. "If it were up to me, I would have taken you somewhere a little more upscale," he confessed.

"I like it here," she said. "This is exactly the kind of food I like, and you can't beat the price."

It was one of those mom and pop diners where they served the kind of grub she mostly associated with comfort food. The kind her mom also liked to make for the two of them, though lately Rita had been taking over cooking chores more and more, since her mom said that after thirty years in the kitchen she was getting fed up and was running out of inspiration of what to cook. Which Rita could certainly understand.

"How is your mom holding up?" asked Samuel. "After what happened this morning to your neighbor, I mean?"

"As well as can be expected," said Rita. "The police have been in and out all day. They were very nice and a big support for us." She still hadn't fully come to terms with what had happened to Morgan. But then they'd only known the man for a couple of months, of course. Now if something like that were to happen to her mom... But since that didn't bear thinking about, she didn't even want to go there.

"They came to the shop today," said Samuel, "asking all kinds of questions."

"They came to your shop? But why?"

She shrugged. "They seem to think I'm a suspect."

"But why? Did you know Morgan?"

"No, I never met the man. But they think I may have been jealous of him..." His face had flushed and he looked as uncomfortable as he had been when he asked her out.

"Jealous? Of Morgan?"

"The thing is... Your colleague Ken talked to them. And he said that I'm in love with you, and that I thought that Morgan was a rival and so I killed him."

She uttered a startled laugh. "But that's preposterous! Morgan was old enough to be my dad. I wasn't even remotely interested in him, and I can assure you he wasn't interested in me." She balled up her napkin. "That Ken. I think it's about time I had a word with the kid. Do you know he's been following me around? Even checking out the apartment? Parking in the parking lot and staring at us with a pair of binoculars. It's just too much."

"He does seem to have an unhealthy interest in you. Probably the reason he accosted me in the parking lot."

"He's just a kid. Maybe he should try and find himself a girl his own age."

"I'm sure the police don't really believe I would do such a thing, though," said her dinner date as they patiently waited for their food to arrive. "They're just crossing all the T's and dotting the I's like in any investigation. If someone tells them that I'm a likely suspect, they're duty-bound to check it out."

"Yeah, I guess," she said. "I hope they catch whoever did this soon. It's a horrible feeling to know that the man you've been living next to has been murdered. For the same token these people could have targeted me and my mom instead."

Samuel grimaced. "It doesn't bear thinking about," he said, which was really sweet of him especially since he didn't even know her or her mom.

Then an idea struck her. "Why don't you drop by the apartment later tonight? After dinner? I'll introduce you to my mom and she can see for herself that you're not some kind of ogre. Then maybe if we go out again, she won't give me such a hard time."

He perked up considerably at these words. "Oh, absolutely."

She realized she had intimated there might be a second date in the future and wondered why she had said that. Maybe because she felt surprisingly at ease around the guy? Almost as if she had known him longer than just the one day. He was certainly easy to talk to. Like a friend she had known for years.

"Look, Mom's bark is much worse than her bite. She just had a tough time having to raise me all by herself, and with not a lot of money to spend. So she developed this dislike of all men. And now with this whole business with Harvey…" She bit her lip, and remembered how she had told herself she wouldn't go there. Discussing her ex-boyfriend definitely was not first-date material—or whatever this dinner was.

"Harvey is your ex-boyfriend?" asked Samuel, eager to find out more about her.

She nodded. "Yeah, he's also the father of my baby," she said, figuring that if she was going to tell him about Harvey, she just as well might go full hog and tell him about the baby, too. See how fast he would run.

"Oh, so you're... pregnant?"

She nodded again. "Six weeks. Harvey wasn't happy when I told him, which is the main reason we broke up, although there are other reasons." She should have said the reason *he* broke up with *her*, but since she still wasn't fully recovered from that, she couldn't bring herself to say the words.

"That's horrible," he said earnestly. "So he's not... intending to get involved?"

"No, looks like he's out of the picture. For good."

"That's shameful," said Samuel with some heat. Clearly, he had read between the lines and had assessed what kind of a person Harvey was. "Absolutely shameful."

"It certainly was a great shock to me," she said.

"Will you be all right? Raising the baby all by yourself, I mean?"

"I'll be fine. Mom will pitch in, and together we'll make sure this little fella—or gal—will want for nothing."

Contrary to what she had expected, he didn't want to cut the dinner short, or didn't seem inclined to run to the hills at all. Quite the contrary. This glimpse into her life seemed to have opened the sluice gates for him, and he told her about the girl he had been engaged with for a while until she had decided to get involved with his best friend at the time. "They're married now. And he's not my friend anymore."

"I'm sorry," she said with feeling. Looked like they had both suffered some of life's setbacks. The food, when it came, was exactly as tasty and nourishing as she had thought, and as they chatted about this and that, she felt more and more at ease with this man. The incident of the collision was all but forgotten, and if this kept up, she might even accept an invitation for a second date—or a real first one. And she had just ordered coffee and a piece of cherry pie when she happened to glance out of the window and saw to her consternation that a familiar figure was watching them from inside a parked car, and filming them on his phone. It was none other than Ken—her annoying twerp of a colleague!

"This is too much," she said. Samuel looked over, and when he saw Ken, growled something she didn't understand.

Moments later he was outside and dragging the kid from his car and confiscating his phone.

Deeply embarrassed, Rita followed him out and confronted her colleague.

"Ken, what the hell!" she cried.

"He was filming us all through dinner," said Samuel, holding the phone out of the kid's reach. "And taking pictures, too. Dozens of them." He flicked through the phone some more. "Correction—hundreds of them. All of you. At work, at home, out shopping with your mom. This guy has been stalking you."

"Ken, what were you thinking?!"

"I'm worried about you, all right?" said the teenager as she pulled his jacket straighter after Samuel had let go of him. She noticed he sported a black eye. He gave Samuel an indignant look. "Someone needs to look after you, with all the people being murdered around you, and the creeps chasing you."

"What creeps!"

"Well, that Harvey for one thing, and now this creep."

"Samuel is not a creep," she said. "Harvey… well, all right. I guess Harvey is a creep." Served her right for going out with him in the first place, and getting pregnant. And hoping he would marry her even though he was clearly not one of the good guys. She fixed the kid with a serious look. "You can't follow people around like that, Ken. You just can't."

"I'm not following people around," he said. "I'm following you."

"Well, you can't do that, all right? Will you promise me you'll stop doing this?"

"Oh, all right," he said. "But then who's going to protect you from the creeps of this world?"

She smiled. "I can assure you that I don't need protecting, Ken."

"Says the woman whose neighbor was found stabbed to death this morning," he grumbled.

"Just stop it, all right? Because if you don't... I'll have to talk to Rose."

He looked up. "You wouldn't do that."

"Just make sure you don't follow me around anymore, understood?"

"Fine," he said reluctantly. He cast a dirty glance at Samuel, who was still holding onto his phone. "You're not going out with this guy again, though, right? I can tell you right now that he doesn't deserve you."

"Ken, you will get back in your car and you will drive away," she said, not mincing words. "And if I ever see you chasing me around again, I will talk to Rose."

"Okay, fine!" he said, holding up his hands. He grabbed his phone from Samuel's hands. But as he glanced at the screen, he uttered a cry of dismay. "You deleted all of my photos! And my videos!"

"Of course I did," said Samuel. "Stalkers shouldn't be rewarded."

"Who are you calling a stalker, creep?" said the kid.

"Ken!" she cried. "Get in your car right now!"

"Yes, Rita," he said, and quickly crawled behind the wheel. They watched him drive off.

"He'll be back," said Samuel.

"No, he won't," said Rita. "He's learned his lesson now." And if he hadn't, she would tell Rose and she would give him a speech that he wouldn't likely forget. The kind of speech that would make him change his ways for sure. Rose had that capacity. When she spoke, people listened.

She returned inside with her dinner date, and for the rest of the evening tried to put this whole business with her neighbor out of her head. Though she did mention that she had been invited to the reading of the will the next day. Something that seemed to surprise Samuel even more than it had her.

"What do you think he will have left you?"

"No idea," she said. "Probably a small legacy. Some trinket to remember him by." Mom and Morgan had become really good friends over the course of the last couple of weeks, so much so that Rita actually thought that they might get involved at some point, which would have quite the turnaround for the books if that happened.

Too bad they'd never know if that was ever in the cards.

CHAPTER 29

After paying a visit to the MacKereth women, we circled back to Uncle Alec's place, since Harriet had expressed the wish to shoot some more ASMR videos of the chief in his hot tub. When we arrived, the party was in full swing, and his jacuzzi filled with people—but Odelia's uncle wasn't among them. The noise level was impressive, and Harriet felt it wasn't ASMR, so she didn't bring out Gran's phone again.

The garden party was certainly a resounding success—though I'm not sure if the organizer—or non-organizer—would have agreed with this assessment, as all he seemed to want was to be left alone. One thing was for sure: the chief had managed to make the topic of the jacuzzi top of mind. To the extent that every person who left the party did so with the fervent wish to own a jacuzzi like the chief's themselves. The only one who denied having a jacuzzi wish was Dolores, but that was because she had made it clear that from now on she was going to be a regular guest at her boss's hot tub—she even told him she wouldn't mind dropping by on a daily basis. Something the chief didn't seem to endorse. At least if his words 'Please God no!' were to be believed.

Like any employer, Uncle Alec sincerely appreciates his staff—but from a distance. And as long as he doesn't have to entertain them after hours. Except the annual obligatory team-building event, of course.

"I still wonder how Alec managed to buy himself no less than two jacuzzis," said Chase as we were walking back home.

"Maybe he took advantage of a deal?" Tex suggested. "Buy one, get the second—"

"Free?" asked Marge. "Now that is what I call a great deal!"

"Not free, but at a discount. Fifty percent off maybe?"

"Don't they have a third one for eighty percent off?" asked Odelia.

"I doubt it, babe," said Chase. "They don't like to put these high-priced items on sale too much. Though you may want to keep an eye on the promotions. You never know."

By now, both Odelia and Marge knew all about the wish their respective husbands had of gifting them a jacuzzi, though clearly between dream and reality gaped the chasm of the financial outlay such a purchase required. But now that they had become aware of Uncle Alec's double-jacuzzi situation, I got a feeling that for the rest of the summer there would be a lot of time spent over at Charlene's place, and that the money they saved on the jacuzzi could be spent on something else—like a couple of extra bags of premium kibble for instance—or a lot of bags, since jacuzzis are pricy. Which begged the question once again of how Uncle Alec and Charlene could afford such an expense, on top of their trip to the Maldives they recently took.

"I think Uncle Alec got a big pay raise when he married Charlene," Dooley reiterated his earlier theory.

"I doubt it," said Odelia.

"You doubt what, babe?" asked Chase.

"Dooley thinks that Charlene must have giving Uncle Alec a big fat pay raise, since she controls the police budget."

"It's not as straightforward as that," said Chase as he eyed Dooley with a kindly gaze. "Charlene may be the mayor, but that doesn't mean she can spend the town's budget any way she pleases. There is a budget committee, and also regular audits and oversight involved. So even if she wanted to double or triple her husband's salary, she wouldn't be able to pull it off without attracting a lot of scrutiny and censure. Also, there would be a big scandal if she did, and her political career would be over, and also Uncle Alec's career as chief of police. In other words: it just wouldn't be worth it."

"It would if they can buy a dozen jacuzzis," Brutus added.

Odelia had to smile at this. "Wait until they buy a pool," she told our friend. "Tongues will surely start wagging."

"They're already wagging now," said Marge as she consulted her phone. "The video that Harriet shared has gone viral, and now the whole town knows that my brother likes to soak in his hot tub and they think he's getting divorced."

"Lots of hearts and hugs," said Tex, who was also on his phone. "Looks like Alec has a lot of support now that he's getting divorced."

"But he's not getting divorced!" said Marge, grabbing her husband's phone and putting it back in his pocket. "Didn't you hear a word he and Charlene said? It's all just speculation on Harriet's part, and now everyone believes that there's going to be a high-profile divorce when nothing could be further from the truth."

"No, I don't think I've ever seen a happier and more united couple," said Odelia. "They're really happy together, and I also love how Charlene is prepared to give Uncle Alec space."

"That's the advantage of getting married at a later age," said Marge. "They're more relaxed and confident in their affection towards each other."

"Just like us," said Tex, as he placed an arm around his wife's shoulder.

"And like us," said Chase, as he did the same with Odelia.

"And like us!" said Brutus as he tried to put a paw around Harriet's shoulder. But since it's tough to walk with three limbs and because Harriet doesn't like it when people put their paws on her when she's walking along the street, the gesture, no matter how well-intentioned, was short-lived.

"I think it's really cute that Uncle Alec and Charlene each have their own houses," said Dooley. "Though I'm afraid that if they don't spend enough time together, they might drift apart and eventually get divorced anyway. What do you say, Max?"

"Well, I'm not a marriage expert, Dooley," said Max. "So I really couldn't say. But it seems to me that they're both smart people and so I'm sure they'll figure it out."

"Perfect answer," said Brutus with a grin. "Spoken like a true politician."

"No, but it's true," I said. "We don't know what's going to happen in the future, so there's nothing we can say right now."

"I know what to say," said Harriet, and that wasn't a surprise, since Harriet always knows what to say, even if she doesn't have anything to say. "That my video was clearly a huge success, and so I'm going to get busy shooting more of them. Beginning with Dooley sleeping with his eyes open." She turned to our friend. "I'm going to shoot a video of you, Dooley, and if you tell me I shouldn't, because of privacy or whatnot, let me assure you that it's all for a good cause. The people watching these ASMR videos are all feeling better, their heart rates are dropping, and so is their blood pressure. So you're being instrumental in healing people."

"I am?" asked Dooley, much surprised.

"Absolutely! In fact, you're preventing people from dying, since they'll feel better and their bodies are working better. So you're in the business of saving lives, Dooley."

"Ooh, I like that," said Dooley, perking up considerably. He hadn't been a big fan of being filmed before, but now he was all for it.

"What is your next video going to be?" asked Brutus. "Apart from Dooley, I mean." He thrust out his chest a little, and it was clear that he was hoping that he would also be featured prominently on his girlfriend's video channel.

"I was thinking of filming cat choir," said Harriet. "I think the sound of cats singing in harmony will soothe a lot of people's nerves. Today's world is so stressful that there can never be too much soothing going on. I'll ask Shanille's permission, of course, but I'm sure she'll agree with me that cat choir is doing the Lord's work in spreading sweetness and joy."

"So... you're going to be filming yourself?" asked Brutus, who seemed slightly disappointed.

"Absolutely," Harriet confirmed. "It's my YouTube channel, sweetness. So if I can't be the star of my own channel, I wouldn't be doing a good job, now would I? And you," she said proudly, "can be my videographer. Isn't that great?"

Brutus cut a pained look in my direction before responding, "That sounds swell, baby cheeks. Just swell."

CHAPTER 30

The moment he saw his neighbor appear in his backyard, Ted Trapper made a beeline for the hedge and accosted the doctor. "Tex!" he loud-whispered. "Pssst! Tex! Over here!"

Tex came sidling up, a curious expression on his face.

"I've been calling you non-stop for hours!" Ted complained.

"You have?" The doctor took out his phone. "Oh, you're right. I'm sorry, buddy. I turned my phone off at the party."

"Party? What party?"

"The jacuzzi party over at my brother-in-law's place," said Tex. "Weren't you and Marcie invited?"

"No, we weren't," said Ted, his sense of injury growing deeper by the minute. "I also sent you several messages. Are you telling me you didn't see those either?"

"When you're in a hot tub it's better not to take your phone, Ted," said his neighbor. "So I just turned it off."

"You were in a hot tub?"

"Absolutely. One of Alec's new hot tubs. He's got two, you know. And it was wonderful. Though there were too many people, of course. Pretty much half the town was there." He tsk-tsked lightly. "Too bad you weren't there, buddy."

"I was too busy dealing with something over here," said Ted, feeling much aggrieved knowing that the entire town had been invited to enjoy the chief of police's hot tub and he and Marcie hadn't. It wasn't fair, he felt. And coming upon the pee incident, his sense of grievance was strong—very strong.

"So what did you want to talk to me about?" asked Tex as he placed his arms on the hedge that divided his backyard from his neighbor's. "Something important, was it?"

"It's that video!" said Ted as he directed a surreptitious look at the house.

"Video? What video?"

"Well, that YouTube video!" When Tex still gave him a blank look, he elucidated, "The video of me peeing on my rose bushes!"

Tex laughed. "You were peeing on your rose bushes? But why, Ted?"

"Because I'd read online that it's a surefire way to make sure that your plants will get the hydration they need."

"Couldn't you simply have sprayed them with the hose, like everybody does?"

"I did, but the peeing makes the plants hold on to the water much better." Or at least that was the theory he had seen proposed online. Now he was getting his doubts whether it was true or not. Marcie, at least, hadn't endorsed the theory. Quite the opposite. The moment she had seen that video she had shouted the house down, and had demanded he got it taken down ASAP, before their friends, family, and neighbors saw.

"I'm not sure I've ever heard that particular theory," Tex confessed. "Though of course it could be true," he allowed.

"Look, the thing is that someone shot a video of me

peeing, and Marcie saw it and she wants it taken down—*I* want it taken down. So can you take it down?"

"Me? Shouldn't you get in touch with the YouTube people for that?"

"I did, but you know how it goes. You fill out a form and who knows when they'll get back to you. So can't you delete it?"

Tex stared at him. "You think I shot that video?"

"It has to be you," said Ted. "Or at least a member of your family. It was shot from right behind the hedge, frog perspective. Personally I think it was Vesta, but it's hard to know for sure. On the same channel, a second video has appeared, of your brother-in-law singing in his hot tub. It also says he's about to get a divorce and to send a lot of good wishes his way. So my money is on Vesta. Or Marge. Though I can't imagine Marge would ever do such a thing."

"I could always ask," said Tex thoughtfully. "But you know Vesta. She never does what you ask her to."

"Reverse psychology, Tex," Ted suggested. He had given the matter some thought, and he figured that the only way to get Vesta to remove that video was either to conk her over the head and steal her phone and delete that video himself. Or to make sure she removed it of her own free will. "You need to tell her that the video is amazing, wonderful, super— just the best thing you've ever seen. And since Vesta hates you and everything you say, she will immediately delete the video."

Tex's face had sagged. "You're mistaken, Ted. Vesta doesn't hate me. In fact, she loves me. I'm her favorite son-in-law."

"You're her only son-in-law. And you know she does hate you. So if you say black, she'll say white, just to spite you."

"She loves me with all her heart and I will prove it," said Tex stubbornly, and he bellowed, "Vesta! Can you come out here a moment?" He awaited his mother-in-law's arrival with a triumphant smile on his face. "I'll prove it," he repeated.

"I don't care what you do," he said. "Just as long as that video is removed from her YouTube channel, that's all I'm asking. When my boss sees that movie, he'll freak out."

It wasn't the policy of Kruger & Sons, the accountancy firm where he worked, to have their personnel feature in weird and embarrassing videos on the internet. It might very well affect the future of his career—if he would even have a future.

Vesta came ambling up. "What is it?" she asked, shooting Ted a dirty look for no reason at all.

"Jacuzzi," said Tex, enunciating clearly.

Much to his surprise, Ted saw the old lady's lips curl up into a wide smile. "You got it?"

The doctor nodded.

"Oh, Tex!" She slung her arms around her son-in-law's neck and actually gave him a smacking kiss on the cheek!

"See?" said Tex. "I'm Mister Popular around here."

"Be that as it may," he said. "Can you please get rid of that video of me peeing, Vesta?"

"I didn't put it online, so I can't put it offline," said Vesta, which sounded quite reasonable, he had to admit.

"But then who put it there?" he asked, getting a little desperate at this point. "If it wasn't you, who made it?"

"I have absolutely no idea," said Vesta, and went so far as to give Tex an actual wink! Clearly, those two were up to something. And then he had it. He pointed a finger at them.

"You're in on this together, aren't you? You shot that video, and you put it online just to spite me. To *spite* me!"

"I have no idea what you're talking about," said Vesta virtuously. "And now if you'll excuse me, I've got to get ready for the watch. We're riding tonight, you see, catching crooks and fighting crime for the benefit of all of Hampton Cove." She gave his chest a pat. "And that includes you, buddy boy."

If looks could kill, Vesta would have been struck down as if by lightning bolt, but unfortunately it didn't work like that.

"She put that video online and you know it!" he said the moment Vesta was out of earshot.

"I'm sure it's all one big misunderstanding," said Tex vaguely, and then he, too, walked off, leaving his neighbor to fume in silence. He walked back to the house, but not before checking his precious roses. And he had to admit they looked a lot better than they had before. His pee therapy, no matter how controversial, was working. His mistake was that he should have applied the therapy at night, when Vesta wasn't looking.

Live and learn.

And so he returned to the house, to face his wife's wrath, and to check his email, hoping the good people at YouTube had written back to announce they had checked the video and had found it to be in contradiction of their terms of service.

CHAPTER 31

Nicholas had been sniffing behind a big tree in the park, as was his habit, when he finally found the spot he had done his business only hours before—his very own tree—the one tree in the park that he really could call his own—and lifted his hind leg. That was the trouble with living rough in the park, he sometimes felt: there was simply no place that you could truly call your own, since there were so many dogs—tourists as he called them—who came there on a daily basis and all of them thought that the park was theirs and treated it as their personal property. Whereas the reality was that the park was his. It was the place where he lived and worked, and so if there was anyone who could claim it as his home, it was him.

Though as things now stood, it looked as if these could be his very last moments spent in the park and living rough. If Cesar's plans went off without a hitch, very soon they would be able to rent an apartment for the two of them to live, and maybe, just maybe, even buy their own house in the suburbs, just like Cesar had always promised.

Nicholas had been Cesar's constant companion for going

on five years now, and so that dream was a long time coming. But he had never lost faith in the man, knowing that even though Cesar had been kicked around by life so often, he had a good head on his shoulders and a certain shrewdness.

After Nicholas had relieved himself against his favorite tree, he passed by the small congregation of dogs that called themselves dog choir. He glanced at them with a touch of disdain, since he couldn't understand how a bunch of dogs could lower themselves to take part in such a sad spectacle. Modeled after cat choir, the unofficial gathering of the cats of Hampton Cove, a couple of the town's dogs had felt they also needed to organize a regular gathering. For them, it wasn't as easy as it was for cats, since most dog owners like to keep their mutts behind lock and key, and don't allow them to go wandering off unsupervised, like cat owners do.

Many was the time a dog owner had arrived in the park and had grabbed their mutt and taken off again, making a big stink and muttering things about being worried sick.

Cesar was never worried sick over Nicholas, since he knew from experience he always came back. They were like an old married couple and knew each other's quirks and idiosyncrasies. Nicholas knew Cesar snored, for instance, but didn't mind. And Cesar sometimes complained that Nicholas had a habit of sleeping on his stomach, and when it was raining, would tuck underneath his coat, but he didn't mind.

He left dog choir to their own devices and headed in the direction of the bench that Cesar had singled out as his home turf. He approached the man and saw that he had already turned in for the night, sleeping on his back as he sometimes did, hands on his chest. And since his paws were a little cold, he jumped up on the man's chest and settled in for the night. It wasn't long before he became aware of something wet and warm under his paws. And when he got up and looked down, he saw a mysterious red substance leaking from his human.

Odd, he thought. Now what was that about? He knew that Cesar had a habit of sneaking a bottle of red wine from time to time and imbibing a little too much when the mood struck. But he didn't see a bottle, and still the liquid kept coming, now dripping on the bench.

And then he had it.

Cesar... had been stabbed!

* * *

HARRIET HAD BEEN PLAYING first fiddle while Brutus had been relegated to videographer, ensuring he got her entire performance on film, when all of a sudden there was a sort of disturbance or altercation. When we looked up, we saw that a familiar dog had burst into our circle and was shouting something. It took a while before Harriet could be convinced to halt her performance, so that we could understand what the doggie, whom I now recognized as Nicholas, had to say.

"You have to help me!" he cried. "It's Cesar! He's been stabbed!" And then he ran off again, paused, looked behind him, and urged, "Well? Aren't you coming!"

Shanille lowered her arms and gestured to me and Dooley. "Off you go. Duty calls. Chop chop. Not you, Harriet. You need to finish that song first. And let's take it from the top!"

And as Dooley and I hurried after Nicholas, behind us the choir resumed its rehearsal, with Harriet singing at the top of her lungs as she always does, her voice piercing the air like a dagger slicing the febrile fabric of the night. In their houses, neighbors were already collecting their shoes so they could throw them in our direction. In other words: business as usual.

But not business as usual for Nicholas, for when we finally arrived at the bench where he had taken us, we saw that Cesar, the vagrant whose acquaintance we had made that afternoon, was lying on the bench, and if I wasn't mistaken, he wasn't sleeping but had been delivered into the arms of death!

Dooley and I jumped up onto the bench, and after a careful examination of the man, both had to conclude life was extinct.

"We have to tell Odelia, Max," said Dooley as we evaluated the situation.

"What you have to do is save him!" said Nicholas.

"I'm afraid there's nothing we can do for him," I told him. "Your human is dead, Nicholas."

"No, but that's impossible!" said the doggie, extremely agitated, I saw, as was to be expected. "He was fine when I left him. He can't be dead!"

"Tell us exactly what happened," I told him, knowing that a witness statement is always best when delivered as soon as possible.

"He was sitting on the bench, and I went for a pee. When I returned, he was lying on his back, so I jumped up on his chest. But then I felt something wet and sticky. At first, I thought it was wine."

"Wine isn't sticky," Dooley said.

"It was blood," said Nicholas, with a horrified and slightly dazed look on his face. "Blood!"

A substantial amount of the stuff had dripped down from the bench onto the ground below. "Did you notice anyone suspicious?" I asked. "Anyone lurking around here today?"

"Nobody," said Nicholas determinedly. "If there was, I would have noticed."

"This morning you told us that you hadn't noticed anyone hanging around the Rock Tower either," I said. "But I got the impression you weren't telling us the whole truth." And I had a feeling that the death of the vagrant just might be connected with the death of the billionaire this morning, and I was determined to get the truth from Nicholas this time.

He hung his head. "You don't think this had something to do with what happened this morning, do you, Max?"

"I'm convinced that it's too much of a coincidence," I said. "So what didn't you tell us this morning, Nicholas?" When he didn't immediately respond, I urged, "Anything you tell us might help us catch the person that did this."

He finally nodded. "Okay, fine. First off, the apartment door wasn't open when we arrived. It was locked."

"So how did you get in?"

"In a previous life Cesar used to be a burglar and an ace safe-cracker. He kept the tools of his trade and…" He gave us a shamefaced look. "From time to time he would break into people's apartments to pinch this and that—never a lot."

"Okay, what else?" I asked, for I had a feeling there was more.

"Well, the moment Cesar had given his statement to the police, he made a phone call. Turns out the killer had dropped a card of some kind—possibly a hotel key card."

"Cesar saw the killer?"

"I think so. It wasn't long before he started getting messages. In the end, he asked for one thousand dollars to be delivered here in the park. The person agreed to bring it but said it was the first and last payment they would make."

"So Cesar saw the killer this morning, and he blackmailed them," I concluded. "Why didn't you tell us, Nicholas?"

"Because I didn't know that Cesar was going to blackmail this person, did I? Not when I talked to you guys. That all came later on."

"But you were hiding something. I could see it in your eyes."

"I've always been a lousy liar," said the mongrel. "Okay, so I didn't actually see the killer, since I had trouble mounting those stairs—six flights is a lot!—but I smelled them."

"You smelled the killer?"

"Well, yes. At least I think it must have been the killer. I smelled something in that apartment, and it wasn't the dead man, that much I knew. And then when Cesar started texting and calling, I knew he must have seen the killer when they left the dead man's apartment. My best guess is that he caught a glimpse of the person on their way down those same stairs."

"And you smelled them."

Nicholas nodded. "Though I couldn't tell you who it was."

"And so Cesar started blackmailing the killer." We all looked up at the dead man. "And paid for it with his life."

CHAPTER 32

Uncle Alec arrived first, and judging from the look on his face, he still hadn't forgiven Harriet for posting that video of him in his hot tub. The look he gave her was not the look you would give the beloved cat of your beloved niece. In short order, the coroner also arrived, and Chase and Odelia. Personally, we had no involvement in the prompt arrival of the constabulary on the scene. It was a late-night dog walker who had come across the body of the dead man and had raised the alarm. And a good thing, too. By the time we would have arrived home, poor Cesar would have been lying out there for perhaps going on an hour, and this way the police were much quicker off the mark.

The dog walker was being interviewed by a police officer, taking down his information, while Abe Cornwall, our county coroner, examined the body. The frizzy-haired expert finally shook his head and rose to his feet.

"Well, he's dead, all right," he announced.

"I know he's dead, Abe," Uncle Alec growled. "But what made him so is what I would like to know."

"In a bad mood, are you, chief?" asked the coroner. "Can't

say I blame you. Going through a divorce like that must be tough on a man. And such a nice woman, too. A real catch."

"I'm not getting divorced!" the chief shouted, and I got the impression it wasn't the first time that day he'd spoken these words.

"Oh?" said Abe, quirking his bushy brows, that were easily as electrically wired as his hair. "But I saw it on the internet. And you know what they say about the internet, chief. It's all true, and even if it isn't, someone out there will believe it."

"Well, it's not true. And if I catch the person that put that video online," he said, balling his hands into fists and giving Harriet a look that could kill, "they'll be sorry for not deleting it when I specifically told them to!"

"Did Uncle Alec ask you to delete his video?" asked Brutus.

"Of course not," said Harriet. "He's joking. He loves the fact that I made him famous. Singing in his pool like that. Pretty soon now he'll be on *The Voice* as the Singing Chief."

"I like that," said Brutus. "Like the Singing Detective."

"I have to say that I really enjoyed the video, though," said Abe. "Especially the singing. Though the jacuzzi wasn't too shabby either. When can I come and visit? It said to pay you a visit underneath the video. Take a dip in that hot tub?"

Uncle Alec's jaw was tensing so bad I got the impression that pretty soon his teeth would shatter from the per-pound pressure, but he managed to control himself with a tremendous effort. Since he didn't trust what would come out of his mouth, he merely sufficed by pointing at the dead man.

"Oh, right," said Abe. "I almost forgot about the poor bugger. Stabbed in the heart, I would say. Pretty big knife."

"Like the knife that killed Morgan Sears?" asked Chase.

"Who?"

"Nathanial Tindell," Odelia clarified.

"Ah, yes. The elusive billionaire." He thought for a

moment. "I'd say so. I'd have to get him on my slab first to make sure. Speaking of my slab, I cut open that Tindell dude, and it was as I told you this morning. Big old knife wound to the chest. Cut straight through the heart muscle. Death would have been pretty much instantaneous. As for this guy..." He gestured to his assistants. "Wrap him up, fellas."

"He's not a turkey, Abe," Uncle Alec growled.

"Keep me informed about that hot tub," said the coroner, paying no mind to the chief's bad mood. "I love a nice hot tub, especially in the early evening. Let's say around five? Best time to work up an appetite before we sit down for dinner."

And with these words, he took off his gloves and removed himself from the scene.

"Only Abe could think about dinner at a time like this," said Uncle Alec disapprovingly. He sighed deeply. "So looks like we've got a second murder in less than twenty-four hours. Must be some kind of record, people."

"Same killer, you think?" asked Chase.

The question was directed at Odelia, and not his boss.

"According to the cats, yes," said Odelia. "They talked to the man's dog, and he says that Cesar saw the killer this morning, and blackmailed them for the sum of one thousand dollars. Looks like the killer decided not to pay."

"And did the dog tell them who the killer is?" asked Uncle Alec hopefully.

"No, but he did say he picked up the scent."

"Fat lot of good that does us," said her uncle moodily.

"It may be useful at some point," said Odelia. "But we'll have to find the killer first, and organize a line-up."

"A line-up for a dog!" cried Uncle Alec. "No way."

"An informal line-up," Odelia suggested. "We could bring in the suspects that we have identified so far. Ken Torres, Harvey Furniss, Samuel Dickenson, and Bella Fuller."

"We should talk to all of these people again," said Chase. "Check their alibis for…" He checked his watch. "When did Abe say he died?"

"He didn't," said the chief, and hurried off after the coroner. "Abe!" he yelled.

The coroner turned. "Right now is not a good time for our hot tub date, Alec," he quipped with a twinkle in his eye.

We watched as the two men talked for a moment, then the chief came hurrying back to our little huddle. "Been dead for about an hour, he reckons. Which would make time of death around midnight."

"What's going to happen to Nicholas now?" asked Dooley. "He can't be all alone, Max. He's such a nice dog."

I hadn't gotten the impression that Nicholas was a very nice dog, since he had lied to us when it mattered most, but it was true that we couldn't leave him at the park, alone to fend for himself. So we raised the matter with Odelia, who put it to her uncle and her husband. And since Odelia felt that she already had enough pets to contend with, Uncle Alec was selected to take care of the dog for the time being, until a different solution could be found.

Judging from the man's face, he was not happy with this.

"He's so judgmental, isn't he, Max?" Harriet complained later, as we were en route to the old homestead. "Complaining about the hot tub situation, and now about the dog. Uncle Alec is becoming grumpy in his old age."

"Maybe we should remove that video after all," said Brutus.

"Nonsense," said Harriet. "It's the one thing that has brought a little happiness in his life. A little ray of sunshine. We can't take that away from him. No, let's keep that video up and make sure as many people as possible get to see it."

"What about Ted Trapper's video?" I asked. "Shouldn't we take it down?"

"Why? Ted has discovered a new way of watering his plants, and they're all the better for it. And besides, that video is the most-watched one of all the videos I've shot today, so that means it's hitting the spot."

"Ted certainly hit the spot," Brutus grinned. "His aim is true." But when Harriet gave him a critical look, he quickly shut up.

"We better get going, snow bunny," she said. "We have those snails to film."

Dooley and I stared at her. "Snails?" I asked stupidly.

"Very ASMR, Max," she said. "Snails crawling over things? People can watch them for hours—which is convenient, since it takes those snails hours to go from point A to point B."

"Buster has told us about a great spot where snails gather," said Brutus sadly. "And now Harriet wants to film them. For hours."

"Let's go," said Harriet briskly. "Snails wait for no one."

"And here I thought they waited for everyone," said Brutus with a sigh, but still slunk after his mate.

"Looks like it's going to be a long night for Brutus and Harriet, Max," said Dooley as we wended our way home.

"A very long night," I said.

"But on the bright side, they're making people happy with their ASMR videos," he said. "So that is very gratifying."

"I'm sure it is," I said, and I thought of Ted Trapper and Uncle Alec, who could both drink Harriet's blood. At least those snails wouldn't mind if they were being filmed.

"I wonder when she will film me. Though I probably won't even know, since I will be asleep."

Oh, dear. "I just hope she won't film me," I said. The last thing I needed was to wake up in the middle of the night to find myself gazing into the lens of a camera and being captured for posterity in a most embarrassing position.

CHAPTER 33

So far Vesta hadn't seen the need to reassume control over her phone. Even though she missed the device, she felt that the advantages of Harriet filming her videos outweighed the disadvantage of having to do without her phone. The videos the cat had shot were all fantastic. That annoying Ted Trapper being filmed peeing was her favorite, of course, and she couldn't stop laughing at the comments that people posted underneath the footage, as read on her daughter's phone.

And of course, Alec's hot tub video was just the best.

"I didn't even know he could sing," she told her daughter as they watched the video together for the umpteenth time.

"Badly," said Marge. "Very badly."

"'The Musical Chief,'" Vesta read. "Very funny. Though they probably should call him 'The Unmusical Chief' since Alec can't sing."

If her son splashing in his hot tub was funny, though, the one about the dog poo was even funnier. For some reason, Harriet got it into her head that filming dog poo was very ASMR and that people would find it relaxing and entrancing.

"I have to say that it *is* fascinating," Marge allowed.

"It's in bad taste, that's what it is," said Tex as he turned off the television.

As usual, they had watched TV far too long and would probably feel it in the morning when they had to get up. But then they shouldn't make such great shows, she thought.

"When are you going to remove them?" asked Marge.

"Ted asked us to," said Tex. "But your mother told him that she didn't put them online."

"I *didn't* put them online," said Vesta. "Harriet did."

"With *your* phone," Marge pointed out.

"So? It's a free world. If Ted is free to pee in his backyard, Harriet is free to post about it."

"It's his backyard, Ma," said Marge, being the fusspot that she usually was. "Ever heard about privacy?"

"There are laws," Tex added, Mr. Fussypants to his wife.

"I'll take them down soon," she promised. "But first let's enjoy them a little longer. It's not every day that you get a YouTube channel that suddenly blows up. Just look at these numbers. Ted's pee video has already racked up twenty thousand views! Amazing. And Alec five thousand. Those are some pretty amazing numbers."

Just then, a new live video started playing, simply called 'Snails.'

"Now will you look at that?" she said. "Harriet is real busy today. Now she's filming snails."

It wasn't as sexy as Alec singing in his hot tub or Ted peeing, but it was definitely... interesting.

"What is it?" asked Tex.

For a moment they all watched as a snail slowly—ever so slowly—crawled over a leaf.

"I've got a hunch this won't rack up twenty thousand views," said Tex after a moment. "Nothing's happening."

"That's the point of ASMR, honey," said Marge. "Nothing

happens and that's very relaxing. Looks like Harriet is finally hitting her stride."

"It looks like she's doing a great job," said Vesta, well pleased with the cats. "If she keeps this up, we'll have quite the moneymaker on our hands. We might even be able to pay for the cats' food and then some."

"The point of having cats isn't to make sure they pay for themselves, Ma," said Marge.

"I know, I know. But wouldn't it be nice if they did?" She yawned and stretched. "Okay, it's time for beddy-bye. This girl needs her beauty sleep."

And since Marge and Tex also felt it was way past their bedtime, the three of them mounted the stairs, with Marge carrying a soundly sleeping Grace, since Odelia and Chase had been called out for some murder that had been committed in the park, so the little girl was staying with them.

Vesta waved her daughter, son-in-law, and great-granddaughter off and entered her room. Moments later, she was out like a light. Which is why when she woke up again, she was feeling a little disoriented. For a moment, she thought there was someone in the room with her, but then she figured it was simply her imagination. So she fell asleep again, and this time pulled through all the way to the morning, when the sun tickled her eyelids and announced a new day.

The moment she opened her eyes, she saw that her phone was lying on her nightstand, which was odd, since Harriet and Brutus had taken it last night to shoot some more ASMR videos.

The moment she picked it up, it vibrated with a message, and when she tapped to open it, she saw that her friend Scarlett had sent it.

"Looking good, girlfriend!" the message read.

She smiled, but then wondered what Scarlett meant. She saw she had also added a link, and when she clicked on the link, much to her consternation, she saw that it was a video… of herself!

As she watched the video, she realized that it had been shot last night, in this room, in this bed, with her as the star. She was fast asleep in the video, from time to time grunting a little, and smacking her lips. The worst part was that a little thread of drool hung from those lips and trailed all the way to the pillow. It looked absolutely horrible!

The title of the video was 'Very Old Woman Sleeping—Very Relaxing—Very ASMR!!!,' and the video had already racked up an astonishing fifteen thousand views.

Aaaargh!

* * *

Turned out that Dooley wasn't the only member of our household Harriet had filmed last night. Her YouTube channel was filled with fresh content, with several familiar faces featuring prominently. There was Dooley, as announced, who was a restless sleeper, and liked to twitch his nose and even his paws and tail from time to time, which was very cute, I had to say. Then there was me, sleeping peacefully and not moving a muscle—fully dead to the world, which was also the name of the video dedicated to my person. Tex had also been captured for eternity, and so had Marge, Gran, Odelia, Chase, and even Grace. All in all, I got the impression that not everyone was happy with this. At least if the cries of horror and shock emanating from the stars of Harriet's new videos were any indication.

"I want this off the internet!" Gran cried as she came storming into the kitchen. "Calling me an old woman! How dare you! I'm not old! This is a gross violation of my right to privacy!"

Harriet didn't seem the least bit contrite. "But you said that privacy is a flexible concept, Gran," she argued. "When I put the videos of Ted Trapper online, and also of Uncle Alec. You even told me to keep up the good work."

"That was before you put a video of me online!" Gran bellowed, and I could see that she didn't fully appreciate the ASMR effect her video seemed to have, judging by the number of likes and the many comments that had appeared under the video.

"But you're a big hit, Gran," said Dooley. "A really big hit. People really enjoy watching you sleep. I know I've enjoyed watching you sleep for years, and now we get to share the experience with others."

"Well, I don't care if people like it or not," said Gran. "I want this video gone!"

"All you have to do is take your phone and delete the video," said Chase as he munched on his breakfast. He was the only one who didn't seem bothered even the slightest about the videos having been shot of himself being asleep. But then Chase slept like a baby. He didn't stir, snore, or even move a muscle. He just lay there, on his back, like a Roman statue. Contrary to Odelia, who kept twisting and turning in her sleep all night. A nervous sleeper, just like her mom. But then I guess we're all different, and our personalities are reflected in the way we sleep.

"Oh," said Gran, as she hadn't considered that all of these videos had been shot on her phone, so all she had to do was simply delete them.

"Don't delete my channel, Gran," Harriet begged. "It's such a big hit, and it's doing so much good for so many people. This ASMR is such a blessing. Lots of people have said so."

Oddly enough, the video that got the most views was the one of cat choir, with Harriet in the starring role. I very much doubted people found it relaxing, though. More nerve-wracking. But then people also like thrillers, horror movies, and watching car crashes.

Gran wavered. If she removed her own video, but kept all the others online, she could be accused of being a hypocrite. If she removed all the videos—the entire channel, in other words—that would mean having to remove her favorite video of Ted peeing and her son taking a dip in his hot tub. A tough decision!

"I like my video," said Grace, who was eating her breakfast cereal like the big girl that she was. "It's very funny. I didn't even know I licked my lips like that when I sleep. Or wrinkled up my nose."

"You're a nervous sleeper, just like your mom," I said. "And that's fine."

"Daddy sleeps like a rock," said Grace. "And Mom like a jitterbug. And Grandma Marge blinks in her sleep, as if she's watching her own private movie, and Grandpa Tex sleeps with his mouth open. And you, Max," she said, pointing a finger at me, "you're very creepy. You don't move at all!"

I smiled. "I didn't even know that about myself, so Harriet's video has really opened my eyes."

"Of course it has," said Harriet. "This may very well be the best thing I've ever done." She raised her voice so Gran heard her loud and clear. "And I fully intend to keep doing it! The world needs more ASMR and I'm going to give it to them!"

"Oh, all right," said Gran, throwing up her hands. "Have it your way. But film me again without asking for my permission, and you're grounded, young lady. That means that pet flap *will* be locked!"

"But... that means we won't be able to leave the house either," said Dooley.

PURRFECT JACUZZI

Gran nodded. "You should have thought of that before you decided to make a fool of me!"

"We won't film you again, Gran," Harriet promised. She lowered her voice and added, "People prefer cat videos, anyway."

"I heard that!" Gran cried. "And I'll have you know that fifteen thousand views is nothing to sniff at. I'm a very popular YouTube personality! Even asleep!"

Odelia walked down the stairs, yawning. "What's with all the screaming and shouting? Did someone else die last night?"

"Your grandmother is on the internet," said Chase. "And she doesn't like it." He showed his wife the latest videos, and she had to smile. "I didn't know I twisted and turned so much in my sleep. It's a miracle how you don't wake up, babe."

"Earplugs," said Chase confidently. "It's the gift that keeps on giving."

She leaned on his broad shoulders as they watched the videos Harriet had shot overnight. "What an amazing job you did, Harriet. Your channel is really taking off, isn't it?"

Harriet looked proud as a peacock. "And the best is yet to come," she promised. "I've got a great ASMR video lined up for later today."

"Oh? And what is it?" asked Odelia.

"It's a surprise," said Harriet. "Let's just say it's a species that is known for their sleep-inducing habits. Watching them in their natural habitat will put anyone to sleep in seconds!"

Odelia smiled and gave her a kiss on the top of her head. "Can't wait, sweetie."

And neither could the world, if the viewing numbers on Harriet's channel were to be believed. She was finally on her way to becoming a huge star!

CHAPTER 34

We had a busy day ahead of us, with the reading of Nathanial Tindell's will at the man's lawyer's office, but also more interviews lined up in connection with the murder case. It seemed reasonable to assume that the two murder cases were connected, and so Odelia and Chase figured that if they solved one, they would solve the other, with the killer in both instances being the same person.

Unfortunately for us, the examination of Cesar's cell phone had offered us no clue as to who he had been blackmailing. The person he had called was an old associate, but he wasn't talking, due to a sense of loyalty to Cesar. In all likelihood, this person had brokered a deal with the killer and set up a meet.

"Blackmailing a murderer is probably not a good idea, Max," said Dooley.

"No, I would say it isn't," I agreed.

We were in Chase's squad car, on our way to the Star Hotel, where Nathanial's ex-wife and son had checked in.

They were going to be present at the reading of the will and had agreed to sit for an interview first. It was more or less a formality, as it had already been established that they both had been in LA at the time, where they had lived since the divorce. Mrs. Tindell, or Buttress as she was now being called, had quickly remarried and moved in with her new husband, another billionaire. It would appear she had gone from one mogul to the next. Though this one wasn't in the drone manufacturing business but the semiconductor line of work.

"Cesar shouldn't have done it," was Dooley's opinion. "Then he would still be alive."

"That's the trouble when you stick your nose in things that don't concern you," said Harriet. "It might get chopped off."

"In this case it wasn't his nose that was chopped off," said Brutus, "but his life that was cut short."

"Well put, pumpkin," said Harriet appreciatively. "I'm going to put that in my next video."

I looked up in alarm. "You haven't secretly filmed the dead man, have you?"

"And what if I have?" asked Harriet haughtily. "There's nothing more restful than looking at a dead body, Max. It may not be something us cats enjoy, but I can assure you that humans find it extremely relaxing."

I shivered a little. "How can looking at a dead body be enjoyable to anyone?" I cried. "Except to a psychopath."

"I'll have you know that I posted a snippet of the upcoming feature, and people responded very favorably. A lot of them said it was the most relaxing thing they had ever seen."

"Good thing he had his eyes closed," said Brutus. "I'm not sure that if he had had his eyes open people would have reacted the same way. Now they simply think he's asleep."

"I don't think it's right," I told Harriet. "Don't post that video, please. It will get you into all kinds of trouble."

"What trouble?" she asked. "I'm in this to help people, Max, and when I look at all the great responses I get, I feel gratified and blessed."

"So, so blessed," Brutus murmured as he cut me an apologetic look.

I shook my head, but since Harriet is one of those cats who always does exactly as she pleases, I knew it was useless to try and convince her to remove this video from her line-up.

We had arrived at the Star Hotel, and Chase immediately drove his car into the underground parking garage. Getting out, I hoped that Harriet wouldn't start filming the concrete pylons in the underground cavern. It might be relaxing, but in bad taste, I found. Concrete is so… concrete.

But fortunately, she didn't linger but briskly followed us to the elevator, and moments later we were riding up to the lobby, where we set foot for one of the small conference rooms, where Nathanial's ex-wife and son were waiting for us.

They had already poured themselves coffee, for the room smelled of the invigorating brew. I could see Odelia perking up at the scent. She and Chase introduced themselves, and decided for the moment to ignore us, since a lot of people find it a little strange when a police detective is joined for an official police interview by no less than four cats.

The adults in the room all took a seat at the conference table, and the four of us settled down in a corner of the room. I could see Harriet messing around with Gran's phone again, and I got the impression she was about to film another one of her hit ASMR videos. Though I could have told her that putting an official police interview online was probably against the law and might get her in some serious trouble.

Hope Buttress was a handsome woman in her early fifties with platinum hair and a perfectly made-up face. She was dressed in a nice gold-thread business suit, and on the floor next to her chair, I saw a Hermès Birkin bag, so she was probably a major client, since the well-known French luxury brand only offers the Birkin to their very best customers.

Her son was a young man in his early twenties, and was both clean-cut and polite, which was a relief, since I had expected him to be some kind of troubled youth with an attitude problem. There was nothing of that going on here, though, as he answered all of Chase and Odelia's questions without fault, and was both saddened and concerned about the death of his old man.

"I spoke to him just last week," he said. "Even though Mom and Dad divorced, we still got along great."

"Did you see him often?" asked Odelia.

"Yeah, I traveled here every month or so to stay with him for a couple of days, if school allowed. Or he would fly out to LA and we would meet up and do something together. Visit a theme park when I was younger, or go out bowling or playing tennis. Dad knew a lot of people out there, so he always found something for the two of us to do. He was a great dad."

"He was a great man," his mother chimed in as she placed a loving hand on her son's arm. "And we'll always keep him in our hearts."

"So you were both in LA when Mr. Tindell was murdered?" asked Chase as he opened his notebook and clicked his ballpoint pen. Odelia had opened her digital notepad and held her stylus poised for anything that might be of interest to the investigation.

"Yes, when Nathanial and I divorced, I moved to LA and I've lived there ever since," said Hope. "My second husband,

Darrell Buttress, owns a house there, so it was only natural that we would move in with him."

"If you want, you could ask him," said Carter. "He'll confirm that we were there at the house, won't he, Mom?"

She smiled. "I don't think that's necessary, sweetie. I'm sure the police will have checked the airlines by now to make sure that we didn't travel here by plane yesterday."

"I would never kill my father," said Carter matter-of-factly. "I loved him very much, and we got along really well, in spite of the divorce and the distance."

"We don't suspect you," Chase assured the young man. "But it's our job to talk to all the people involved."

"We understand," Hope assured us. "Of course we do, and we hope that you will catch the person who did this."

"Is it true that the same killer has struck again?" asked Carter. "A bum this time?"

"It's possible the two cases are connected," said Chase, as usual keeping his cards close to his vest. "Mrs. Buttress, is there anyone you can think of who may have wished to hurt your ex-husband?"

"Well, he was in charge of one of the biggest companies in the defense industry," said Hope. "And we all know that the defense industry is in the business of creating weapons to defend our country against its enemies, both foreign and domestic, so I'd say you have your pick of people who wanted to get rid of a man as brilliant and innovative and as talented in keeping us all safe as Nathanial was."

"The Russians, the North Koreans, the Iranians, the Chinese," Carter summed up. "You name it, they probably had every reason to get rid of my dad."

"That was one of the reasons for our divorce," Hope revealed. "After Carter was born, I felt that maybe Nathanial should get out of the drone business, as it wasn't safe for his young family. That he should transition to a different line of work. One that wouldn't put a big target on all of our backs. But he steadfastly refused, and said that drones were his life and he couldn't think of doing anything else."

"He could have created commercial drones," Nathanial's son suggested. "But Dad said there wasn't as much profit to be made in commercial drones. He said drones for the defense industry were the future, and he was probably right."

"But see where it got him," said Hope. She sighed deeply. "If only he had listened to me, he might still be alive."

"And you wouldn't have gotten divorced," Carter pointed out.

"Well, we'll never know," said his mother as she flicked a piece of lint off her Chanel blouse. "He made certain choices, and I made mine, and that's just how life is. You make a choice and then you live with it."

"Can you think of anyone in particular who might have formulated certain threats against your ex-husband, Mrs. Buttress?" asked Chase.

"You'd have to ask Bella Fuller," said Hope. "She was more up to date on Nathanial's connections than I am. Even though we tried to keep things civil, we rarely spoke, so I'm afraid I wasn't privy to what was going on in his life."

"I'm not aware of any specific threats either," her son admitted. "Dad didn't like to talk about such things."

"He tried to protect you, sweetie," said his mom.

"Dad was very considerate," said Carter.

"He loved you very much."

"He did. And I loved him."

A pair of deep blue eyes gazed innocently at Chase, and I could tell that the kid would miss his dad very much. I now saw that Harriet hadn't filmed the interview but an ant crawling underneath the table.

"Ants are very ASMR," she assured me. "People can watch them for hours."

"I'm sure they can," I told her, even though I had my doubts that her ant video would attract quite as many viewers as her Peeing Ted videos or Uncle Alec's hot tub singing sensation.

The interview seemed to have come to an end, and all those present rose from their seats.

"Will you also be present at the reading of the will?" asked Hope.

"Yes, we will be there," Chase assured her.

"We've already arranged with the lawyer that a small portion of the inheritance should go to the man who was killed in the park last night," said Carter. "To arrange the funeral, and also to support his family."

"Did you hear that, Max?" asked Dooley. "They're going to give some of those billions to Nicholas!"

"I very much doubt whether Nicholas will get a single cent from these people," I said. "Dogs aren't family, Dooley."

"But he will get something, won't he? He *should* get something, since he's all alone now."

"He won't be all alone. Cesar had family. They will take care of him." Or at least I hoped they would. If not, life for the little doggie would become very difficult indeed. Though he was safe with Uncle Alec and Charlene for now. The police chief was the only member of our family who didn't have a pet yet. Though he did have his beloved jacuzzi, of course. But even though jacuzzis are great, they don't have a lot of love to give, and I had a feeling that Nicholas, even though he had lied to us, had all the makings of a very loving companion.

CHAPTER 35

The big meeting took place in the lawyer's office where Nathanial Tindell did his lawyerly business, which I could imagine would have made him one of their best clients, since a business leader of his renown must have provided them with a lot of business to chew through. It was exceptional that the police had been formally invited to attend the meeting, but then I got the impression the lawyer in charge was afraid there would be 'unpleasantness,' since he had specifically asked Chase to be present and maybe bring some extra manpower along with him. Why this was, was anyone's guess, but it added to the suspense that surrounded the meeting.

As announced, Nathanial's ex-wife Hope was there, and their son Carter, but also Rita MacKereth and her mother Georgia, the personal assistant Bella Fuller, and a man whose face looked vaguely familiar, until I remembered we'd seen him at the house where Nathanial lived—it was the faithful butler. Scanning the faces of the others who were seated in front of the lawyer, I recognized Nathanial's CEO Jason Bourne and a few people I didn't know but who also worked for Nathanial in some capacity and had been his fellow travelers along the long road to success over the years.

Odelia had strictly forbidden Harriet from filming the meeting, but she didn't seem too bothered by this dictum, for the moment the doors were closed and the lawyer took his position behind the desk, she started filming.

"Lawyers are the best soporific known to mankind," she whispered when I gave her a questioning look. "Everybody knows this. Legalese is the best way to put a person to sleep in a heartbeat!"

"If Odelia finds out, she won't be best pleased," I whispered back.

"What she doesn't know..." Harriet returned. Since she was going to post the video on her YouTube, I couldn't see how she thought she'd get away with it, but then Harriet was in a creative mood, and your true creative rarely bothers about the consequences of their flights of creativity.

The lawyer, a smallish man in his early sixties with a kind, pink face and round-framed glasses on his nose, cleared his throat. He raked those present with a pair of pale blue eyes for a moment before getting down to brass tacks. "I have here before me the last will and testament of Nathanial Jeffrey Tindell the Third," he announced, causing his listeners to shuffle in their chairs and prick up their ears. I could tell that for most of them the main question foremost in their minds was, 'What's in it for me?' but then I guess these will readings mostly revolve around such quandaries.

"The date on the will is marked as Friday last," he said, causing an intake of breath amongst both Nathanial's ex-wife and her son. "When Nathanial personally paid a visit to this very office to draw up this latest will and testament, rendering the previous will, made up fifteen years ago, null and void."

Hope Buttress and her son shared a look of dismay, and I got the impression that strange goings-on were afoot.

"The bulk of the estate of Mr. Tindell goes to Rita MacKereth," the lawyer read, "who inherits the house, the grounds, and all its contents. She also inherits one hundred percent of the shares that Mr. Tindell held in Iron Eagle, Inc."

Suddenly, a chair clattered to the floor. Hope Buttress had risen to her feet and was staring daggers at Rita and her mother. "This is an outrage!" she bellowed. Her face had gone puce, and she had lost the equanimity and quiet charm that had been a hallmark of her persona until now. "Who are you?! Why did Nathanial do this to us—to his only son!"

"Please take a seat, Mrs. Buttress," the lawyer begged, and cut a glance to Chase to intervene if things got out of hand. Chase nodded and put the officer he had placed near the door on notice that if things got rough, he had to step in.

Mrs. Buttress took a seat, but she now resembled a coiled spring, and I got a feeling that she would attack Rita the moment she was pushed. Her son just sat there, looking stunned, and chewing his fingernails in the process.

The lawyer steepled his fingers on the desk and eyed Rita with a benevolent eye across moon-shaped glasses. "I've known Nate Tindell for thirty years, and in all that time he never revealed to me what he revealed last week. Obviously, it was a secret he didn't want to share, but for some reason felt he had to. Do you remember your father, Miss MacKereth?"

Rita shook her head. "No, I don't. He died before I was born."

"That isn't necessarily true, though, is it, Mrs. MacKereth?"

Rita's mom sat up as if stung. "Of course it's true. He passed away in the first weeks of my pregnancy. Which is why Rita has never known her father."

"But she did know her father," the lawyer assured her with a benevolent smile. "For he lived right next to you for several months. You knew him as Morgan Sears, but by now you know his real name was Nathanial Tindell."

Rita looked confused. "I don't understand." She turned to her mom. "Morgan was... my dad?"

Rita's mom shook her head decidedly. "Of course not. Such nonsense. Don't you think I would recognize the father of my child? And besides, he died, like I already told you."

"He didn't die. He left you," said the lawyer. "There's a difference. And since you didn't want to admit to your daughter that her father had left his unborn child and her mother at such a vulnerable moment in their lives, you made up the story that he had died, when all the while you didn't know what had happened to him. He came into your life, and then he left again, suddenly and unexpectedly."

"Nonsense," said Rita's mom, but the cautious glances she threw in her daughter's direction told a different story.

"Nathanial revealed the truth to me when he was in my office last week to draw up this new will," the lawyer explained. "He was already married at the time, with a baby boy on the way, but he had to be in New York on business, and a friend invited him to stay a couple of weeks at his house in the Hamptons. That's when he met you, Mrs. MacKereth, and he fell in love with the beautiful and irreverent girl you were—looking much the same as your daughter does now, so many years later. He engaged in a torrid and quite passionate affair, but after his Hamptons sojourn was over, so was the fling, for he couldn't desert the woman he had promised to marry, since she had informed him that she was pregnant, and being the honorable man that he was, he felt he needed to do the right thing. And so he left as abruptly as he had arrived. What he didn't know was that you were also pregnant and would deliver his baby daughter a few short months later."

"You can't convince me that Morgan Sears was the man I met that summer," said Rita's mother stubbornly. "He looked nothing like that boy I fell in love with."

The lawyer now took out a picture and handed it to the woman. "This is a picture of Nathanial that summer, taken here in Hampton Cove," he said, "by the friend he was staying with."

Rita's mother gasped as she studied the picture and brought a startled hand to her face. "But... that's him! That's Ricky!"

"He gave you a false name, as he didn't want his fiancée to find out he had been unfaithful to her," the lawyer explained. "But you can confirm that this is Rita's father, yes?"

The woman nodded, tears having sprung to her eyes. "Yes, this is Ricky," she said hoarsely.

Her daughter took her shoulder and pulled her close. "Oh, Mom," she said. "Why did you tell me he died?"

"Because he was dead to me," said her mother in broken tones. "And he still is."

"Only now he really is dead," Brutus murmured.

"I can't believe you didn't recognize him," said Rita.

"People change," said her mother. "And Ricky changed a lot. For one thing, he didn't have any hair anymore."

It was true that the person we saw in the picture as it was passed around the room looked very different from the person Nathanial had been. And it was also true that without hair, the man looked virtually unrecognizable.

"So that's why you liked Morgan so much," said Rita. "Because unconsciously he reminded you of my dad."

"I don't believe this," Hope Buttress raged. "You're telling me that this woman is Nathanial's illegitimate child?"

"That's correct," said the lawyer. He took off his glasses

and polished them. "And since Nathanial felt that he had treated Miss MacKereth and her mother extremely unfairly, he wanted to do something for them."

"And so he left them his entire fortune?" the woman cried. "So what about his real son? Where does that leave him?"

"Unfortunately, certain rumors had come to Nathanial's attention," said the lawyer. "Rumors that didn't reflect positively on either you or your son, Mrs. Buttress."

"What rumors? What are you talking about?"

"The rumor that your husband had become the main investor in D-ROHN, Iron Eagle's main competitor, and was doing everything in his power to destroy Iron Eagle."

"That's absurd," said the woman. "Absolute nonsense!"

"Nathanial hired a detective to look into the matter and to check if the rumors were true, and he discovered they were. Darrell Buttress owns a controlling share in D-ROHN Enterprises and was dead set on taking over the position of Iron Eagle as the Department Of Defense's main drone supplier, effectively putting Iron Eagle out of business. Also, when Nathanial discovered his own son was being groomed by his stepdad to become D-ROHN's next CEO, he realized he had nurtured a viper to his bosom, and vowed to cut you both off and leave his estate to his daughter, whose acquaintance he had recently made and who had made an extremely favorable impression on him. In fact he had grown quite fond of her."

"This is preposterous!" Hope cried. She had risen from her chair once again. "I'm going to sue," she told the lawyer. "And I'm going to contest this will if it takes every last cent I own!"

And with these words, she stalked out of the room, followed by her son, who cast a curious glance at his half-sister.

For a moment, silence reigned, and then the lawyer

settled back and relaxed. It looked as if the most difficult part of the reading was over. The rest of the session was devoted to announcing different smaller sums and legacies to be dispensed amongst Nathanial's former staff and collaborators, who were all very grateful.

Rita and her mom just sat there, looking absolutely gobsmacked, and I could see why. They had arrived expecting nothing except maybe a small legacy or gift. And now they were leaving as the main beneficiaries of one of the largest fortunes ever to have been amassed in the history of the country. It was quite the turnaround for them.

"I don't understand, Max," said Dooley. "So Rita is Nathanial's secret daughter?"

"That's correct," I said. "And since he liked her more than his son, he decided to leave her pretty much everything in his will."

"But… why didn't he tell her?"

"I'm guessing that he was going to tell her when he felt the time was right. But someone intervened before he could."

"But why? Who killed him?"

"If it's true that the person who benefits the most is the killer, then Rita must have done it," said Harriet.

"I very much doubt it," said Brutus. "Just look at her. She obviously had no idea about any of this."

He was right. Rita's face revealed her complete surprise. If she had known about this, she was an extremely gifted actress, and I didn't think she was capable of such subterfuge.

"No, someone else must be behind this whole business with the killings," I told my friends.

"I think the lawyer did it," said Dooley. "He was the first one to learn about the new will, and so he decided to murder his client and write himself into his will."

It was true that the lawyer had also received a small sum, but hardly enough to warrant murdering a man over.

Which is when I remembered that we hadn't used our star witness yet. Nicholas would recognize the killer because he had olfactorily witnessed the person. But when I told Odelia, and she contacted her uncle to ask for Nicholas to assist us in our inquires, he sadly informed us that the dog had run away.

Clearly he hadn't been as bowled over by the chief's jacuzzi as the rest of Hampton Cove. So where was he?

CHAPTER 36

"This is a joke!" Hope Buttress fumed as she threw her clothes into her suitcase. "We're getting out of here—now!"

"I don't understand how he could do this," said her son as he was busily packing his own bags. "Hire a detective to spy on us? How could he!"

"It just goes to show that I was right about the man all along," said his mother as she grabbed her watch from the nightstand and put it on. "I was right to divorce him and I was right to make sure he paid for what he did to this family."

"Did you know he had a daughter, Mom?" asked her son.

She looked him straight in the eye. "No, I did not. Of course I didn't."

"Right," he said, but she could tell that he still wasn't fully convinced.

"If I had known, don't you think I would have told you?"

"But you must have suspected something when he spent that summer in Hampton Cove, right? So what happened? Were you on a break or what?"

She rolled her eyes. "God, this is all such a long time ago. Do you honestly expect me to remember every little detail of our relationship?"

"It's important, Mom," he reminded her. "Especially in light of this new will that has suddenly popped up."

For years Nathanial had promised them that his son was the main beneficiary in his will, and now this. "Yes, we were on a break," she said. She couldn't believe she was forced to rehash this ancient history again. "I had a brief fling with an old boyfriend of mine. Nathanial found out and freaked out. So he left for New York and vowed never to return. I begged him to come back, but for weeks I didn't hear from him. Then when I told him I was pregnant, he suddenly resurfaced one day. I apologized, I told him that the boyfriend and I were definitely over, and we kissed and made up."

"And in the meantime he'd made another woman pregnant," said Carter.

"Well, it appears that way," she said as she slammed her suitcase shut. "He never told me."

"Because he didn't know," said Carter. "He must have found out not so long ago, and decided to spend some time with the girl, and that's when he hired this detective to look into Dad's connection to D-ROHN."

"What's done is done," said Hope. "But I can assure you that once our lawyer looks into this business, they'll make sure this new will is thrown out and the old one restored."

"Can they do that?"

"Of course they can. What do you think we pay them for? That girl," she said as she planted her hands on her hips, "won't know what hit her."

"I guess," said Carter, and much to her chagrin she saw that he seemed to be wavering. So she took him by the shoulders. "Hey, I need you to be strong for this, you hear me? We're not going to win by being weak and spineless."

"Of course, mom," he said. "It's just that…"

"It's just what?"

"Well, she is my sister, isn't she?"

"No, she's not. She's an accident. Something that should never have happened. And we're going to make sure that this doesn't go any further. Your dad may have gone soft in his old age, but that doesn't mean we have to. We're going to get our hands on what is rightfully ours, is that understood?"

"Yes, Mom," he said.

Just then, there was a sort of ruckus at the door, and she groaned. "Now what?" She stalked over to open it, and was surprised to find four cats staring back at her, and also one dog. The moment she opened the door, the dog entered the room and started sniffing at her son. The moment he did, he sank down on his haunches and started barking furiously.

"Aren't those the same cats that detective brought along to the meeting?" asked Carter.

"I don't know and I don't care," she said. "Cats and dogs shouldn't be allowed in a hotel like this. So I will personally kick them out and I will be complaining to the manager. Out, you," she told the dog, who was yapping for all it was worth now, and jumping up against Carter's leg.

"He's cute, isn't he?" said Carter as he picked up the dog.

"Don't!" Hope yelled. "It will bite your nose clean off!"

"No, it won't," said Carter, who always did like pets way too much. The consequence of a lenient upbringing, and she only had herself to blame.

"Put that mongrel down and kick him out," she said.

"Oh, but he's not a mongrel, is he," said Carter. "He's a cute little dog. Aren't you, dog? You're the cutest."

But the dog kept on barking all the while and didn't seem all that happy to be picked up.

"Just put it down and get rid of it," she said. "Before you're crawling with bugs and fleas and all kinds of other vermin."

"I don't think it's infected," said Carter, who was way too nice for this world.

"And I'm telling you it is. Just look at its fur. It's got pieces missing, for crying out loud!"

"Oh, you poor thing," said Carter. "You do have pieces of fur missing, haven't you?"

"It also needs a wash," said Hope. "It stinks to high heaven!"

"Do you want me to give you a wash, doggie?" asked Carter.

The dog gave vent to its frustration by barking even louder.

In the end, Hope simply snatched the animal from her son's hands and unceremoniously threw him out of the room before slamming the door shut in its face and that of those horrible cats.

"Good riddance!" she cried. "And now let's go home." She stared off into the middle distance, taking on the pose of a warrior queen of old. "And let the battle begin!"

CHAPTER 37

"And? Was it him?" I asked.

Nicholas, who had landed on his paws after Hope had thrown him out of her room, nodded. "Yep, it was him, all right."

"But how can that be?" asked Brutus. "He was in LA when his dad was killed. He only arrived in town this morning, for the reading of the will."

"I don't know," said Nicholas. "But I recognize the smell. It was definitely him at the apartment yesterday morning. And now that I think about it, his smell also lingered around Cesar last night, so he must have killed him, too." A grimace had appeared on his furry face and he growled and showed his teeth. "Let me have a piece of him, Max," he said as he turned to the closed door. "Let me dig my teeth into that man."

"Maybe not," I said. "What will happen is that they will call hotel security on you and have you kicked out. Or, worse, maybe locked up in the pound. And then where are we?"

"Nowhere," he admitted. He sighed. "But there has to be

something we can do, Max. That man in there murdered my human!"

It had taken us a little while to track down the dog, but finally, Harriet had the bright idea to return to the park, to the same bench Cesar had been stabbed at last night. The bench had been cordoned off with yellow crime scene tape, but that hadn't stopped people from placing flowers on it and turning it into a commemoration site for the dead man. Underneath the bench we had found Nicholas, and when we told him we needed him to do something for us, he had flat out refused, and said he would stay there indefinitely—close to Cesar.

Only when I told him I thought we might have a shot at identifying Cesar's killer did he relent and come away with us.

We had returned to the lawyer's office, and Odelia had let us in. But after he had taken one sniff, he had determined that none of those present had been the person present at the scene of Nathanial's murder. And since the only people who had left the lawyer's office were Hope Buttress and her son Carter, we decided to pay them a little visit, just to make sure. I didn't believe for one second either of them was involved, since they had been on the other side of the country at the time, but then I do believe in being thorough. And that position has paid dividends in a big way over the course of my so-called career.

I glanced over to Harriet and Brutus—the two-cat movie crew. "Did you get all of that?"

"We did!" said Harriet. "Though I'm not sure how relaxing people will find it. I don't think it's the best ASMR video we've done so far, Max."

"It's not an ASMR video," I told her.

"Then what's the point?"

"The point is we show this to Chase, and hopefully he'll

be able to figure out how Carter Buttress managed to be in two places at the same time."

We left the hotel through the lobby, with the receptionist not even surprised to see four cats and one dog crossing in front of his desk. He had seen us before and knew who we were. It took us some time to get back to the lawyer's office, where Odelia and Chase were still convened and talking to Rita MacKereth and her mother. Rita still looked stunned by the news that Nathanial was her dad, and so did Georgia.

"I honestly had no clue," said the woman. "He looked... familiar, you know. Like the kind of person you meet and you have this feeling you've known them all your life."

"In this case, you did know him all your life," said her daughter. "Or at least part of your life."

"I just wish he had told us who he was," said Georgia. "We could have talked about what happened. And maybe then I could have been less angry with him—and men in general."

"So he didn't know you were pregnant at the time?" asked Odelia.

Georgia shook her head. "I didn't even know myself. I only found out after he had already left town. And since I had no way of contacting him, I just figured he'd left and wasn't interested in us anymore. And since I didn't want Rita to know her dad wasn't interested in her mother, I made up this story that he had died. It seemed like the best thing to do."

"But when he started making a career for himself, didn't you realize that this was the same man you had briefly dated?" asked Odelia.

"I don't really follow the business press," said Georgia. "*Forbes Magazine* and all of that. So I had no idea of his stellar rise to the top. And I'm not interested in drones either, so…"

"The only people Mom knows are the actors that star in

her favorite soaps," said Rita as she gave her mother a hug. "Isn't that right, mom?"

"At least you can rely on them to always be there for you," said the woman.

Odelia looked down at us. We had been trying to attract her attention, but understandably she was more interested in hearing from Rita and her mom. Partly to write an article about this fairy tale story, but also in connection to the investigation into the deaths of Nathanial and Cesar.

"What is it?" she asked as she crouched down next to us.

"Nicholas has identified the killer," I said.

"He has?" asked Odelia as she gave the dog a loving pat across the head. "Who is it?"

But when I told her, she found it hard to believe too. "I'm sorry, but Nicholas must have made a mistake. There's absolutely no way Carter is the killer. He was in LA yesterday morning, and also last night. We have several witnesses who confirm he was at his dad's house. Servants, but also neighbors who saw him. Chase contacted his LA colleagues and they sent two officers down to the house owned by Carter's stepdad. They said he was definitely there."

"But how can that be?" asked Nicholas. "I swear it was him. I never forget a smell, and it was this guy—one hundred percent."

We all shared a look. "How can a man be in two places at the same time, Max?" asked Dooley.

"He can't," I said.

Harriet showed Odelia the video, and she shrugged. "All I see is a dog attacking a man and being kicked out of the room." She handed back the phone. "This doesn't prove anything." She gave me a smile. "Looks like it's back to the drawing board for you, Max. Your friend is wrong. Carter Buttress is innocent."

CHAPTER 38

Uncle Alec had called a meeting in his office, and Odelia and Chase had both been summoned. The chief wanted to know if any progress had been made in the case of Nathanial Tindell's murder and that of Cesar. Unfortunately, they had to disappoint the police chief.

"No progress whatsoever?" asked Odelia's uncle. "How can that be? I thought the reading of the will might have led to a clue as to who benefits from the murder."

"Oh, we know who benefits," said Chase. "Rita MacKereth and her mother."

The chief goggled at them for a moment. "Come again?"

"Turns out that Rita MacKereth is Nathanial's daughter," Odelia explained. She still found it a little hard to believe herself, as did Rita and her mother, but the lawyer had assured them that it was all above board and that nobody, no matter how many fancy lawyers they hired, could possibly contest that will. It was ironclad. Also, there was DNA evidence that Rita was the billionaire's daughter, just in case Nathanial's ex-wife went to court as she had promised.

"A summer fling led to a pregnancy," said Chase. "And

when Nathanial found out years later, he decided to get to know the daughter he didn't know he had a little better, and also her mother. It led to him drawing up a new will."

"But why disinherit his son?" asked the chief.

"Turns out that Nathanial's ex-wife married a major investor in Nathanial's rival company," Odelia explained. "Also, Nathanial claimed that his son had been spying on him. He offered the kid a job in his LA branch and he temped there a couple of months. He was training him to rise through the ranks of his company and eventually take over Iron Eagle from his dear old dad. But as it transpired, Carter's stepdad had the same idea, and was using the kid to spy on his competitor, with certain critical information that he immediately passed on to Nathanial's main rival."

Uncle Alec whistled through his teeth. "I don't believe this. So Nathanial's own son was a spy for the competition?"

"The competitor launched a new type of drone a couple of months ago that has certain features that Nathanial's team of engineers came up with first," said Chase. "So that got him thinking that someone had been spying on his R&D team. He put in-house security on the case and they found irrefutable evidence that Carter Buttress had accessed the schematics of the new drone, which at the time were highly classified and still in development. The upshot was that D-ROHN managed to bring a drone to market that was almost identical to the one that Iron Eagle had in development. Nathanial was understandably upset with his son and his ex-wife. He quietly transferred his son to a department where he wouldn't have access to sensitive information, and also changed all of his passwords so he wouldn't be able to snoop around anymore."

"Why didn't he confront him?"

"He was still his son. And since he figured the kid had

been pushed by his mother and stepdad, he didn't want to make a big stink about it."

"He didn't want to jeopardize the relationship with his boy," said Odelia. "But it certainly made him think."

"So that's the reason he took a step back from his company?" asked Uncle Alec.

"That's right. That and the discovery that he had a daughter. It made him re-evaluate his priorities. And so he decided to get to know his daughter before revealing himself to her as her dad. Only he never got the chance."

"How did he find out he had a daughter?" asked the chief.

"Quite by accident," said Chase. "The same friend who had invited him to stay with him all those many years ago was still living here, and when Nathanial was over to pay him a visit, he happened to drop by the pet clinic where Rita works. When he saw her, he was struck by the remarkable resemblance to the woman he had once loved, before his sense of honor and duty had made him return to the mother of his son. It wasn't long before he discovered that she was the daughter of his old girlfriend. Finding out her date of birth wasn't hard, and so he quickly put two and two together and figured there was a good chance that he was Rita's dad."

"He couldn't be one hundred percent sure, though," said Odelia. "She could have had other boyfriends at the same time as she was seeing him."

"That's where the DNA test came in. He asked the same detective agency he had on retainer to dive into the matter. It wasn't hard for them to get a sample of Rita's DNA."

"Probably by breaking into the girl's office," said the chief.

"That's exactly what they did. They took DNA from a plastic water bottle and compared it to Nathanial's. It was a match. And that's how he knew he had a daughter. From that moment, he became obsessed with getting to know her. But he knew he couldn't just barge in and reveal who he was. Georgia's aversion to men is a well-known fact. So he had to be careful."

"And pretend to be the friendly neighbor."

"Well, the ruse worked," said Chase. "Rita and her mom thought that Nathanial was the kindest, greatest person they had ever met. Rita saw him as a father figure and Georgia thought he was possibly the only man who wasn't evil."

"Little did she know that he was exactly the reason she had gone off men," said Uncle Alec. "Okay, but that still doesn't explain who killed the guy. Or Cesar Tinker. Tell me that at least you have some clues?"

"We have several suspects," said Chase. "There's the competitor who may have decided to sink Iron Eagle's stock by permanently retiring its boss. There's Ken Torres, jealous of any man who caught Rita's eye. Or Rita's ex-boyfriend Harvey Furniss, who's the violent, jealous type."

"There's also Bella Fuller," said Odelia. "Nathanial's loyal personal assistant who he treated very badly. At least if Nathanial's cats are to be believed."

"Any evidence?" asked the chief.

"None," said Chase sadly. "Plenty of alibis, though. Some of them solid, some not so much."

The chief leaned forward. "How about Georgia MacKereth?"

"What about her?" asked Chase.

"For the murder, I mean. If she realized that Nathanial was her ex-boyfriend, maybe she finally let all that anger she'd been harboring for years out and killed the man?"

"But she swears she had no idea that he was her old boyfriend," said Chase.

"But what if she did?"

It certainly was a theory they needed to follow up on, Odelia felt. Though judging from the expression on the woman's face when the will was being read, she had absolutely no idea who Morgan Sears really was. Still, it behooved them to talk to her again and check her alibi.

"And now for the most important thing," said Uncle Alec as he took out his phone and placed it on the desk. "I want you to get rid of this video."

"What video?" asked Chase.

"This video!" said the chief, and held up the phone and pressed play. It was the video of him in his hot tub, singing a pleasant tune and clearly having a ball.

"Have you asked your mother, boss?"

"I have, but she says it's out of her hands!"

"But it's her phone, isn't it?" asked Odelia.

"It is, but she claims the cats have taken it and they're refusing to give it back." He flicked through some more videos that had accrued on the channel. "My god, they have been busy, haven't they? Will you look at that?"

"Stop!" Odelia cried suddenly. "Can you back up one video?"

Her uncle played the video in question, which was called, 'ASMR of lawyers talking—very effective! Extreme relax!'

"But… that's the reading of the will!" she said. "I specifically told her not to film that!"

"And she did," said her uncle. "Now will you finally do something about this? If this keeps up she will film every last person in Hampton Cove and put the footage online!"

"She filmed us sleeping last night," said Chase with a grin. "Pretty fascinating stuff. For instance, I had no idea that Tex snored so much."

"Tex is a big snorer," Uncle Alec confirmed.

"She also filmed Gran," said Odelia. "And she wasn't happy about it. Said it ruined her reputation."

"Oh, it'll ruin her reputation if she doesn't get her phone back and finally starts deleting these videos," the chief warned. "And now get lost, the both of you. And find me that killer!" Out of sheer habit, he darted a look at the floor, and seemed surprised to find the cats were absent. "Where's Max?"

"No idea," said Odelia. "He claimed to have cracked the case."

"He did?" asked her uncle. "So who does he think did it?"

"Carter Buttress. But that's impossible, as he's got several witnesses confirming on record that he was in LA yesterday."

Her uncle frowned and did not look happy. "Looks like the famous Max is wrong for a change. How about that?"

CHAPTER 39

After leaving the lawyer's office, where we hadn't been able to convince Odelia that we had cracked the case, we decided to go for a stroll through town. Harriet was still on a kick to shoot more ASMR videos, and I had to think. Odelia was right, of course. If Carter was in LA when his father was murdered, and later that night Cesar, he couldn't be our killer. But in spite of the evidence, our own star witness was still very much convinced that the young man was the killer.

We passed by the barbershop, and Harriet insisted we enter and shoot a video of Fido Siniawski cutting hair.

"There's nothing more ASMR than hair being snipped and gently fluttering to the floor," she explained.

In the short time she had been making these ASMR videos, she had already become an expert. And so she held out the phone, with the assistance of Brutus, and moments later was recording the hairdresser as he expertly snipped off the tips of Charlene Butterwick's long locks and fashioned them into something more akin to a modern style. In front of him stood a picture of Jennifer Lawrence, whom Charlene must have picked to be modeled after. It was a popular thing that Fido's clients picked a famous movie star or maybe just a model from a magazine and asked him to cut their hair just like that.

And it had to be said he was doing a pretty good job. Though of course Charlene would never look like Jennifer Lawrence, not even if her hair was exactly the same. And that was something people didn't seem to understand. They figured that if they wore the same clothes as a star and their hair was the same, and they used the same products and ate the same food, they would magically look like that star. Unfortunately, that wasn't the case, or otherwise the world would be full of Jennifer Aniston or Scarlett Johansson or Margot Robbie lookalikes.

"And?" asked Fido. "What do you think?"

He had been looking in the mirror for a moment when he suddenly became aware of Harriet and Brutus filming, and uttered a shriek of surprise. Unfortunately, his trimmer had been hovering right over the crown of Charlene's head, and when he jumped a foot in the air, a sort of spasm must have afflicted his right hand, for he sliced off a nice chunk of the mayor's hair in the process, right down to the skull, making her look like a punk rock chick—but not the pretty kind.

This time it was Charlene's turn to shriek when she saw what Fido had done to her hair, which now featured a middle part—taken to the extreme.

The shrieks continued unabated, both from the mayor and her hairdresser. The moment they both turned angry eyes at us, we felt it was probably time to go. And so we hurried out the door. And not a minute too soon, for Fido, seeing his reputation ruined, hurled a pair of scissors at us!

"We better not go back there for a while," said Brutus.

"At least we've got our video," said Harriet proudly. "I can feel it in my bones, you guys. This is going to be a big hit!"

I could have told her the hits would come when Charlene issued a court order to have us all locked up at the pound!

We passed by the General Store, and Harriet immediately disappeared inside, eager to shoot a video of the fruits and veggies, which she said were extremely ASMR. And since I had lost my appetite for ASMR, I decided to keep Kingman company. The spreading piebald was lounging in front of the store, as usual, and seemed reluctant to engage us in conversation. When I glanced around, I saw why this was. A very pretty feline was hanging out across the street, seated on the balcony of the Star Hotel, sunning herself.

"She's been there all morning," he told me with a wistful sigh. "But will she look at me? Of course not. So close and yet so far."

"She probably belongs to a guest at the hotel," I said.

"A tourist, Kingman," said Dooley. "She will be in and out of your life in days, so better don't get emotionally invested."

We both stared at our friend. "My god, Dooley," said Kingman. "That's probably the most mature thing I've heard you say."

"It was on General Hospital," Dooley said shyly. He isn't used to getting a lot of compliments. "When Doctor Virginia Scooter falls in love with a visiting cardiologist, her best friend tells her she can't fall in love because the specialist will be out of her life soon and her heart will be broken. To which she says that since the specialist is a cardiologist he's exactly the right person to break her heart, since he's the only one who can put it back together again. Gran thought it was pretty neat." His face sagged. "Too bad Gran is upset with us now."

"Vesta is upset with you guys?" asked Kingman.

"Yes, Harriet filmed her sleeping, and she didn't like it."

"Oh, I saw that video," said the voluminous cat with a grin. "It's quite the big hit, isn't it? Pretty much everyone who's dropped by the store today has been commenting on it. Wilbur even said that Harriet should visit him in his sleep and film him. It would do wonders for his bottom line."

"Too bad people seem to get so upset," said Dooley. "The videos are supposed to lower your blood pressure and your heart rate, but all they're doing is the exact opposite."

"Yeah, most of these ASMR victims are in urgent need of some ASMR themselves," I muttered as I glanced across the street and saw Hope Buttress and her son come out of the hotel and step into a taxi. And as we watched, suddenly a dog accosted the duo and attached itself to the seat of Carter's pants. He screamed bloody murder and tried to get the dog off but the canine had locked on tight and wasn't letting go.

I recognized him as Nicholas, and he was obviously taking revenge for the death of his master.

"Oh, no," said Dooley. "Nicholas is going to be in so much trouble, Max."

"He certainly will be," I said as we saw how the bellboy came out of the hotel, and also the receptionist, and then a burly security man. All of them tried to separate man and dog and finally, with a sort of rending effect, they managed. The dog had most of the kid's pants in his mouth, though, and was determined to hang on to it. Chased by the hotel personnel he took off and we saw him disappear around the corner, going well and not slowing down, which couldn't be said about the trio chasing him, who soon gave up.

"A vigilante dog," said Kingman admiringly. "Now there's something you don't see every day."

"Poor Nicholas," said Dooley. "He's so sad over the death of his master that he's lost his mind."

"Maybe not," I said. We all eyed the Buttresses as they returned to the hotel, possibly to make a complaint. "Maybe Nicholas is the smartest one of us all."

Inside the store, there was a sort of commotion, and as

PURRFECT JACUZZI

we looked up, we saw that Harriet and Brutus came sprinting out of the store, with Wilbur on their tail.

"And don't come back!" the shopkeeper yelled as he shook his fist.

"God, what did they do now?" I said.

"Looks like Harriet's idea of ASMR is a little odd," said Kingman with a big grin. He was pointing to an orange that was lying on the floor. It had teeth marks all over it, and I had a feeling that Brutus had held the orange between his teeth while Harriet filmed it, to make sure she got it from a nice angle. And since no shopkeeper likes it when his wares are being mauled, Wilbur must not have looked kindly on this original way of featuring an orange in Harriet's latest video.

And it was as we decided to follow Harriet and Brutus and make sure they didn't get into any more trouble, that I suddenly saw a man walking down the street who shouldn't have been there. He looked like any regular tourist and seemed to be enjoying himself tremendously, his hands full of shopping bags and dressed like every other tourist, with expensive sunglasses perched on his nose, a baggy pair of board shorts, and a very snazzy and costly loud shirt.

Which is how I knew I had finally cracked the case!

CHAPTER 40

Stuart Love enjoyed the quaint town of Hampton Cove. He appreciated the people, the cozy restaurants, and the beach—pretty cool surf, dude! But most of all, he liked that nobody here recognized him. His friend Carter had advised him to keep a low profile for a couple of days, and that's precisely what he intended to do by making the most of his vacation.

He took plenty of pictures of the cozy streets downtown, spent ample time surfing at the beach, and generally behaved like any other tourist would. While strolling along Main Street, snapping shots of the cats that strutted the sidewalk as if they owned it—the most curious sight he had ever seen!—he noticed something extraordinary: a cat with a smartphone!

He laughed incredulously. "What the heck..." he muttered as he held up his own phone to capture a picture of the cat for his Insta. As he aimed his phone at the cat, the feline—a Persian, if he wasn't mistaken—pointed her phone at him, assisted by a second cat, a black bruiser of a cat, and snapped a picture of him!

"I don't believe this," he said, chuckling with delight. "Wait till the folks back home catch wind of this. They'll think I've landed on the far side of the moon, where animals talk and the streets are lined with chocolate fountains and lemonade rivers."

As he filmed the cat, the cat filmed him, and they circled each other for a while until he suddenly noticed he was being watched. Looking up, he found himself face to face with his old school chum, Carter Buttress!

"Carter," he said, surprised. "What are you doing here?"

"What am *I* doing here?" asked Carter, who didn't look happy to see him. "The question is, what are *you* doing here? Didn't I tell you to lie low for a couple of days?"

"Well, I am," Stuart pointed out. "That's why I'm here."

"You're telling me you're in the one place you shouldn't be? The only place I specifically told you not to go?"

"Huh?" Stuart said. He vaguely recalled Carter mentioning something like that, but he couldn't remember the name. "I thought it was someplace in California," he said. "A place I've never heard of, by the way. But this is the East Coast, buddy boy."

Carter appeared to be in the throes of some powerful emotion, standing there, balling his fists and turning red in the face. Stuart recognized the phenomenon. His friend had always had a pretty volatile temper. He just hoped he wouldn't explode, with so many people looking on. Two of those people seemed extremely interested in the pair of them. They were a man and a woman, and as they approached, the man took out a police badge and held it up for Stuart's inspection.

"Cool badge, bro," Stuart said. "I didn't know you guys had cops in this part of the world."

"You're under arrest on suspicion of the murders of Nathanial Tindell and Cesar Tinker," said the cop. Even though he thought the cop was just pulling his leg, he proceeded to utter the exact same words to Carter. Judging from the look on his buddy's face, the cop wasn't kidding at all. So when Carter suddenly broke into a run and sprinted away from them as fast as his legs could carry him, he figured that maybe something else was going on.

"Hey, Carter!" he yelled after him. "Where ya goin', bud?"

"Christ," said the cop, cursing a little. Then he broke into a run himself, in pursuit of the other man.

The woman just stood there and gave him a pleasant smile.

"So are you a cop also?" he asked, just to make sure. At this point, he was starting to wonder if he was awake or still in his hotel bed, sleeping and dreaming of this funny town where cops looked like supermodels and cats used their phones to film perfect strangers on the street. Most likely he was fast asleep, he finally decided.

"I'm a civilian consultant assisting the police in their inquiries," the woman told him, which is how he knew for sure this was a dream. Who had ever heard of pretty blond babes assisting the police in their inquiries? Except in TV shows, of course. But that was Hollywood, and not even remotely close to reality.

"That sounds great," he said, and since he kind of liked this blond babe, he decided that if he was dreaming, he might as well enjoy it. "Wanna go for a drink later? I'm new in town, you see, and I don't know anyone here—yet."

"But you're under arrest, Mr....."

"Love," he said. "Stuart Love."

She stared at him. "Are you serious?"

He shrugged. "Hey. It's a blessing and a curse."

"I'm afraid there won't be any dates for you in the near future, Mr. Love. Only the one the judge will set for your trial."

"Trial? What trial?"

"You are involved in a conspiracy to commit murder, Mr. Love, so you can see how that won't go over well with the judge."

He stared at the woman, and then slowly pinched himself. When he still hadn't woken up, he figured he should probably pinch a little harder. So he did, but it didn't make a lot of difference. The cats were still filming him, and the pretty babe was still keeping a close eye on him and uttering strange and unsettling words like trial and arrest and murder. Not the kind of thing a fun-loving tourist likes to hear, in other words!

He saw his buddy running full-tilt across the street, followed by that beefcake cop. And as he ran, Stuart saw Carter's mom walk out of the lobby of the hotel her son was passing at high speed. She seemed as surprised as he was by the events that were in motion. "Carter!" she yelled. "What's going on!"

But then she saw Captain Beefcake, and her lips formed a perfect O. And then she did the most outrageous thing: she placed a pair of sunglasses on her nose and hailed a cab driving slowly down the road. When it stopped, she quickly got in and instructed the driver to take off as fast as he could. Or at least that's what Stuart assumed she must have said, for the driver stepped on it, and the cab took off hell for leather.

"Darn it," said the hot babe, and took out her phone, then started babbling into it to call for backup and to signal to whoever she was talking to that they had to flag down the cab with the license plate that had just picked up the mother of his best friend since high school.

"Lady," he said finally, having once and for all ascertained that he was wide awake and this was really happening, "can you please tell me what the heck is going on?"

CHAPTER 41

It certainly was a strange scene: a cab carrying one suspect in this direction, a second suspect being chased by Chase, and a third suspect having absolutely no clue what was going on, and ogling Odelia in a way that, if Chase had been present, he would have found extremely annoying. Meanwhile, Harriet and Brutus were filming everything on Gran's smartphone.

"How is this ASMR?" I asked Harriet. "People chasing each other, a suspect being arrested? I don't think your audience will find this even remotely relaxing."

"It's all part of the ASMR experience, Max," she professed as she kept her eye on the ball—in this case, the tourist under arrest, who bore a remarkable likeness to Carter Buttress, even though his name seemed to indicate he wasn't the man's twin brother. "ASMR is a big family with lots of different little brothers and sisters. This is what I would categorize as Law and Order ASMR. People like to feel that the strong hand of the law is protecting them and their loved ones. It makes them feel safe. It makes them feel good. And so in that sense, you could make a case that this is the ultimate ASMR."

"But I thought ASMR was supposed to be relaxing?" asked Dooley, who must have read up on the subject.

"Maybe in its initial inception," said Harriet. "But we're expanding, Dooley. We're taking ASMR in new and exciting directions."

"Oh, okay," said our friend. "So this is the new ASMR as opposed to the old ASMR that is all over the internet?"

"Just you wait and see. Before long, my ASMR will be the new ASMR and the rest will have gone out of style completely."

"I see," said Dooley, though judging from the look on his face, he didn't see at all, and neither did I. But then I'm not an expert on internet fashion, and clearly Harriet was.

Brutus was starting to buckle a little under the weight of having to keep that smartphone straight. "How much longer?" he asked. "My arm is getting tired."

"As long as it takes, snow pea," said Harriet, relentless in her pursuit of the perfect video to create the effect she was looking for.

Just then, Carter Buttress was passing us by for the third time, soon followed by Chase. And since Odelia must have felt that this was all taking an awfully long time, she stuck out her foot and the man went flying, landing right on top of Wilbur Vickery's tomatoes, squashing them in the process.

"Pure ASMR!" Harriet cried happily. "Tell me you got that, stud muffin?"

"All of it," Brutus said proudly. "In vivid HD!"

"This is going to be such a big hit," Harriet said with a happy sigh.

Chase was quick to collar the young man and to attach a pair of shiny new handcuffs to his wrists. He then repeated the procedure for Carter's tourist lookalike, and since at this point several police cars had arrived on the scene, both men were taken away. A police patrol had captured Nathanial's fleeing ex-wife, and we saw that the lady now sat in the back of a police car, also being taken to the police station.

"Looks like we've got them all," said Odelia happily, and I got the impression she wasn't referring to Pokémon but the trio of suspects now safely in custody.

Chase stood panting a little from the exertion. "Why do they always have to run?" he lamented. "Can't they just come quietly?"

"I guess criminals are allergic to being arrested," said Odelia, as she patted the burly cop on the back. "You should really work on your condition, babe."

They calmly walked in the direction of the police station, but not before Odelia had grabbed her grandmother's phone from Harriet's and Brutus's paws and checked the footage they had shot. "Excellent work, you guys," she said. "Mind if I take this? Thanks."

"But..." Harriet stared in abject dismay at our human, walking off with her phone in her hand. "But but but!"

"Looks like you'll have to take a short break in your ASMR activities," I said.

"But she can't do that!" Harriet cried, having recovered from the shock of watching her phone being confiscated in such an unceremonious fashion by the long arm of the law. "She can't just take my phone!"

"It's not your phone," I pointed out. "It's Gran's phone. And I guess Gran wants it back."

"So she should buy herself a new one. That's my phone now! I need it for my channel!"

"Well, isn't that a pity?" said Brutus, giving me a wink.

"I've got so many ideas for new videos!" Harriet cried. "I was going to film the ducks pooping in the park. ASMR people love watching ducks poop! It's very relaxing!"

I couldn't imagine what was so interesting about watching a duck poop, but then like I said, I'm not an expert on ASMR. Possibly there is something extremely relaxing about it. I know I find it relaxing when I've just had a nice bowel movement. Makes me feel very happy inside.

Wilbur Vickery must have noticed that his tomatoes had borne the brunt of the fall from grace of Carter Buttress, for he now came storming out of his store to examine the damage. When he saw that every last one of his tomatoes had been reduced to tomato sauce, he grabbed at his hair and started jumping up and down in despair.

"You can always use them to make spaghetti sauce," I suggested, but of course he didn't pay me any attention at all.

Kingman had emerged from the store again. He glanced up at his human and looked surprised. "What did I miss?"

"Only the arrest of the murderer of Nathanial Tindell and Cesar Tinker," I said.

"Oh, so they made an arrest? Who was it?"

"Nathanial's son," I said.

Kingman shook his head. "Kids these days. I blame the parents."

"That's exactly what he did, and why he killed his dad."

Kingman took up position in his usual spot in front of the store. "Okay, better tell us all about it, Max. And don't leave out a single detail, no matter how seemingly insignificant."

CHAPTER 42

"So why did you do it, Carter?" asked Chase.

Odelia, seated next to her husband, studied the young man's face and wondered how he was going to respond to the allegations that had been leveled against him. Would he deny? Would he confess? They had a lot riding on this moment, as they didn't really have a lot of solid evidence, apart from the fact that Max had spotted the man's lookalike prancing about the streets of Hampton Cove and had immediately put two and two together and hurried to alert Odelia.

The kid hung his head. "Bella told us Dad was about to change his will," he said as he studied his fingers. "So we knew it was only a matter of time before he assigned the bulk of his fortune to this girl he met. She figured Dad was head over heels in love. Off his rocker. Quitting his job, moving in next to the girl, and making an appointment with his lawyer. If we acted fast, she reckoned we could still make sure Iron Eagle landed in our laps and not that of this Rita MacKereth." He spat out the name, as if it was the most repulsive thing he had ever heard, which quite possibly it might have been.

"But you were too late."

"No one was more surprised than I was that Dad had changed his will before we got a chance to get to him," said the kid with a shrug. "Looks like he had kept even Bella out of the loop this time. Maybe he suspected that she had been leaking information to us for years. Information that we then used to inform Dad's main competitor, my stepdad."

"So you didn't know that Rita was his daughter?"

"No idea," he said. "Turns out he hadn't told Bella about that either."

"So you flew here on your friend's I.D. and murdered your dad."

He nodded. "Since we were kids together, people have thought that we were twins, Stuart and I, even though we're not related. We just look very much the same. And so it wasn't hard to travel with his identification."

"Only you hadn't counted on him traveling with yours."

"I told him to lie low for a couple of days until this whole business with my dad blew over—just in case someone had seen me. But of course, he had to go and take a vacation to the last place he should have gone—Hampton Cove. Stuart is a great guy, but he wasn't first in line when The Creator doled out the brains. In fact, he's a little dumb—and I say that with the greatest affection, since he really is a great friend."

"Did he know that you were going to use his I.D. to come here to murder your dad?"

"No, he didn't. He wouldn't have said yes if he did."

"So what did you tell him?"

"That I'd been blacklisted by the airline for smoking in the toilets. He immediately believed it and thought it was pretty cool that he could be instrumental in helping me avoid a punishment he felt was unjust."

"Wasn't he surprised that he could travel without a problem if your info was on the blacklist?"

Carter smiled. "Like I said, Stuart is no genius. He had probably forgotten all about it when he booked that flight."

"So take us through what happened, Carter."

The kid sat back. "Look, my dad and I have always gotten along great, all right? Even though I didn't see him a lot, there was no acrimoniousness between us. But when we heard that he was going to leave his inheritance to a girl he had never met before, some enterprising gold digger, I was furious."

"Who is this 'we' you keep referring to?" asked Odelia.

The kid looked caught, but then relented. "I may have mentioned to Mom what I was about to do."

"And did she encourage you?"

"She wasn't happy about Dad's decision," he said, prevaricating a little. "But I want it on record that it was my decision and my decision alone to take matters into my own hands to safeguard my future." He tapped the table with his index finger. "That company is mine. I'm the designated heir to the Tindell fortune, not some woman from the sticks."

"Is that how you see your half-sister?"

"Well, you can't deny that she and her mother are a pair of gold diggers. How else would you explain Dad leaving everything to them?"

"Maybe because he got to know them and appreciated them?" Odelia suggested.

"Nonsense. They manipulated him into signing everything over to them. They're a couple of hustlers, pure and simple. And so I did what I had to do. Only it was too late."

"Why did you kill Cesar Tinker?" asked Chase.

"Because he saw me. And blackmailed me. He wanted a measly thousand to begin with, but I knew that if I started paying him off, it would never stop, and I'd end up paying him for the rest of his natural life—so I decided to cut it short," he added with a grin. When Chase gave him a look of disapproval, he added, "Hey, he had it coming! He shouldn't have been so greedy."

"I think greed is the one thing that motivated your actions," said Chase. "Pure greed and resentment that someone else would manage to gain the affections of your dad."

"You can think what you want," said Carter with a shrug. "But I know that what I did was right. It's the way Dad raised me: do whatever it takes to get what's owed you. So I did."

"I very much doubt that your dad's lessons extended to murder," said Odelia.

"So what's going to happen now?" asked Carter.

"That depends on the judge," said Chase.

"You have to release my mom. She didn't know I was planning to do this."

Chase gave him a wry smile. "We have our doubts about that, Carter. I think she knew perfectly well what you had planned. In fact, I think you planned this together."

"But why? She's married to the second-richest man in the country. She doesn't need the money."

"I think she wanted to get back at your dad for cheating on her all those years ago," said Chase. "And for having the gall to leave you out of his will, after he had made promises to train you to become Iron Eagle's next CEO. So when Bella told you about your dad meeting the MacKereth women, you both felt getting rid of him was the best solution."

"Mom is innocent," he insisted. "You will release her now, or I'll retract my confession."

Chase patted the tape recorder. "Too late."

"I'll tell the judge you coerced me."

Chase pointed to the camera hanging in a corner of the room. "Nice try, kid."

He got up, and so did Odelia. They had what they wanted: a full confession to both murders.

"At least let Stuart go," he said. "He had no idea what was going on. All he did was switch I.D.'s with me."

Chase nodded. "That, I can believe."

Carter nodded. "Look, I'm sorry about what happened, all right? But like I said, Dad only had himself to blame."

Chase's lips formed a hard line. "Keep thinking that, kid. But you and I both know it isn't true. The truth is that you couldn't stand that your dad's fortune would go to someone else. Nothing but pure greed motivated your actions—and I, for one, hope that you will get the punishment you deserve."

And with these words, they both left the room.

CHAPTER 43

I was enjoying some peace and quiet before the storm. As often happens on a Saturday, the family was coming over to enjoy a barbecue in Tex and Marge's backyard. Only, as things stood, Uncle Alec and Charlene hadn't yet confirmed their presence, still a little miffed after the jacuzzi incident. And the hair incident. Likewise, Gran seemed unhappy with recent events, especially the fact that Odelia had taken her phone from Harriet but had failed to remove the offending video of her sleeping from the device. All in all, it looked very much as if the event would be canceled, and even though I enjoy the nice morsels of meat Tex likes to dole out on these occasions, I wouldn't be sad if it *were* canceled. All this arguing and throwing arguments back and forth is not my cup of tea.

"Do you think the barbecue will happen, Max?" asked Dooley.

"I very much doubt it, Dooley," I said. "Uncle Alec and Charlene are probably in one of their jacuzzis right now, and Gran is still upset about the invasion of privacy Harriet perpetrated on her, so it looks as if it's all up in the air right now."

"Where is Gran's phone?" asked Dooley.

Harriet smiled. "In a safe place."

"But where is it?"

"In a very safe place," Brutus confirmed.

"Gran tried to stifle my creativity, and if there's one thing that the constitution of this great nation protects, it's the right to take a video of anyone at any time," said Harriet.

"I doubt that's the case," I told her.

"No, but the founding fathers wrote about it," she assured me. "That everyone should have the right to have a YouTube channel and post whatever videos they want for the edification of their audience." I could have told her that YouTube didn't exist at the time the founding fathers were busy doing their founding, but I got the impression she wasn't really interested in my spurious arguments.

Next door, I could hear strange sounds, and as the four of us shared a look of curiosity, we decided to go exploring. But first, Harriet had to retrieve Gran's phone from its hiding place. For a moment, she disappeared into the house, then came out again, carrying the phone between her teeth. "Ready, tootsie roll?" she asked her camera-cat.

"Absolutely," said Brutus proudly. Ever since their YouTube channel had started going from strength to strength and was racking up the numbers to an amazing extent, he felt that they were making a difference and was proud to be a part of this endeavor.

We passed through the opening in the hedge and came out on the other side, only to find that Ted Trapper was at it again: tinkling on his rose bushes.

At his feet, Rufus sat, looking sad.

"He's at it again, you guys!" he cried. "Tinkling away, while Marcie has told him that he shouldn't!"

Harriet gave her partner in crime a wink. "Get ready, set, go!"

And the filming recommenced, with Ted soon to star in his second pee video, no doubt becoming another viral hit.

And as Brutus pressed Record, suddenly Marcie stepped from behind a bush, followed by Gran, Odelia, Chase, Marge, and Tex. Marcie grabbed the phone from Harriet, and immediately Ted stopped his tinkle in progress, giving his wife a curious look. "It's good for the plants," he repeated his earlier explanation.

"I know, honey," said Marcie. "I know. And you keep tinkling away as much as you like." She held up the phone. "Now that we've confiscated this, we can finally do whatever we like in our own backyard, without fear of being ridiculed online or exposed to the eyes of a billions-strong audience!"

She handed the phone back to Gran, who took it gratefully. And then, before our very eyes, she ceremoniously opened the YouTube channel that Harriet and Brutus had worked so hard on and proceeded to delete the video of Ted peeing, of herself sleeping, and in short order, all the videos that had caused so much embarrassment these last couple of days.

"Hey, what are you doing!" Harriet cried, extremely dismayed that her highest-scoring videos were being deleted. "You can't do that!"

"Hundreds of thousands of views," said Brutus solemnly. "Gone, with a click of a button."

"Is that all of them?" asked Marge as she looked over her mother's shoulder.

"I think so," said Gran. "You better take a look. My eyesight isn't as good as it used to be."

"Ted's video," said Marge as she checked Harriet's channel. "Your sleeping video, my sleeping video, Tex, Odelia, Chase, Alec's hot tub video…"

"Maybe leave that one up," said Gran.

Marge smiled. "Maybe I should leave that. My brother does only have himself to blame."

"He should have shared his jacuzzi with us," said Odelia.

"I love my godfather very much," said Chase. "But you're absolutely right. That was a very selfish thing of him to do."

"Okay, so I've removed all of the offending videos," said Marge, handing the phone back to her mother.

"But Gran!" Harriet cried. "All the effort I put into those videos!"

"You should learn once and for all," said Gran as she wagged a reproachful finger at her cat's face, "that you can't make absolute fools of people without asking them permission first. So no more shooting videos of the people you know and love, is that understood?"

"It was a trap," said Brutus. "Ted peeing? It was a trap to lure us and to grab that phone."

"Darn tootin' it was a trap," Marge murmured.

"You can still shoot videos of snails and ants," said Odelia. "As much as you want. But that's it. Nothing else."

"Oh, that's just great!" said Harriet. "Who wants to watch snails and ants? People want to see the good stuff! Not some stupid ants and snails."

"Like watching paint dry," Brutus added.

"But that is ASMR!" said Dooley. "It's watching paint dry, and grass growing, and snails moving from one place to another. I've looked it up online."

"Oh, Dooley," said Harriet with a sigh.

"Yes, Dooley, what do you know about true ASMR?" asked Brutus, peeved that his super channel had suddenly lost its biggest draws.

"So it's all right that I pee on my rose bush?" asked Ted, who hadn't really followed the conversation all that much. "It's just that I've read it's very good for the plant, you see."

His wife gave him a kiss on the cheek. "You pee away, honey."

Ted gave her a look of extreme gratitude. "Oh, great!" He glanced around and made to resume his activity, but Gran shouted, "Hey! Urinator! What do you think you're doing!"

"Well, healing my plant," said Ted.

"Not while we're watching!"

"Oh, right," said our neighbor.

And so we all returned to our own backyard. And lo and behold: Uncle Alec and Charlene had shown up, carrying a bottle of wine for their hostess. Our eyes immediately went up to Charlene's hair, and I saw that Fido must have fashioned her with a wig, for she didn't look like a punk chick anymore. Right behind them was Scarlett, and Tex rubbed his hands. "Looks like we've got a party!" he cried, and went to drag his grill set out of his garden house to fire it up and get that party started.

"Who is The Urinator, Max?" asked Dooley once we were settled on the porch swing once again. "Is he like The Terminator?"

"Absolutely," said Brutus with a wink in my direction. "Ted Trapper was sent from the future to get rid of the mother of the leader of the human resistance, one tinkle at a time."

"I knew it," said Dooley. "I just knew it!"

"Too bad they removed all of our best videos," said Harriet. "Or else we could have featured The Urinator as the star of our channel. Now all we have are ants and snails."

"It's all right, baby," said Brutus, rubbing her back consolingly. "At least they didn't delete the entire channel. We will build it back—bigger and stronger than ever."

"Marge said we couldn't make embarrassing videos again, though," said Harriet. "And turns out that's the only kind of videos that people like to watch." She thought for a moment.

"She didn't tell us that we couldn't film videos of other pets, though. So what if we turn our ASMR channel into a pet blooper reel? Film funny cat and dog videos."

"Sweetie, that's brilliant!" said Brutus.

I could have told them that the internet was already swarming with pet blooper reels, but they were so happy to have hit upon this brilliant new idea that I felt it would have been cruel of me to pop their bubble. And so I decided to let them enjoy their new endeavor. And it has to be said, they probably could film plenty of funny scenes, considering the wide circle of pets we counted amongst our acquaintances and friends, and the stunts they frequently got up to.

"We'll call our channel Pet Pranks," said Harriet.

"Or Pet Pratfalls!" Brutus suggested.

As we waited for Tex to deliver those first few delicious treats, Dooley was lost in thought. After a while, he came out of it. "Max?"

"Mh?"

"So this Urinator, how does he vanquish his enemies?"

"Dooley, we're about to have dinner," I said plaintively. "Let's keep it clean, all right?"

"No, but I really want to know, Max. The Terminator overpowers his enemies with his sheer force. But how does Ted think he'll be able to get rid of the mother of the leader of the human resistance?"

"I'm sure he has his ways," I said as delicately as I could. Too bad Brutus had to go and put ideas in my friend's head.

Dooley lapsed into thought once more, and when he re-emerged, he had hit upon a fresh idea. "I think his pee must be toxic. Like acid? So when he pees on something, it simply evaporates!"

"Great thinking, Dooley," I said.

"But that means that he shouldn't pee on those poor rose bushes! They'll be destroyed!"

"I'm sure they'll be fine," I said as I yawned. The anticipation of food always makes me sleepy. Probably to prepare my stomach for the big job ahead. I closed my eyes for a nice nap, but before long I was awakened by Dooley tinkling in a corner of the porch. "Dooley, what do you think you're doing!" I cried.

"Assisting The Urinator, Max," he said. "He can't hack it alone, so we all have to pitch in and give him a helping tinkle!"

Harriet and Brutus were filming the scene, and declaring it the best thing they had ever seen. I very much doubted whether this was the case. I didn't think anyone would be interested in watching a cat take a tinkle. But then *they* were the self-professed Martin Scorseses of the pet world, not me.

I closed my eyes, but soon became aware of strange goings-on, and when I opened them again I saw that Harriet and Brutus were filming *me*!

"Why are you filming me?" I asked, perplexed.

"Because you're a natural, Max," said Harriet. "It's all in the eyes. You can do nothing and still the audience will be fascinated. I don't know why, but you've got this raw talent." She sighed deeply. "Max, will you be my fetish actor? The Leonardo DiCaprio to my Martin Scorsese?"

It was the first time anyone had ever used the F-word to my face, and so I did the only thing I thought was prudent: I jumped off that bench and legged it.

"Max!" Harriet yelled after me. "Don't go! The world needs your talent!"

"Yes, Max," said Brutus. "Come back! You need to star in our next movie! It's about a big red cat named Brick!"

"He's big and red and vanquishes his enemies with the power of his big brain!" Harriet added.

"I'm not red—I'm blorange!" I yelled back.

And so I made for the hills. Okay, so I didn't head to the

actual hills, since I'm not really all that crazy about physical exertion. Instead, I legged it to the pet clinic where Rita MacKereth works. When I got there, I hurried straight into her office, where I knew I would be safe from these rabid filmmakers, and hid under her desk.

A pair of eyes peeked down at me, and as she picked me up and put me on top of her desk, I muttered an apology. And then she did the most outrageous thing: she gave me a big hug!

"I never thanked you for looking out for me, Max," she said.

"Oh, it's nothing," I said, wondering what she was going on about.

"If you hadn't been there, and alerted Odelia about Carter Buttress's doppelganger walking around in Hampton Cove, my father's killer would never have been caught."

"Oh, that," I said. "That was nothing. Just being in the right place at the right time, I guess."

There was a rustle at the door and Dooley walked in, looking around a little shyly. "I guess I don't want to be filmed anymore either, Max," he confessed.

"We're safe here, buddy," I said, and invited him to jump up onto Rita's desk, too.

"Well, aren't you simply the cutest?" she said as she tickled him under the chin.

She put us both down on the floor and pointed us to a nice basket in a corner of the room. It was occupied by Shelley and Patrick the hedgehog, whose acquaintance we had made before.

"What are you doing here?" asked Patrick.

"Still not very keen on cats, I see?" I said.

"Cats are the vermin of the pet world," he stated brusquely. He paused. "Though I guess you guys are all right."

"Thanks, Patrick," I said. "Coming from you, that's a big compliment."

"We heard all about you catching Morgan's killer," Shelley explained. "Rita is so happy about what you did."

"She is," Patrick confirmed. "Over the moon, in fact."

A second doggie came wandering into Rita's office, and I recognized him as Nicholas. He was glad to see us. "Hey, you guys," he said. "Popping in for a visit, are you?"

"We escaped Harriet and Brutus," Dooley said. "They want to turn us into the stars of their new YouTube channel. They want to feature Max as a crime fighter called Brick and me as his loyal sidekick, The Urinator."

This had Patrick in stitches. "The Urinator! That's hilarious! Do they want you to do all your stunts yourself?"

"I hadn't thought about that," said Dooley. "But I think so." He sagged a little. "That probably means I'll have to drink a lot since Harriet will want to have a lot of takes of every scene, and I will have to tinkle every time. But I can't tinkle in front of an entire crew, Max. I just can't do it!"

"You won't have to," I assured him. "Because we're not going to star in any of Harriet's videos."

"Oh, good," he said, relaxing a little. "I really don't think I'm cut out to be a superhero."

"You can say that again," said Patrick with a chuckle.

"And I think both Max and Dooley are superheroes," said Nicholas. "They singlepawedly caught Cesar's killer."

"Thanks, Nicholas," I said, touched by his words.

"Do you live here now?" asked Dooley.

The doggie nodded. "Rita has decided to adopt me."

"She's adopting a lot of pets," said Shelley. "First me, then Patrick, and now Nicholas. The house will be filled with pets."

"The house?" I asked.

"We moved," she explained. "From that grotty apartment to the house where Rita's dad used to live. It's much nicer."

"I'll say," said Patrick. "The place is so big she can start her own zoo."

"The only drawback is those cats," said Shelley. "Mia and Tia. They're not very friendly. But we're working on that."

"They're also liars," I warned her. "They told a lot of lies about Nathanial saying bad things about Bella Fuller and calling her all kinds of names, when clearly that wasn't true."

"Bella did reveal confidential information to Nathanial's son," Nicholas pointed out. "So that wasn't very nice of her."

"No, she shouldn't have done that," I said. Though Bella had told Odelia that Carter had tricked her into revealing things she shouldn't have, as she thought she could trust him. He was, after all, the boss's son, and Iron Eagle's future CEO.

At any rate, it was sure nice to know that Nicholas was being taken care of after the ordeal he had suffered, and even though Dooley and I had no ambitions whatsoever to join Rita's growing pet household, it was good to have options, just in case Harriet tried to turn us into YouTube stars again.

Rita's boss Rose entered the office and seemed surprised to see us lounging in the corner of Rita's office. "I swear to God," she said, "every time I walk in here there's more of you guys."

"Max and Dooley are visiting," said Rita. "They belong to Odelia Kingsley."

"Oh, right," said Rose, and crouched down to give us both a cuddle. "Thanks for what you did," she said, adding her voice to the growing choir of gratitude for our modest contribution to the capture and arrest of Carter Buttress.

I guess it is nice to be appreciated, especially if you don't have to make a fool of yourself online in exchange.

Another person walked into the office, and I recognized him as Samuel Dickenson, the honey salesman. He was carrying a large bouquet of flowers and handed it to Rita, who took it with a big smile. "Ready for our date?" he asked.

"You bet," said Rita. "Third one is the charm, Sam."

Rose rolled her eyes. "Oh, get a room, you two!"

She walked out again, and Rita and her new boyfriend shared a smile. Moments later, Ken came walking in, but when he saw Samuel, he immediately walked out again.

"Still in love with you, huh?" said Samuel.

"Yup," said Rita. "But at least he's stopped following me around like a puppy dog."

"Improvement!"

They both laughed, and Samuel shared a loving kiss with his new girlfriend.

And since the five of us all cringed at the sight of this, we echoed Rose's sentiments by yelling, "Get a room!"

Humans. Even when they're not being filmed for an ASMR video, they can't help but embarrass themselves in public.

EPILOGUE

Scarlett was thoroughly enjoying herself. Once a week or so she liked going to the beauty parlor and order the full treatment: nails, hair, skin, massage, and of course her favorite, the steam room. And she had just spread her towel and stretched out in the sauna cabin, preparatory to having all of those pores of hers open and cast away any dirt that might have accrued there, when she saw a figure move in front of the small window in the wooden door. Odd, she thought. Almost as if someone was watching her. And that someone was a cat. But that couldn't be so, of course, since cats weren't allowed in the beauty parlor, and definitely not in the steam room. Besides, cats are beautiful by themselves and don't need a treatment to improve on Mother Nature.

And so she lay back down on her towel and closed her eyes. She had invited Vesta to tag along, but her friend had claimed she had things to do. Her loss. Soon she was feeling thoroughly relaxed, and getting the full benefit of the dry heat.

. . .

On the other side of the sauna door, a pair of cats were filming every drop of sweat glistening on Scarlett's corpus.

"This is the ASMR video to end all ASMR videos!" said the white Persian to her companion, a big black cat. "Humans love sweat. They can't get enough of it. The more the better."

"I know, right?" said her companion. "The sweat is real!"

"Oh, sugar muffin, this is gonna be the biggest hit we ever scored! We'll call it 'Old Lady Sweats A Lot! Very Relaxing!'"

Just then, someone suddenly appeared behind them. It was their human Vesta Muffin, and she didn't look happy. And as she grabbed her phone, she had a suggestion for a new title for the video: 'Old Lady Swears A Lot! Not Very Relaxing!'

Looked as if the world of ASMR was about to say goodbye to two of its biggest proponents and promising new stars.

THE END

Thanks for reading! If you want to know when a new Nic Saint book comes out, sign up for Nic's mailing list: nicsaint.com/news

EXCERPT FROM PURRFECT CHICKEN (MAX 87)

Chapter One

Dooley had been staring deeply into the small pond of the garden they were visiting and wondering if the fishies that inhabited the pond were happy there or not. It wasn't as if he could ask them, since fishes are a notoriously aloof type of species and not all that prone to conversation. Nevertheless, he wished them well and hoped they would be treated correctly by the people this pond belonged to—whoever they were.

He glanced up at the house and wondered when Odelia and Chase would be finished in there. They had announced they had an important mission to tackle and had invited Dooley and his best friend Max to tag along, just in case... Dooley had immediately asked the pertinent question: what case? But to his disappointment, no answer had been forthcoming, and so he was left feeling like the third wheel, with Max wandering to and fro and glancing here and there in the hopes of encountering someone to talk to, just like Dooley himself.

EXCERPT FROM PURRFECT CHICKEN (MAX 87)

It had to be said that both he and his friend were cats of a sociable nature and enjoyed shooting the breeze with any pet or creature whose acquaintance they happened to make. It was exactly the reason Odelia liked to drag them along when she was out on a case or chasing a story. But mostly she made sure they were briefed well in advance so they knew in what direction they needed to steer their socializing. But today there had been none of that.

They had been awakened by the buzzing of Chase's mobile phone located on the nightstand. The cop had picked up and exchanged a few terse words with the person on the other end. The upshot had been that he and Odelia had hit the shower and had practically run out of the house, but not before roping both Max and Dooley into this new mission of theirs and dropping their daughter Grace off at the little girl's grandparents next door.

Having enjoyed the company of these colorful fishes for as long as he could stand, Dooley decided to rejoin his friend, who was sniffing at a rose bush that offered a visually pleasing and colorful palette. "Still no sign?" he asked hopefully.

Max shook his head. "Nothing yet," he said and pressed his nose into a particularly gorgeous flower. When he retracted the organ, it was sprinkled with pollen and Dooley laughed.

"Max, your nose!" he said.

Max crossed his eyes to look at his own nose, which is always a tough proposition, unless you're cross-eyed, of course. "What is it?" asked his blorange friend. "Is it a bug? A bee?"

"It's only pollen," Dooley reassured him. "I'll get rid of it for you, shall I?" And so he wiped the pollen off Max's nose with his paw, smearing some of it across the big cat's whiskers in the process, giving Max a pretty funky look.

EXCERPT FROM PURRFECT CHICKEN (MAX 87)

"I hope everything is all right," said Max, indicating that he, too, was concerned about the lack of information from their human.

"I'm sure it is," Dooley said. "Otherwise, she would have invited us in."

It's a rare household where cats aren't welcome, but then it takes all kinds of people to make the world go round. The moment the door had opened and the woman standing at the door had seen Max and Dooley, she had made a face and made it clear in no uncertain terms that as far as she was concerned, cats had no place in the general constellation of things and definitely had no place in her nice little home. And so it was to their surprise that Odelia had told them to stay put.

"I think she did it," said Dooley now.

"Who did what?" asked Max, giving one of the flowers a gentle poke. It danced back and forth for a moment, before welcoming the two cats to take another whiff of that same pollen that it had freely shared with Max a moment before. Unlike the owner of the house, flowers aren't very discerning and are open for anyone to partake in their gorgeousness.

"Well, the lady who didn't want to invite us in, of course," said Dooley. "It's usually a clear sign of psychopathy, Max."

"What is?" asked his friend, unusually slow on the uptake today.

"Being anti-cat, of course. People who don't like cats... it's a bad sign, Max. A very bad sign indeed." Which was why he was so worried that Odelia and Chase were locked up in there with the cat-hating person. For all they knew she might have murdered them by now.

"She won't harm Odelia," Max assured him. He might be slow on the uptake, but he had correctly assumed that his friend was worried not so much about their lack of access to

EXCERPT FROM PURRFECT CHICKEN (MAX 87)

the house but Odelia's safety. "And besides, Chase is in there with her, and he won't let anything happen to his wife."

That was true enough. Chase was as protective as they came, and not only that, but he was also a deft hand at self-defense techniques. When it came down to it, he could protect both himself and Odelia against any crazy person's bad intentions.

Dooley returned to his former spot near the window, hoping to catch a glimpse of what was going on inside, but unfortunately for them, the woman had drawn the curtains, which was an odd thing to do since night hadn't yet fallen.

Just then, the pet flap located in the kitchen door flapped once, and a small doggie came prancing out, looking happy and relaxed. The moment it spotted the two cats trespassing on its domain, though, it immediately started barking up a storm.

"It's fine," Dooley hastened to assure the tiny canine. "We're here because we've been invited by your human."

The doggie didn't seem to accept this explanation, though, for it kept yapping up a storm, moving back and forth with jerky movements as some of those tiny dogs do. Its entire body was shaking with indignation at the sight of Max and Dooley.

"Our humans are inside," Max explained. "With your human. And since she didn't want us to set paw in the house, she asked us to wait outside."

"A likely story!" the doggie cried as it regarded them with unwavering hostility. "If my human had asked you to wait outside, she would have told me. I am the official guard dog, after all," it added, puffing out its chest for a moment, to show that it took its job very seriously.

"Look, if you want, we'll take up position in the front yard," Max suggested. "Or on the sidewalk, even. But before we do that, can you tell us one thing?"

EXCERPT FROM PURRFECT CHICKEN (MAX 87)

"What?" asked the doggie suspiciously.

"What's your name? My name is Max," he hastened to add. "And this is my friend Dooley."

"We live just around the corner," Dooley added. "On Harrington Street."

The doggie wavered. Clearly, it didn't want to get overly familiar with them, but on the other hand, it didn't want to come across as uncivilized either. So finally, it relented and declared, "My name is Huey. And you'd do well to get lost, Max and Dooley. This is my backyard, and you have no business here."

"Of course," said Max. "We're leaving already, Huey."

"You wouldn't happen to know Fifi, would you?" asked Dooley. "It's just that she's our neighbor, you see, and she knows a lot of dogs on the block."

The doggie stared at him, still with that same suspicion etched on his furry features. He was pretty much the same size as Fifi, who was a Yorkshire Terrier, though if Dooley had to guess, he would have pegged Huey as a miniature poodle.

"Yes, I know Fifi," he said. "And you're telling me that she's your neighbor?"

"We live right next door," said Max.

"Oh," said Huey, and for a moment didn't seem to know how to respond to this. If the saying that a friend of a friend is my friend also is applicable, he probably should have changed his attitude towards them. But instead, he decided to double down on his lack of neighborliness by spitting, "I don't believe you! Fifi would *never* be friends with a pair of cats!"

"And yet she is," said Max in those same kind tones he had used since Huey had burst onto the scene—quite literally. "Our very good friend. And so is Rufus, who is our other neighbor."

EXCERPT FROM PURRFECT CHICKEN (MAX 87)

"We hang out all the time," Dooley added.

"Oh," said Huey, and once again was forced to take this information and process it. And since he had a very small head, Dooley figured it might take some time before his synapses worked their magic. Finally, he shook his head. "I still don't believe you. I know Rufus very well, and he's never mentioned either of you before. So if you can please leave now?"

"Of course," said Max, and gestured for Dooley to follow him. But before they had taken the path that led from the backyard to the front of the house, another canine popped out of the pet flap. It was the spitting image of the first one, but this one sported a goofy expression that the first one sorely lacked.

"Ooh, kitties!" the second poodle cried as it gamboled up to them. "Pretty kitties! Wanna play?"

"We don't play with cats, Dewey," said Huey haughtily. "And now you better return inside before mistress finds you missing and gets very upset."

"But I want to play with the kitties!" Dewey cried with dismay. He darted a yearning look in Dooley's direction, and even though the latter felt that here was their chance to fraternize with the locals, Max insisted that they make themselves scarce before Huey took umbrage.

"Let's go, Dooley," he said, and they continued their trek up the garden path.

"Don't go!" Dewey yelled. "We never meet any friends! Let's play a game!"

"We do *not* play games with cats," said Huey. "Get back inside, Dewey!"

"I don't wanna," said the poodle unhappily. "I wanna stay here and play with my new friends."

"They're not our friends," Huey specified. "They're

EXCERPT FROM PURRFECT CHICKEN (MAX 87)

strangers—not to mention they're cats, and we both know what mistress thinks of cats."

"She don't like them," Dewey said.

"Exactly. So let's both return inside before she finds out we've been talking to these two and gets very upset."

"We don't want mistress to get upset," Dewey admitted.

And after darting a final longing glance in their direction, the doggie entered the house again through the pet flap and was soon gone, followed by Huey.

The flap flapped once, and then all was quiet again in the backyard.

"That was weird," said Dooley as he followed his friend to the front of the house.

"You can say that again," said Max. The moment they were standing next to Odelia's car, he lowered his voice and said, "Don't look now, but we're being watched."

Immediately, Dooley turned his head.

"I said, 'Don't look now!'" said Max.

But Dooley had already spotted the doggies staring at them from behind the plate glass window. They were Huey and Dewey, and they weren't alone. He counted no less than three miniature poodles in total, and all of them were staring at them. Some with abject hostility, like Huey, others with a sort of strange yearning, like Dewey.

"They don't look happy," said Dooley, and suddenly felt for the canines.

"No, they don't look happy at all," Max concurred.

Just then, the front door opened and Odelia and Chase came walking out. The relief Dooley felt to see their humans alive and well was so great that he momentarily forgot all about those poodles and their curious behavior.

Moments later, they were back in the car and driving in the direction of town. Mission accomplished? Oddly enough, both of their humans were strangely quiet. And even though

EXCERPT FROM PURRFECT CHICKEN (MAX 87)

Dooley was itching to ask them what they had discovered, he knew better than to ask. For Max had placed his paw against his lips in a bid to make sure he kept quiet.

And so it was that they arrived at the offices of the *Hampton Cove Gazette*, with Dooley burning with curiosity and Max just sitting there in the backseat of the car looking like a sphinx. Odelia opened the car door to let them out, and they both jumped down to the sidewalk. But if they had expected that Odelia would park the car and accompany them inside, they were in for a surprise. The moment they had stepped out, the door closed again, and their humans drove off!

They watched them go, and it was a testament to Max's perturbation that even he made a noise of utter confusion. "Well, I never!" he cried.

Chapter Two

Donald Weaver glanced from behind the curtain and fixed his clear blue eyes on the house across the street. When he didn't see a sign of his neighbor Miranda Gobbs, he grunted with satisfaction. Suddenly, a voice rang out behind him.

"Donald, are you ogling Miranda again?"

Immediately, he let the curtain slip from his grasp and jerked his head back, feeling caught. "Of course not. I was just looking out for the mailman. It wouldn't be the first time he forgot to ring the bell."

"Well, just make sure Miranda doesn't see you. She's liable to file another complaint."

"She won't," he assured his wife. "Since I'm not spying on her, and I have never spied on her. The woman is simply mad, that's all there is to it."

"Mh," said Darlene but didn't look convinced. She had

EXCERPT FROM PURRFECT CHICKEN (MAX 87)

brought a tray into the living room. It contained two cups filled to the brim with piping hot coffee, accompanied by a liberal assortment of home-baked cookies. He took the tray from her and there was some rattling as he put it down. He grimaced. "What is it?" his wife asked, concern in her voice.

He rubbed his elbow. "That darn arthritis is acting up again. When are we finally going to follow Doctor Poole's advice and move to a warmer climate? He said that if we'd just go and live in Florida all of my pain would disappear. And so would yours, by the way."

Donald's joints had been giving him a lot of trouble lately, and the thought of moving to a warmer climate appealed to him a great deal.

"You know we can't," Darlene said softly as she took a seat at the table.

"We could if we sold this place."

"Well, I don't want to sell this place," she said adamantly. "There's Ruth to consider."

Darlene's sister was living in a facility for people with a disability and wouldn't be able to survive without her loving sister to be there for her.

Donald glanced up at the big clock over the television and wondered where the time had gone. He still had plenty of errands to run in town and already it was past eleven.

"I wonder what the Kingsleys were doing across the street," said his wife thoughtfully.

"I was wondering the same thing," he said.

She smiled. "So you *were* spying on Miranda."

"I wasn't!"

They were both quiet for a moment, and as he dug his teeth into a crispy cookie, Jim came hurrying up and put his paws on his knees, begging for a bite.

"You know that chocolate isn't good for you, sweetie," he said.

EXCERPT FROM PURRFECT CHICKEN (MAX 87)

"Give him a biscuit," said Darlene. "From the tin." She handed him the tin filled with dog biscuits, and he dug one out for the tiny doggie and held it up. Jim's ears were wiggling excitedly, and he released a happy yip, his body vibrating with anticipatory delight. As Donald handed their sweet pet the biscuit, Jim deftly took it between his tiny teeth and hurried off with it, darting a glance across his shoulder as if afraid they might change their minds and take the delicious treat away from him again.

Both Donald and Darlene chuckled at the sight of their canine companion's behavior. With dogs in the house, you didn't need a television. They provided free entertainment.

Darlene turned serious again. "I just hope she hasn't filed another complaint."

He gave her a thoughtful look. The last time Miranda had called the police to her home, it had been to launch a complaint against her neighbor for spying on her. Now it was certainly true that Donald glanced in on the woman from time to time, but what neighbor doesn't? He had eyes in his head, and he wasn't afraid to use them. But actually spy on her? Using binoculars or even filming her? That was just a load of nonsense. So when the police had paid them a visit and had searched the house for those self-same binoculars or the camera that Miranda said he had been using to spy on her, they had found absolutely nothing.

No camera, no footage on his computer, nothing out of the ordinary. It had certainly soured the relationship between the Weavers and Miranda Gobbs to some extent, and ever since the incident, as he and Darlene still referred to it, Donald's desire to put as much distance between themselves and Hampton Cove had grown substantially.

If only he could find a way to get away. And convince Darlene of the same.

"If she had filed another complaint," he said as he took

EXCERPT FROM PURRFECT CHICKEN (MAX 87)

another nibble from his cookie, "the Kingsleys would have been on our doorstep already."

"Unless they've decided to call in the cavalry like last time," countered Darlene. "It took a couple of days before they showed up at the house, remember?"

Of course, he remembered. It had been possibly the darkest day of his life. Being accused of a crime he didn't commit, and to suffer the humiliation of having police vans parked in front of the house and officers crawling all over the place. The whole neighborhood had stepped out, to take up position outside, wondering what was going on. One of their neighbors had even asked if they were Russian spies, or maybe burying dead bodies in the basement. And ever since that fateful day, people had started looking at them strangely. Crossing the street when they passed, or looking away when they met in the shop. Almost as if Donald had been tainted with suspicion, even though he hadn't done anything wrong.

And it was all because of that crazy woman across the street. Miranda Gobbs. From the moment she had moved in, they hadn't gotten along. And now, of course, it was full-out war. A war he was determined to win, even though he hadn't told Darlene yet.

He had a plan. A plan to make sure that Miranda never bothered them again.

Chapter Three

Dooley and I had returned to the heart of town after being dropped off by Odelia, and I had to admit we both felt a little discombobulated. First, Odelia dragged us along on one of her investigations, literally picking us up from the bed and putting us in the car so we could assist her and Chase. Then, when we arrived on the scene, we weren't even allowed in the house, which was inhabited by one of the

EXCERPT FROM PURRFECT CHICKEN (MAX 87)

worst cat haters I've ever met. To top it all off, we were chased out of the backyard by a dog, and when all was said and done, Odelia didn't even give us the benefit of the details of her case. No blow-by-blow account of her interview with the woman—she didn't even tell us what was going on and what the case was about!

"That wasn't very nice of Odelia, Max," said Dooley as we watched our human drive off.

"You can say that again," I said.

"That wasn't very nice of Odelia, Max."

I stared at him.

"You told me to say it again," he explained.

I smiled and patted him on the back. The world may have gone crazy, but at least Dooley was still his old self. "I say we go and pour out our lament into a listening ear," I suggested.

"Pour what into what ear?" he asked.

"Let's tell Kingman what just happened," I said. "A sorrow shared is a sorrow halved."

We found Kingman in front of the General Store, where he likes to sit and watch the world go by. And talk to any and all cats who are willing to lend him a listening ear. When he saw us toddle up, a wide smile stretched his cheeks from ear to ear. "Now there is a sight for sore eyes," he said. "I was just asking Harriet and Brutus where you guys had gone off to."

"Harriet and Brutus are here?" asked Dooley, looking around.

"Inside," said Kingman, with a nod in the direction of the store entrance. "Wilbur has put some chicken nuggets on display and put out some tasters."

"I love a good taster," I said, glancing eagerly in the direction of the store.

"Go on, Max," said Kingman with an amused look at me. "You know you want to."

EXCERPT FROM PURRFECT CHICKEN (MAX 87)

"It's been a strange morning," I told our friend, "and I feel like I could use a pick-me-up."

And so Dooley and I both entered the store, looking for that taster Kingman had described in tantalizing detail. We found Harriet and Brutus at the end of the store, where the meat section is located. The little dish with the tasters was too high for them to reach, and they were mewling piteously to anyone who would listen and might be induced to drop a chicken nugget to the floor. And so it was that the four of us sat underneath that tasting dish, looking up with anticipatory relish. The person who finally showed up wasn't a helpful customer, though, but Wilbur Vickery himself. And if he was inclined to give us a taste of those chicken nuggets, he didn't give any indication. Quite the contrary. "Out," he said in a voice that brooked no contest. "These tasters are for my customers, not a couple of freeloading cats. Do you understand? Out!" He was pointing to the exit, and since I got the impression we wouldn't be able to change his mind, we slunk off in the direction indicated.

"I didn't know Wilbur to be this stingy," Brutus grumbled.

"He's a grinch," Harriet chimed in. "A regular grinch!"

"One little piece of chicken," said Dooley. "That's all I ask. Just one little piece."

"I'm hungry," I grunted unhappily. After our fruitless trip with Odelia, the only thing that could buck me up was food, but clearly food was not to be had—at least not right now.

"He's very protective of his chicken," said Kingman with a nod. "Hasn't even given me a taste, can you believe it? Usually, I'm the first one he thinks of when he has something to offer his clients, but today he won't even let me come near that chicken of his."

"Maybe it's special chicken?" Dooley suggested.

We all laughed. "Chicken is chicken, buddy," said Brutus. "It all tastes the same."

EXCERPT FROM PURRFECT CHICKEN (MAX 87)

Harriet groaned. "Don't talk about the taste of chicken, snuggle pooh. I can't stand it."

"Talking about chicken," said Brutus, as he put his nose in the air and sniffed. "That smells mighty delicious, you guys." We all followed his example and inhaled the delicious smell of grilled chicken.

"That's Wilbur," said Kingman. "He's gone and bought himself one of those grills. Apparently, the smell of grilled chicken doubled one of his competitors' turnover, so now he's determined to try the same thing."

"It's like the smell of baked bread in a supermarket," Brutus knew. "Drives up the profits twenty percent, or so I've been told."

"I certainly could be induced to fill up my shopping cart with chicken-related items right now," said Harriet as she eagerly licked her lips.

"This is torture," Brutus groaned. "He can't do this to us, can he? Aren't there laws against this sort of thing? Animal protection laws?"

"I don't think there's a law against grilling chicken," I told our friend.

"There should be!" he cried unhappily.

"And to think he doesn't even give you first dibs," Harriet told Kingman.

"Yeah, I don't know what's gotten into him all of a sudden," said Kingman. "He's become unusually stingy lately. Doesn't even give me first dibs at any new kibble he gets. Says he doesn't need my services anymore."

"Or our services," said Brutus gloomily.

For the longest time, we had been Wilbur's unofficial tasters. He would put out bowls with the good stuff, and if he saw that we imbibed it with relish, he would order more for his customers. If we didn't touch the stuff, he knew that it was junk and would send the supplier packing. It was a fool-

EXCERPT FROM PURRFECT CHICKEN (MAX 87)

proof system and a win-win for all concerned, except maybe the suppliers whose wares he returned… until now.

"I've been feeling the fallout," Kingman lamented. "Used to be that every cat in Hampton Cove dropped by the General Store to shoot the breeze and partake in my little haul, and now they avoid me like the plague." He gave me a pleading look. "I hope you won't start avoiding me also? I have so much more to offer than just the best kibble in town, you know. My scintillating conversation, for one thing, and my fascinating personality for another."

"We won't avoid you," I told the big cat as I placed a reassuring paw on his shoulder. "I promise."

But judging from the look on Brutus and Harriet's faces, selecting a different venue from now on sounded like a good idea. And Harriet's next words confirmed this. "We haven't seen Buster in a long time, have we, scrumptious?" she asked Brutus.

Brutus gave her a keen look. "No, we have not, starshine!"

And without another word, they both hurried off in the direction of the hair salon, leaving us to stare after them.

"See?" Kingman cried. "One by one, they all desert me!"

"We won't desert you, Kingman," said Dooley. "Will we, Max?"

"No, we won't," I promised.

"Even if you don't offer free food anymore," Dooley added, "we will still keep visiting you. Because we enjoy your silly conversation and your painful personality."

"God give me strength," Kingman groaned.

ABOUT NIC

Nic has a background in political science and before being struck by the writing bug worked odd jobs around the world (including but not limited to massage therapist in Mexico, gardener in Italy, restaurant manager in India, and Berlitz teacher in Belgium).

When he's not writing he enjoys curling up with a good (comic) book, watching British crime dramas, French comedies or Nancy Meyers movies, sampling pastry (apple cake!), pasta and chocolate (preferably the dark variety), twisting himself into a pretzel doing morning yoga, going for a brisk walk, and spoiling his feline assistants Lily and Ricky.

He lives with his wife (and aforementioned cats) in a small village smack dab in the middle of absolutely nowhere and is probably writing his next 'Mysteries of Max' book right now.

www.nicsaint.com

Printed in Great Britain
by Amazon